THE BUTTERFLY
WHISPERER

By the Author

Love On The Red Rocks

The Butterfly Whisperer

Visit us at www.boldstrokesbooks.com

THE BUTTERFLY WHISPERER

by

Lisa Moreau

2017

THE BUTTERFLY WHISPERER

ISBN 13: 978-1-62639-791-0

This Trade Paperback Original Is Published By
Bold Strokes Books, Inc.
P.O. Box 249
Valley Falls, NY 12185

First Edition: January 2017

CREDITS
Editor: Shelley Thrasher
Production Design: Stacia Seaman
Cover Design by Melody Pond

Acknowledgments

This past year I had the pleasure of meeting Radclyffe, Bold Strokes Books (BSB) publisher; and Sandy Lowe, BSB Senior Editor, at the GCLS Conference in DC. The first thing I did after arriving at the conference was hunt down Rad (I can call her that since we took a selfie together, which I'm pretty sure means we're BFFs). I thanked her for giving my stories a home and an outlet to reach more people than I ever thought possible. Even though I accosted her early one morning at the coffee machine, she took time to chat with me. She expressed a genuine interest in my experience as a new BSB author, and I was happy to report that it's been amazing and that I love being a part of her incredible publishing company. The next thing I did was track down Sandy, who—despite the disappointing absence of a highly anticipated Australian accent—is very impressive. I probably didn't properly relay this to her, but she does an incredible job and is a joy to work with. Her input and suggestions on my book proposal made it a better, stronger story. When Sandy speaks, I listen. She knows what works, what doesn't, and is pretty darn sharp.

It was a pleasure to work with Shelley Thrasher, editor extraordinaire, again. I'll let you in on a little secret: Shelley makes me look and sound a hundred times better than I actually am, and if it weren't for her I have no doubt I'd be known as the Cliché Queen. Shelley, it might not be evident, but I've learned a great deal from your line edits and hopefully, the next manuscript will be less bloody.

One of the most gratifying, unanticipated experiences of being published is all the new author friends I've made. The most creative, talented, witty, intelligent women have crossed my path since my first book was released. There are too many people to name, but you know who you are. Thank you for your encouragement, advice, humor, and support. Several of you took this new, clueless author under your wing and showed me the ropes, and for that, I'm very grateful. Hopefully, one day I can pay it forward with another newbie BSB writer.

Thanks to my big sis, Carla, and niece, Sasha, for your continued friendship, love, and support. You two are the first people I think about contacting when anything big, small, good, or not-so-good happens to me. A lot of our loved ones have crossed over, but I'm thankful that we have each other.

To the readers of my first book, *Love On The Red Rocks*: thank you for the book reviews, connecting with me on social media, and sending personal emails. Your feedback and support means a lot. Keep it coming!

For all the soul mates who have lost and found each other again.
You lucky dogs.

"If nothing ever changed there'd be no butterflies."
—Anonymous

PROLOGUE

The Big One

New Year's Eve, 1999

It became known as the turn-of-the-century earthquake. For years afterward, no one within a hundred-mile radius of Monarch, a speck of a town along the Central California coast, could last two minutes when first meeting someone without asking, "Where were you when the big one hit?" To them, the earthquake was what they'd come to remember about that New Year's Eve, but to Jordan Lee, it marked the last day she ever saw Sophie.

"Meet me at our tree in fifteen minutes." Jordan gripped her cell phone and pressed it hard against her ear.

"Where are you!? I've been trying to reach you for days." Fear tinged Sophie's voice.

"Please. Just meet me in fifteen minutes." Jordan disconnected before Sophie could protest. She threw the phone into the passenger seat and rested her forehead against the steering wheel. This was by far the hardest thing she'd ever have to do. A lump formed in her throat as tears threatened. She couldn't start crying now. She'd never stop.

Jordan grabbed a flashlight from the glove compartment and headed down the trail along a sixty-foot cliff overlooking the ocean. She and Sophie walked this path often on their way to the butterfly grove. A full moon shone brightly in the indigo sky when Jordan stopped at the edge of the bluff. The beautiful night was almost too perfect, given the circumstances. The sound of crashing waves and squawking seagulls filled the air. She breathed in the scent of sea salt and stared at the moon's reflection in the dark-teal waters below. If Sophie were there she'd say, "When you whisper a wish to a butterfly under a full moon, the great Native American spirit is sure to grant it."

If only that were true.

Jordan peeled her gaze away and quickened her pace down a side trail that led from the bluff to the eucalyptus forest. She wanted to see something before Sophie arrived. Three butterflies circled her head before flying in front, as though leading the way. Jordan followed until she reached a towering tree, which stood in the center of the grove. Thousands of orange-and-black monarchs huddled on the branches, making it look more like an orange blossom than a eucalyptus. She squatted beside the tree and traced her fingertips over the initials SOS. Sophie Opal Sanders. After days of pleading, Sophie had finally agreed to carve their initials into the tree. She said it was like slapping Mother Nature in the face and they'd probably go to hell for it, but she did like the idea of immortalizing their friendship in her favorite tree. So she'd compromised and said they could do it on the bottom of the trunk, where no one would notice. That was three years earlier, when they were fifteen.

Jordan sat on the ground with her back against the smooth bark, her face buried in her raised knees.

"Are you okay?" A melodic voice prompted Jordan to lift her head to a shining face looking down at her. She'd always teased Sophie that she looked like a Disney Princess, with golden hair, expressive blue eyes, and heart-shaped face. Jordan wouldn't have been surprised if squirrels and birds carried on a conversation with her, just like in a fairy tale. When Sophie squatted and rested her hand on Jordan's arm, warm tingles cascaded through her body. Abruptly, Jordan stood and took several steps back. She couldn't be that close to Sophie and say what needed to be said. Sophie stood as well, concern etched on her face.

"I need to tell you something." Jordan winced at the quiver in her voice. She cleared her throat and willed a commanding tone. "I'm leaving. Tonight."

"What are you talking about? Where are you going?"

"I'm going to live with my mother in New York."

"What?! That's crazy. We're graduating in four months. You haven't seen your mother since you were ten."

"Try to understand. And please, please don't ask me why." Jordan stared at the ground, unable to look in Sophie's eyes.

"This is insane. What does your father—"

Thousands of flapping butterfly wings interrupted as the sky filled with orange and black. A sharp jolt shook the earth and knocked them both to the ground. Jordan covered Sophie's body as the land violently trembled and rolled. Falling branches scraped her face, and a heavy object pounded her back. She resisted the urge to cover her head with her hands. It was more important that Sophie be safe. The shaking probably lasted only thirty seconds, but it felt like an hour. When the earth's vibrations subsided, they both sat up in a rubble of leaves and branches, Sophie still entwined in Jordan's arms.

"What...what was that?" Sophie asked breathlessly.

"I...I think an earthquake...a big one. Are you okay?" Jordan was shocked by the sudden tremor, but even more shocked that Sophie was in her arms. This was the closest they'd ever been.

"I think so. Are you? Your face is scratched." Jordan's breath hitched as Sophie grazed her cheek. "Does it hurt?"

Jordan gulped and managed to shake her head, silently praying Sophie wouldn't stop stroking her wounds.

"Oh, my gosh. The butterflies." Sophie lifted a large branch, which revealed several lifeless monarchs underneath. Her eyes immediately filled with tears. "They're dead."

Jordan's heart melted. Not for the butterflies, but for Sophie. "Look at all the ones that survived, Soph. Like the little guy that just landed on your head."

Sophie grinned through a sob. "Really? One is on my head?"

"Yeah, and he looks comfy up there."

"You always know how to make me feel better."

Jordan stiffened as Sophie scooted closer and rested her cheek on her shoulder. It would have been so easy to lean down and kiss the tip of her nose, then her lips. As though reading her mind, Sophie bolted upright and backed away.

"What were you saying before? About leaving?" Uncertainty clouded Sophie's blue eyes.

Jordan stood on shaky limbs and steadied herself with a hand on the tree. Sophie stood as well, careful not to step on any butterflies.

"If you hear anything, if anyone says something, just remember that I'm sorry. I didn't mean for any of it to happen."

"What are you talking about? Sorry for what?" Sophie reached for Jordan's hand, but she pulled away.

"I have to go." Jordan took several steps back. *She couldn't explain. If Sophie knew the truth, she'd hate her. Just like her father did.*

"Why are you doing this?" Tears brimmed in Sophie's eyes.

A sharp stab ripped through Jordan's gut. She hated being the cause of Sophie's sadness. Without another word, she turned and ran down the trail. Sophie's screams echoed through the forest, like a wounded animal in pain, each cry an arrow through Jordan's heart. She ran as fast as she could, stopping only when she reached the edge of the grove. Burning tears threatened as her heart pounded.

If this is what love does to you, I want no part of it ever again.

Fear welled within Jordan as the earth shook beneath her again. It was an aftershock, not a strong one, but enough to remind her of the earthquake. What was she thinking? She shouldn't have left Sophie alone. Jordan rushed back into the forest, relieved to find her sitting under the tree. She hid behind a bush until Sophie got up and walked down the trail. Jordan followed until Sophie was home safe, where she collapsed, sobbing, into her aunt Helen's arms.

As Jordan watched Sophie from afar, her head felt like a pressure cooker ready to explode. The muffled, rapid pounding in her ears mimicked her heartbeat, and she felt light-headed. She wasn't sure what was happening, but it was like someone had sucked all the energy out of her body; her arms went limp, and her knees buckled. Then she saw spots, right before everything went completely black.

CHAPTER ONE

Be Careful What You Wish For

Ten Years Later

Jordan was immediately suspicious. Doug invited her to Le Papillon only when he had bad news. In the dark, discreet restaurant, everyone talked in whispers and rarely caused a scene.

"Why not Frank's Deli?" Jordan inched down Beverly Boulevard and chatted with Doug on her cell phone.

"It's too noisy."

"That's why I like it."

Le Papillon—French for "the butterfly," though they spelled it *Papillion*—always reminded Jordan of Sophie, which left her feeling melancholy. Plus, it was a little creepy that the table centerpieces contained live yellow butterflies in clear-glass containers. Who wanted to stare at an insect while stuffing filet mignon down their throat? Wasn't there a People for the Ethical Treatment of Butterflies group? Not that Jordan cared one way or another, but she was surprised no one picketed the place.

Jordan slammed on her brakes and honked long and hard at a Hummer that cut her off. "Asshole!"

"Jordan? You still there? Le Papillon. Noon." Doug disconnected before she could protest.

"Asshole." Jordan wasn't sure if she was referring to the Hummer or Doug. Who was she kidding? She loved Doug. He was her BFF/business partner/gay wardrobe consultant/amateur psychotherapist. Pathetic to say, but Doug was her only real friend. She didn't know where she'd be without him. They'd met in New York ten years ago at a community college and immediately hit it off. Several years later, they moved to Beverly Hills to start Soul Mate Outreach Solutions, better known as SOS, a matchmaking company. They'd hit it big after an Oscar-winning actress's endorsement and become known as matchmakers to the stars, even scoring an interview with Ophelia, the most influential talk-show host in town. Their long-term success rate was impressive, considering Hollywood couples stayed together as long as it took ice cream to melt on a sunny Southern California day.

Traffic was at a complete standstill. Jordan craned her neck but couldn't see beyond the bumper-to-bumper cars. LA traffic sucked. It could literally take forty-five minutes to drive four miles, mostly because of the brigade of tourists clogging lanes looking for stars' homes. Jordan usually didn't like bumper stickers but couldn't resist the one she'd slapped on the back of her Jaguar that read, WELCOME TO LOS ANGELES. NOW GO HOME.

Sighing dramatically, she glanced at a hairy beast in the SUV next to her. His ears perked up, and he barked once in a deep baritone. Jordan had a feeling he was trying to tell her something, but the hell if she knew what it was. Not that she'd admit it, but her heart melted a little when he looked at her with sad, brown eyes. He was actually pretty cute, in a woolly mammoth sort of way. On rare occasions, she considered getting a dog, one to protect her from robbers and fetch the paper every morning. Dogs did that, right? Or was that only Lassie? Anyway, the dog idea was always short-lived. It was too much of a commitment.

After what felt like forever, traffic finally started moving. Instead of coming upon a wreck or some other plausible cause of the backup, Jordan saw something that made her want to laugh and cry all at the same time. Two lanes were closed on an ultra-busy street because palm trees were being planted in the median. Seriously? The last thing LA needed was more freaking palm trees. They needed open lanes of traffic!

A familiar, strange sensation swept through Jordan as she broke out in a cold sweat. She felt weak and shaky, her head spinning like a merry-go-round. Dread weighed her down as she gripped the steering wheel. Not now. Not here. *God, please don't let me see black spots.* The last thing she needed was to be in a wreck. Jordan pulled to the side of the road and took deep breaths in an attempt to slow her racing heart. She didn't have time for this. She had places to be, things to do. After a few minutes of sitting quietly, she was back on the road, thankful she hadn't fainted…this time.

Jordan pulled into the restaurant valet station thirty minutes late, glad to see Ralph was working. He was a nice kid, whom she trusted not to go hot-rodding in her black Jaguar. The car had been an extravagant birthday gift to herself, but she had to keep up appearances. She couldn't be seen driving around town in anything that cost less than forty grand.

Before getting out of the Jag, Jordan took a quick look in the rearview mirror. Not too bad considering she'd been up and going strong since five a.m. She ran fingers through thick chestnut hair and pinched her cheeks to add natural color. Doug frequently said she could pass for a runway model, which always made her chuckle. Granted, she was five foot eight with a killer body, heart-stopping hazel eyes, and an attractive face, but she'd never thought of herself as gorgeous and certainly wasn't confident enough to strut down a runway.

When Jordan entered the restaurant, Doug was seated and sipping red wine, which was clue number two that something was up, since he rarely drank. After a quick hug she took a seat, immediately wanting the scoop. "Spill it. What's up?"

"What makes you think something's up?"

Jordan raised an eyebrow. "Le Papillon? Wine? What gives, Dougie?"

"Can't we order first?" Doug studied the menu like it was the most engrossing thing ever.

Jordan drummed her fingers on the table and glared at him. He really was a beautiful man. A Caucasian mother and African American father had produced a mocha complexion and striking green eyes. Always impeccably dressed and with a body more buff than that of any personal trainer at Crunch Gym, he could nab any guy he wanted, and often did.

After several minutes Doug peeked over his menu. "Is that a new outfit? Ann Taylor?"

"Yes, and you're stalling."

"Fine," he said, putting down his menu. "I went over the books and even talked to the accountant, and we can't do it. We don't have the capital to open another office."

"Damn. Are you sure? We've been doing so well." Jordan frowned, sat back, and folded her arms across her chest. She dreamed of expanding SOS with an office in San Francisco, Dallas, then who knew where.

"I've crunched the numbers every which way, and we just can't swing it right now. Not in the foreseeable future either. Maybe you could ask your mom for the money?"

Jordan shook her head vigorously. "No way. I don't even know where she is these days. Last I heard it was Paris."

Jordan's mother was a travel photographer. When she was ten, her parents had divorced and Jordan's father had reared her. Even after she'd moved into her mom's New York condo after she left Monarch, she rarely saw the woman. She had, though, given Jordan a nice sum of money to start her own company. That was enough. She refused to ask her for anything more.

"What about borrowing the money from Bibi? Lord knows she's loaded." Doug winced, probably because he knew the reaction that idea would elicit. Bibi was Jordan's for-the-moment girlfriend.

"Hell, no. The last thing I need is to be indebted to her."

"Hey. I meant to tell you that lawyer called again. That's like the third time. He said it was urgent you call him back."

Jordan frowned. Why would a Monarch lawyer be calling her? She hadn't had contact with anyone since she left.

"Oh, God, don't look now, but Patty Parker is heading toward our table," Doug whispered.

"See? We should have gone to Frank's Deli. Stars never go there."

The click of Patty's stiletto heels echoed behind Jordan. "Why, if it isn't the SOS dream team."

"Patty, it's so good to see you again," Jordan lied.

Doug stood and pulled out a chair. "Won't you join us?"

"Aren't you a doll? I wish I could, but I'm with that big hunk-a-man over there." Patty pointed to a nervous-looking Bill Poser sitting at a table. "We're waiting for his parents." Patty smiled coyly. "We're announcing the news…of our engagement!" She squealed in decibels high enough for only a dog to hear. Amazingly, the wineglasses didn't shatter.

"Congratulations," they said in unison.

"Well, I have you two to thank since you introduced us. Listen, I have to get to the powder room, but you're both invited to the wedding. And I hope you'll be coming…together." Patty wiggled her eyebrows before sashaying away, leaving a heavy scent of Chanel No. 5 in the air.

Doug giggled. "She still thinks we're an item? I'm gayer than a picnic basket at the West Hollywood Park, and you're all but missing an *L* tattooed across your forehead."

"You should love that since you're in the closet." Jordan took a swig of Doug's wine.

"I'm not *in* the closet. But when you date actors who aren't out you have to be careful. Oh, and like you go around waving rainbow flags."

"I don't feel the need to advertise my sexual preference. If anyone asked, though, I'd tell them the truth. But no one asks. I think they're afraid of the answer."

"Half of Hollywood is in the closet. Don't ask, don't tell." Doug opened his menu and studied it. "Do you know what you want?"

The yellow butterfly frantically flapping its wings inside the acrylic centerpiece caught Jordan's eye. "Someone told me once that if you whisper a wish to a butterfly, it'll come true."

Doug furrowed his brow. "Butterfly wishes? Seriously?"

Jordan shrugged. "It's worth a try, don't you think?" She grabbed the container, closed her eyes, and said, "I wish that a big pile of money would drop down from the sky and land in my lap." She squinted one eye open and grinned when she saw Doug's horrified expression. "It's not like I really believe it'll work, but you can't blame a gal for trying."

❖

Sophie stared at the items on her kitchen table. Was she a little insane? She checked off the objects on her list: empty box, a white feather, vial of seawater, handful of sand, and a Bic lighter. The lighter was a sad replacement for a candle, but it was all she could find, so hopefully it wouldn't make a difference. She stuffed the items, which represented the four elements of air, water, earth, and fire, into the box. This just proved it. You could find anything on the Internet. Even a soul-mate spell.

Earlier that day she'd Googled "soul-mate love invocation" after reading her horoscope in the *Monarch Messenger*, as she did every morning. Written by Madame Butterfly, the resident psychic, it was always eerily accurate. Hers had read: *Unpleasant surprises have dominated your year, dear Pisces. The death of something or someone lurks heavy on your mind, but do not despair. With death comes a new beginning.*

The death referred to her girlfriend, Cindy, metaphorically speaking. Six months ago, Cindy had walked into their bedroom and said, "I'm leaving you. I've fallen in love with another woman and am moving to Seattle."

Sophie had been speechless. Taking two shaky steps backward, she'd plopped down on the nightstand, right on top of the rose-quartz crystal Cindy had given her for Valentine's Day. How apropos. Love was biting her in the ass—again. She'd gripped the sides of the table and watched her girlfriend of two years stuff her undies into a suitcase. Never trust a woman who wears G-strings. They weren't even comfortable, always riding up her ass. Sophie knew they hadn't been happy for a while. In fact, it'd been months since they'd had sex, but she'd thought they were just in a rut. You know, the infamous lesbian bed-death syndrome. She'd never expected that Cindy was having an affair.

Sophie grabbed the horoscope and read it again. *With death comes a new beginning.*

Well, if a new beginning was coming her way, she wanted to make darn sure the universe knew what she wanted. No more lying, cheating, G-string-wearing women. The Internet instructions suggested reciting the invocation under a full moon, and luckily, one was scheduled for tonight. Sophie grabbed the box from the kitchen table, along with a garden shovel, and headed into the living room.

"Hey, Mr. Limpet. I bet you think I'm nuts, don't you?" The electric-blue betta fish waved his fins rapidly when she tapped on the aquarium. "This will be our little secret, okay?" Sophie dropped two freeze-dried shrimp into the water, with Mr. Limpet jumping like a dolphin to retrieve the treat. "You be a good boy, and I'll be back in about an hour."

A full moon lit the forested path leading from Sophie's cabin to the eucalyptus grove. It was a beautiful night, surprisingly warm for November. This was the best time of the year. Thousands of monarch butterflies migrated along the Central California coast during October to January. It was also the busiest time, since Sophie ran the monarch butterfly sanctuary. Halfway down the trail, she stopped abruptly. Darn. She'd forgotten the printed soul-mate chant. The website had directed to recite the incantation exactly as written, but it was too late to turn back. Hopefully, she'd remember what it said.

As Sophie approached the forest, she inhaled the sweet scent of eucalyptus. This was quite possibly her favorite place on earth—amid trees, surrounded by monarchs, and with the sound of crashing waves in the distance. She walked to the largest tree in the center of the grove and looked up at hundreds of orange dots as monarchs huddled together. Her gaze roamed down the tree to a spot at the base of the trunk. BFFs 4Ever. That's what was carved under her and Jordan's initials. Sophie's heart clenched. What a joke.

She knelt under the tree and began digging a hole. Satisfied that it was deep enough, she placed the box of items in the dirt, covered it, and rolled a large boulder on top. She took a deep breath, closed her eyes, and contemplated what she wanted. Well, she knew what she didn't want, which was a lying girlfriend who would leave her brokenhearted. She wanted to find *the* one, her soul mate, if such a person existed. Sophie opened her eyes and held out her hands. Within seconds a butterfly landed in her palm. She gazed lovingly at the orange-and-black creature, admiring its beauty and endurance. It was amazing how these beings—with such delicate, paper-thin wings—migrated over two thousand miles each year.

Okay, now what was that chant? Sophie gazed at the moon, like it would help her remember. It had a cute rhyme. Something like love be strong...for she done me wrong...no, that was a country song...or maybe...oh, screw it...she'd make up her own.

Sophie gazed at the butterfly and whispered, "Flames of time erase mistakes...bring true love whatever it takes...uh...Be ye far or be ye near, I summon my soul mate to me here...um...by the power vested in the full moon and the Great Native American Spirit, my wish is granted...amen...that's all, folks...with liberty and justice for all... the end."

Sophie made the sign of the cross, though she had absolutely no idea why since she wasn't even Catholic. The monarch flapped its wings and flew into the tree, carrying the whispered wish with him. Sophie stood and looked at the full moon, semi-satisfied with the ceremony. Now she just had to have faith that her soul mate would appear.

CHAPTER TWO

Breaking Up Is Easy to Do

Not the French accent again. Bibi was born in Fresno, for Christ's sake. Ever since she'd played a Frenchwoman in an international instant-coffee commercial, the accent had stuck. And Jordan was fairly certain Bibi wasn't her given name, not that she'd ever admit it. They were sitting on the couch in Jordan's Beverly Hills condo with two cups of hot water and a box of assorted Leif's instant java on the coffee table. Bibi grabbed the box and studied her photo, tapping it a few times with a half-inch fuchsia fingernail.

"I was having a great hair day," Bibi said, doing a bad Brigitte Bardot impression. She ran her hands through luxurious sangria-colored locks. Actually, it was brown with red highlights, but Jordan wouldn't make that mistake again. Bibi's two-hundred-dollar-an-hour hairstylist called it sangria, and because she was the hair goddess of the universe, the description had stuck. Jordan was all for extravagances, but two hundred dollars for a haircut and color seemed excessive even to her. Bibi ripped open the box, squealed, and sucked on one of her fingers.

"Paper cuts are the worst," she whined. Yeah, the worst…except maybe for that Ebola thing. But then again, paper cuts involved bleeding and throbbing. Weren't those the symptoms of Ebola? "I don't know why you don't have a maid."

Jordan chuckled. "My place isn't big enough to warrant a maid. What would she do? Open boxes for me so I don't get paper cuts?" Guilt gripped Jordan when Bibi batted her big brown Bambi eyes. "I'm sorry. Let me see your finger."

She cradled Bibi's hand in her palm and looked at the injured member but couldn't see anything, so she leaned closer…and closer…

Was she looking at the right hand? She didn't see even a pinprick. Where did she keep her magnifying glass? "I don't see anything."

Bibi pulled her hand back and stared at Jordan indignantly. "I stopped the bleeding myself." She grabbed a packet of Café Viennese, poured it into one of the cups, and stirred vigorously.

At times like this Jordan wondered why she was dating Bibi. Okay, so she had beautiful sangria hair, perfect bone structure, and an even more perfect body. Granted, she'd had more than a few Botox sessions, but so had everyone else in Hollywood. She was a semi-talented, spoiled actress, not a great conversationalist, and they didn't have much in common aside from the fact that they were both discreet about their sexuality. In retrospect, maybe Bibi *was* the perfect match. Lord knows Jordan wasn't looking for anything serious. She never was.

Jordan stirred coffee grounds into her cup and tried not to groan. This instant crap sucked. "So where are you off to for the next commercial?"

Bibi had a sweet deal. She got an insane amount of money to travel the world filming ten-second commercial spots. All she had to do was sit on a mountain or at an outdoor café, sip coffee while wearing a low-cut blouse, and say—in a sexy growl—"Mmm, for instant gratification, I drink Leif's." Obviously, sex could sell anything, even a drink that tasted like insect repellent.

"Paris, maybe, but that's not important." Bibi put her cup down and turned to face Jordan. "I want to talk to you about something."

"Oh?" Jordan peered over her cup.

Bibi inhaled sharply, held her breath, and squealed, "Let's move in together!"

Jordan spewed French-vanilla mocha across the room. She couldn't have been more surprised if Bibi had just told her she'd been nominated for an Oscar. "What?!"

"I'm in love with you, ma chérie."

Jordan coughed, cleared her throat, and placed her cup on the table. "We've only been dating two months. You can't possibly be in love with me."

"But I am, and I know you feel it, too." Bibi grabbed Jordan's hands and clutched them tightly to her voluptuous chest.

"I'm not in love with you. I'm sorry." Jordan pried her hands out of Bibi's cleavage, bolted upright, and paced across the living room.

This was why she rarely dated. She could have spent the energy, emotion, and time on something important, like her company. Clearly, Jordan was missing the lesbian U-Haul gene. She'd never lived with a woman and didn't intend to do so. She was a loner and liked it that way. Even a normal lesbian, though—with all genes intact—would have thought Bibi moved too fast.

Jordan stopped and faced the coffee queen head-on. "I told you when we started dating that I'm not looking for anything serious. This isn't going to work."

"What are you saying? You're breaking up with me?" Bibi's false eyelashes blinked rapidly.

"We want different things. And do we really have that much in common? So, yeah, I think we should break it off." This was the part Jordan hated the most—the breakup, which she always seemed to instigate.

Bibi bolted off the couch. "I can't believe you're breaking up with *moi*! It should be the other way around."

"I'm sorry. Really." Actually, she wasn't sorry, but she didn't know what else to say.

"Fine!" Bibi grabbed her three-hundred-dollar Kenneth Cole purse. "You're a cold fish in bed anyway! You have no idea how to please a woman." *Ouch, where'd that come from?* "And for your information, people in relationships sleep over after having sex. They don't slip out at three a.m. You're not…normal!"

Jordan had spent most of her life feeling like a square peg in a round hole. She didn't need a reminder from an angry, overpaid actress.

"Good-bye, Jordan!" Bibi stomped to the front door—as much as one could stomp in seven-inch heels—and slammed it shut on her way out. Geez, what a drama queen.

Jordan stood stiffly and stared at the door. *Cold fish?* Bibi would have to zero in on her biggest insecurity. She'd never felt particularly comfortable with physical intimacy and had learned to fake orgasms better than a bored housewife could. Not that Jordan didn't enjoy sex, but the words "erotic" and "sensual" weren't in her vocabulary. She plopped down on the couch. Whatever. She was better off without Bibi anyway. In fact, she was better off without *any* woman. She'd have more time to spend on SOS, which is all that really mattered anyway. The single, celibate life was the way to go. Jordan took a sip of cold French-vanilla mocha and spat it back into her cup. She needed a Starbucks latte. That was what *normal* people drank.

Jordan grabbed her cell phone as it vibrated on the coffee table. "Hey, Doug."

"Guess who I got you an interview with. Go on, guess."

"I don't know how you could top Ophelia, but let's see…don't say TMZ because they try to twist everything I say into a controversy."

"Nope. It's with the hottest magazine in town. *LA Live!*"

"Whoa, seriously? Good job. When?"

"Friday. I've already told them we have a client-confidentiality agreement, so no personal questions. They want to ask about our process and what makes our match rate so successful."

"That's great."

"I thought you'd sound more excited."

"I am. Totally. It's just…well, I broke up with Bibi. Like literally two minutes ago."

"Good gosh, Jordan. How long did you date this one? It keeps getting shorter each time."

"She wanted to move in together! After only two months."

"I thought that's what you girls did. Isn't that in the lesbian handbook or something?"

"Well, not this girl. Plus, she said she was in love with me."

"Oh, having a gorgeous actress in love with you must suck," Doug said sarcastically. "I've known you almost ten years, and you haven't dated anyone longer than six months. You know what your problem is—"

"I know you took a semester of psychology in community college, but no more psychoanalysis, please." Jordan sighed loudly.

"You purposefully date women you don't even like. You know there's no chance of falling in love, so they're safe. What are you so afraid of?"

"I'm not afraid," Jordan said defensively. "Anyway, I'm swearing off women. SOS is my true love, and anything else just gets in the way."

"Maybe you just haven't met your soul mate yet. Maybe if you didn't date beautiful bimbos—"

"It's not that. I'm just not relationship material. It always ends in disaster. Listen, I gotta go. I'll talk to you later." Jordan disconnected before Dr. Freud could spout any more psychobabble.

Despite all her balking about relationships, Jordan did believe in soul mates, that one special person who feels like…home. She'd experienced that once in her life, with Sophie, but they were just teenagers. What'd they know about love?

❖

Sophie sat on her couch and eagerly tore into the UPS box on her coffee table. Most people got excited about receiving books or clothes in the mail, but not Sophie. What got her heart pumping were one hundred packets of *Asclepias eriocarpa* seeds, better known as woolly pod milkweed. Seventy-five seeds per packet distributed to students up and down the coast meant an increase in milkweed plants, which would hopefully make a dent in monarch conservation. The mass mailing would be time-consuming, but Sophie would do anything to save the butterflies. Without milkweed, they would die off. It was the sole food source for monarch caterpillars and what the butterflies used to lay their eggs. As it was, milkweed was being cut down to build parking lots, shopping malls, and condominiums, which infuriated Sophie something awful.

Her insides twisted into a Celtic knot concerning the uncertain fate of the monarch sanctuary. Frances, the elderly woman who owned the center and surrounding land, had passed away a month ago. She was completely hands-off, which made her the perfect boss. In fact, she'd only stepped foot in the place once, when it opened five years ago. Sophie was appreciative since she had free rein of the sanctuary, where she worked tirelessly to build a thriving milkweed field.

Surely the property would go to Charles, Frances's son, which wouldn't be a good thing. He was a stern bulldog of a man...and Jordan's father. Not that that mattered, but Sophie had had several uncomfortable interactions with him after Jordan disappeared. He'd responded to her many attempts to inquire how to reach Jordan in New York or what had happened with silent stares or slammed doors. No. Having Charles as her boss would not be pleasant. Or worse yet, he'd sell the land to a condo developer. Sophie's stomach soured. She'd never let that happen. Nor would the townspeople. Since the sanctuary had opened, the city of Monarch had embraced the butterfly theme with a passion, maybe going a little overboard at times.

Sophie looked up as someone walked through her front door, which was wide open. One of the many things she loved about Monarch was that you could safely leave your door open without fearing that anything more than a few butterflies or a squirrel would break in. Sophie bolted off the couch and wrapped her arms around Bertha. She was a short, plump woman in her mid-sixties, who gave the best hugs ever. Bertha's mission in life was to brew the best java in town in her coffee shop and look after Sophie. At twenty-nine, she was more than capable of taking care of herself, but it never hurt to have another mom, considering her biological one sucked. When Sophie was ten, her mom had landed in jail for a foiled bank-robbery attempt with her loser boyfriend and then completely disappeared after her release. Sophie had never known her father and had been raised by her aunt and uncle. They were wonderful caregivers, but she didn't feel like she had a real mom until she met Bertha.

"Hey, sweetie. What do you have going on here?" Bertha motioned to the packets piled on the coffee table.

"It's milkweed seeds. I'm doing a mass mailing to several schools in the area."

"Isn't it a little late to plant seeds? Shouldn't you do that in summer or spring?"

"These are *Asclepias eriocarpa*." Sophie smiled at Bertha's frown. "Woolly pod milkweed."

"Oh, yes. I like those. They have white flowers and fuzzy leaves."

"Exactly. These are native to California and can be planted any time of the year. Plus, they're drought-tolerant, which is good considering how little rain we've had lately."

"Well, you can count on me to help mail these out. I know Molly and Mabel would help, too."

"Thanks," Sophie said with a smile. She missed some things about living in a big city, but nothing could replace Monarch's family atmosphere. Not only did she have a replacement mom but also two substitute aunts in Molly and Mabel.

"So, have you heard who'll inherit the sanctuary and land?" Sophie asked. If anyone would know, it'd be Bertha. Her coffee shop was the hub of gossip.

"I haven't a clue. Seems like it'd be Charles, but if so, you'd know by now, I'd think. Maybe Frances didn't have a will and the state will take it over. I'm not sure how those things work."

That would be the best scenario. Sophie could work with a government agency to protect the land for butterfly conservation.

"Now, don't you worry," Bertha said when she undoubtedly saw the concern on Sophie's face. "We'll make sure nothing happens to the milkweed field and sanctuary."

Sophie forced a smile. "Let's get out of this mess, and I'll make us some tea."

"Do you have any coffee instead?" Bertha asked as she followed Sophie into the kitchen.

"You know I only drink your brew. Besides, I don't even own a coffeepot."

Bertha gasped and put a hand over her heart. "Well, I know what to give you for Christmas now. Speaking of which, I'm planning a big shake, rattle 'n' roll New Year's Eve party to commemorate the ten-year anniversary of the earthquake, so be sure to mark it on your calendar."

Sophie grunted to herself. She didn't like to think about that night. It wasn't Bertha's fault for bringing it up, though, since she didn't have a clue as to what had happened. Sophie hated how her body still reacted to the mere thought of Jordan. Her face flushed, her heart pounded, and her mouth had a metallic, sour taste. That was quite possibly the worst time of her life. Sophie had cried for months after Jordan disappeared. Eventually, though, the tears had turned to anger, especially after she'd reached out to her several years ago when hearing about her company in Beverly Hills, with no response whatsoever.

Sophie rose on her tiptoes, reached into the top cabinet, pulled out a box, and handed it to Bertha. "Cindy left this here. What do you think?"

Bertha perched reading glasses on the tip of her nose and studied the photo of an attractive woman sipping a cup of java. "Leif's international coffee. I've seen these commercials. This Frenchwoman does make it look tasty. Oh, wait, it's *instant*?" Bertha looked at Sophie in horror, like she'd suggested they drink cyanide.

"It's not half bad. Nothing compared to yours, of course. Let's give it a try." Sophie grabbed the box and opened it. "Do you want Café Vienna, Suisse Mocha, Caramel Macchiato—"

"Surprise me," Bertha said, sitting at the kitchen table. "Speaking of Cindy, have you heard from her?"

"God, no, and I hope I never do." Sophie leaned against the counter as two cups of water warmed in the microwave.

"It's been what? Six months since she left? Any prospects?"

Sophie shrugged and debated about whether to tell Bertha about her soul-mate ceremony. Bertha wouldn't be opposed to such things, but Sophie decided to keep it to herself. "I did sign up on a singles website but haven't met anyone yet."

"Uh, a website?" Bertha was many things, but up-to-date technologically wasn't one of them.

"The Internet. On the computer."

Bertha gasped and held her breath. "You know what you need!?"

"No, what?"

"You need a matchmaker! I saw it on the Ophelia show. Some bigwig Beverly Hills matchmaker was being interviewed. She could help you find a soul mate."

Sophie knew Bertha was talking about Jordan because she'd seen the interview as well. No matter how much she'd tried to turn it off, she couldn't take her eyes off Jordan. It was the first time she'd seen her in almost ten years, the first time she'd heard her voice again. Sophie had missed that voice. The way it cracked when Jordan got excited and how the cadence was quiet and smooth when she spoke about something that touched her heart. Jordan hadn't changed much over the years, except that she looked even more beautiful. In fact, she was pure perfection. Healthy chestnut curls cascaded around her flawless complexion, which glowed under the studio lights. When Jordan's hazel eyes had gazed into the camera, Sophie could have sworn she was peering directly into her soul. Seeing Jordan again had stirred up all sorts of emotions, which had kept Sophie awake half the night.

"You may not be able to get that swanky company to help you out," Bertha said. "But I bet there are matchmakers around here. You should look it up on that…er…website…thingie."

"That's something to consider." Sophie heaped instant coffee into the cups and stirred vigorously. She placed the drinks on the kitchen table and sat across from Bertha.

Bertha peered into the cup, sniffed it a few times, and said, "Well, here goes nothing." She took a sip and swallowed hard before coughing uncontrollably.

Sophie jumped up and patted her on the back. "Are you okay?"

"Oh, my." Bertha looked horrified.

"That bad, huh?"

"Worse." Bertha cleared her throat and pushed the cup aside. Sophie handed her a glass of water, which she gulped down. "You know, someone at the coffee shop told me that matchmaker went to school here, if you can believe that. A real-live celebrity from Monarch. Did you know her? She must be about your age."

"Mmm…I don't think so." Sophie hated lying, but the last person she wanted to talk about was Jordan.

CHAPTER THREE

The Jackpot

Jordan gazed out her fourth-story office window overlooking Rodeo Drive. When she and Doug were searching for office space, she'd wanted something in West LA or maybe even downtown, but considering more than half of their clients were actresses, it'd been a smart move. They could lunch at La Scala and commiserate over the lack of available straight men in Hollywood before walking around the corner to let SOS add romance to their lonely lives.

"Hey, boss." Doug strolled into her office. They were equal partners, but he had started calling her *boss* after the Ophelia interview, since she'd become somewhat of a celebrity.

"Is Tiffany in yet?" Jordan asked. Doug raised an eyebrow. "Seriously? She's late again?"

Tiffany was their receptionist, a twentysomething anorexic with a red streak in her hair and a famous boyfriend from the hottest boy band in town. Clients found her fun and amusing. Jordan thought she was lazy and irresponsible.

Jordan plopped into her chair. "Are we seriously not going to fire her? She's always late, she types with two fingers, and she dots her *i*'s with a heart. That's so not professional."

Doug chuckled. "Clients love her."

"She's a screw-up. Last week I caught her designing a new tattoo when she was supposed to be doing reports."

"I'll talk to her. So what's Tiffany's new tat gonna be?" Doug smirked.

"I'm not sure exactly. It looked like a guitar inside a heart, but it could've been a penis. It had her boyfriend's initials on it, so it could go either way."

"Too funny. Okay, so I came in here to tell you who our newest client is." Doug paused for dramatic effect. "Sabrina Cooke!"

"*The* Sabrina Cooke? Impressive. She just won a Golden Globe."

"And she's even more beautiful in person. And obviously s.i.n.g.l.e."

"Why are you looking at me that way? First, I'm swearing off women, and second, we have a strict policy about messing around with clients. And it's a good thing ninety percent of them are women, or else you'd be in big trouble."

"You're no fun." Doug sat on the corner of Jordan's desk. "So how are you doing? After the Bibi thing?"

Jordan shrugged and leaned back in her chair. "Fine. I dunno. She…uh…she said I wasn't…normal."

Doug bolted upright, his fists clenched. "Do you want me to beat her up for you?"

Jordan wasn't sure if he was kidding, but from his stance he looked serious. He really was a good friend. Her big, gay protector.

"That's sweet, but I'm pretty sure she could take you. She said I was a cold fish in bed and that it wasn't normal I don't sleep over. You know, after sex."

"You don't stay all night? Cuddle and all that girly stuff?"

"No. It feels too…too…"

"Too much like a relationship?"

"Precisely. That's weird, isn't it? God, maybe I am abnormal." Jordan rubbed her face with her hands.

"You need to do what's right for you. I only hound you about dating because I want you to be happy. And who am I to say you'd be happier with someone than alone?"

"Thanks. And I am happy. Really." She wasn't the type to dot her *i*'s with little hearts or use smiley emoticons, but that didn't mean she wasn't happy. Right?

Jordan put Bibi and relationships out of her mind and got back to work, until the phone started ringing…and ringing…and ringing. Finally, it stopped, which either meant the person had hung up or Tiffany had finally showed up. A few seconds later, the office door swung open.

"You have a call." Tiffany leaned against the door frame and put a hand on her hip. She was wearing a tight black leather outfit more suited for the Roxy Theater than a professional office.

"Who is it?"

"Someone named Fifi or Mimi or something."

Jordan raised an eyebrow. "Could it be Bibi?" Tiffany responded with a blank stare. "If it's Bibi, tell her I'm in a meeting." Jordan continued typing but then stopped when Tiffany didn't make a move.

"You're in a meeting?" Tiffany opened her mouth wide and glanced around the office.

Jordan bit her lower lip. "Just tell her I'm unavailable and take a message."

"So...like...you want me to like...*lie*?"

Oh my God, the girl who bragged about getting arrested for doing it with her boyfriend in the O *of the Hollywood sign suddenly has morals?*

"Like tell her I like can't talk right now. And that's not like a lie."

Tiffany sighed, spun around on her heels, and slammed the door shut. Jordan took a deep breath and shook her head. That girl had to go. She looked at her computer screen and was about to start typing when the phone rang again...and again...and again.

"Tiffany?" No response. "Oh, good God." Jordan picked up the receiver. "SOS, how may I help you?"

"I need to speak to Ms. Jordana Lee." The man sounded serious, professional, and had a voice she didn't recognize. Plus, he'd used her birth name, which was weird.

"This is she."

"Ms. Lee, I've been trying to reach you for weeks. I'm so glad to finally speak with you. My name is Michael Simms, and I'm an estate-planning attorney in Monarch." Jordan's body tensed. Just the mention of the town made her anxious. "I'm afraid I have some bad news. I'm sorry to inform you that your grandmother passed away a month ago. Your father said no one in the family has been in contact with you for quite some time. Otherwise I would have let a family member break the news to you."

Jordan was silent for several seconds. "Mr...Simms, is it? My father is correct. I'm no longer a part of the family. Thank you for your call, but it wasn't necessary."

"Ms. Lee, wait. Don't hang up. Your grandmother had a will. She left you the Monarch Butterfly Sanctuary."

"My grandmother left me a...what? There must be some mistake. I seriously doubt she'd leave me anything."

"She was very adamant about gifting the center to you. So, if possible, I'd suggest you come to Monar—"

"Hold up, Mr. Simms. I wouldn't be caught dead in Monarch." Jordan winced at the poor choice of words, considering the circumstances. "The last thing I need is a butterfly building...or whatever it is. Just give it to my father. I'm sure he's the one my grandmother meant to leave it to."

"Before you make any rash decisions, you need to know some things. The property consists of the sanctuary, which employs a lepidopterist, and sits on two acres of land. It's prime real estate, which is located on a bluff overlooking the ocean. It's quite valuable."

Valuable? He had her attention. "Two acres? Is that a lot? And how valuable are we talking here?"

"An acre is approximately the size of a football field. The sanctuary and land have been appraised at two million dollars."

Jordan coughed loudly into the phone. "Excuse me. Did you say two million? Would it seriously sell for that?" If this were a cartoon, her eyes would be dollar signs.

"Ms. Frances received several offers from Kelstrom. They own the chain of Grand View Hotels and Spas."

"Why didn't she sell it?"

"Your grandmother said it belonged to you."

Okay, this was weird. Jordan had been excommunicated from the family, and she and her grandmother hadn't been close. In fact, she scared the crap out of Jordan. The woman's glare could cut a tin can better than any Ginsu knife ever could.

"So, I'll just sell it. I don't need land in Monarch or a butterfly... thing," Jordan said, thinking aloud. "But are you sure there isn't some mistake?"

"It's all in the will. I think you should come to Monarch, Ms.—"

"No! I'm not going to Monarch. Can't you just handle everything for me?" Jordan looked up as Doug walked into her office. She motioned for him to sit.

"I didn't want to do this over the phone, but there's a stipulation in the will."

Aha. She knew there had to be a catch. "What kind of stipulation?"

"Everything is in the letter from your grandmother. I had hoped to give it to you in person so we could discuss it."

"A letter? What does it say? Can't you overnight it to me?"

Doug mouthed a silent "What's up?" which prompted Jordan to hold up a finger.

"I suppose I could. Should I send it to your office address?"

"Yes, please. But can't you tell me what it says?"

"I'm afraid not. Your grandmother had strict instructions. Only you should open it. I suggest you give me a call after you've read the letter. My contact information will be included in the package. I'm sorry for your loss."

"Thanks. I'll call you soon." Jordan hung up and stared at Doug.

"What was that about? Jordan? Are you okay?"

"Remember when I wished that a big pile of money would drop in my lap?"

"Yeah, so?"

"I think we just hit the jackpot."

❖

Jordan looked at her watch for the fortieth time, wondering what time UPS arrived. For once she was glad Tiffany was late. She didn't want her turning the package away or opening it herself. Doug walked past Jordan's office and stuck his head in the door.

"Nothing yet?" he asked.

"No, and the suspense is killing me." Jordan chewed the nail of her little finger. "What kind of stipulation could there be? We're probably getting our hopes up for nothing. My grandmother wouldn't leave me something valuable."

They both looked toward the front door as it opened. Doug glanced back at Jordan. "I guess we're about to find out."

After signing for the package, Jordan stared at the envelope on her desk.

"Do you want some privacy?" Doug asked.

"No, have a seat. You're more family than my grandmother ever was."

She ripped open the package and briefly glanced at the letter from Mr. Simms before seeing a white envelope that read, TO BE OPENED BY JORDANA LEE AFTER THE DEATH OF FRANCES LEE. She glanced at Doug and took a deep breath. The letter was dated a few weeks before her death.

Dearest Jordana,

If you're reading this, then I am dead. And so be it. This life has dragged on too long as it is. My only regret at being six feet under is that I missed seeing the look on your father's face upon learning that you are the sole heir of my property.

I never was one for sentimental drivel, so I'll get to the point. Until a few months ago I didn't know why you disappeared that New Year's Eve. For all I knew you'd been killed in the earthquake, since Charles never spoke your name again. It wasn't until Rebecca blabbed everything after one too many mai tais at lunch that I knew what had happened.

Whatever the circumstances, we're family and should stick together, which is a lesson I must have failed to impart to my son. The three of us are all that's left, and now that I'm gone it's just you and your father. Since I couldn't bring you two together while I was alive, perhaps I can do so from the grave.

By now you know that you own two acres of land as well as the monarch butterfly sanctuary. You're free to do with it as you wish under three stipulations:

1. *You must live in Monarch and work at the sanctuary for two months.*
2. *Your two-month residence must commence within one week from receipt of this letter.*
3. *You must meet with your father twice within those two months and try to make reasonable amends.*

Michael Simms, my attorney and trusted friend, will periodically check on you to make sure you are adhering to these three items. If you fail to comply, the land and sanctuary will be given to the State of California.

Sincerely,

Frances Lee

Jordan stared at the letter and read the three items several more times. She looked at Doug, took a deep breath, and closed her eyes. "Fuck."

"Wow," Doug said. "Why does she want you to move to Monarch for two months?"

"'Cause she knows I wouldn't step foot in that town unless forced to do so. I guess she thinks if I'm there, then my dad and I will have a better chance of reconciling. But why does she want me to work at the sanctuary if she doesn't care if I sell it?"

"What are you going to do?"

"I have no idea."

Doug grabbed the letter and scanned it. "Who's Rebecca?"

"My stepmother, which is a joke since she's only ten years older than me." Jordan jumped out her chair and paced back and forth. "Okay, let's break this down. We have the property. It is, in fact, ours."

"We?"

Jordan stopped and looked at Doug. "Yes, we. You're more than just my business partner. You're like a brother to me. I wouldn't have survived the last ten years without you."

Doug smiled as his eyes misted. "I feel the same way."

"Okay, enough of this sentimental drivel," Jordan said with a grin. "So, the land is ours to sell if I move to Monarch for two months, work at the sanctuary, and make contact with my father twice."

A wave of nausea washed over Jordan as her heart pounded. She plopped into the chair and put her head between her legs, the room suddenly spinning. She heard a muffled voice, maybe Doug asking if she was okay. Black spots clouded her vision right before she encountered total darkness. The next thing Jordan remembered was feeling puffs of air on her face. As she blinked her eyes open, Doug was frantically fanning her with a file folder as she lay flat on her back. She tried to sit up, but he held her down.

"Don't get up just yet. You fainted." Doug sounded frightened, even though he knew it wasn't anything serious. They'd been through this many times.

She closed her eyes and laid her arm over her forehead. "How long was I out?"

"Just a few minutes. You're lucky you didn't knock your head on the desk."

After she lay still for a couple of minutes, Doug helped her stand upright and sit in the chair. Jordan rolled her eyes and felt heat rise to her cheeks. The fainting episodes were embarrassing and always made her feel like such a wimp. It was the only thing in her life she couldn't control.

"These spells seem to be happening more often," Doug said.

"I'm fine. So, where was I?" Jordan asked, wanting to change the subject.

"You were talking about seeing your dad again. Ten years is a long time. Maybe he's had a change of heart."

"You don't know my father. He isn't the forgiving type. God, I can't go back to Monarch. I just can't. And live there for two months?"

"I'll support whatever decision you make. We've made a success of SOS without your grandmother's money. We don't need it."

Jordan gaped at Doug. "It's two million dollars. Do you have any idea what we could do with that much money?"

"Don't remind me." Doug sighed and gazed out the window as Jordan rested her forehead on the desk.

"You never did tell me what happened with your father. All you said was that he threw you out so you went to live with your mom in New York."

Jordan groaned loudly. She lifted her head and looked at Doug, who was staring directly at her. It wasn't that Jordan didn't want Doug to know the whole sordid story. If anyone would understand it'd be him. She just didn't want to relive the memory. The compassionate look on his face, though, urged her on.

"It was a few days before New Year's Eve," she said. "I was a senior in high school, about to graduate in four months and excited about going to college. I came home one day to a very angry father and stepmother sitting at the kitchen table…with my journals."

"They read your diaries?"

"Oh yeah. All five years' worth."

"So what'd you write?"

"They were mostly filled with feelings and fantasies about my best friend."

"Who I take was a girl?"

"Most definitely. I had a huge crush on her." Jordan ran her fingers through her hair. "Well, actually, it was more than that. She was my first love." *And last.*

"Seriously? *You* were in love?" Doug pointed at Jordan in disbelief.

"Geez, you make me sound like some sort of robot incapable of having a human emotion."

"Sorry. I'm just surprised you never mentioned her before. So, your dad freaked over you being gay? Is that when he threw you out?"

"He said I was a disgrace to the family, that he never wanted to see me again, and that I was going to hell. He tracked my mom down in New York and shipped me to her a few days later. I got my GED, took a few business classes at community college, and that's where you and I met." Jordan's stomach clenched and a hard lump formed in her throat. *Damn. This shouldn't still be so hard.*

"Bastard. How could he do that to his own child?"

"I wasn't a boy."

"What?"

"My father always wanted a son. He made that fact clear from the moment I was born. He'd have badgered my mom into getting pregnant again, but she was too wrapped up in her career. I always wondered if he would have reacted the same way if I were his son."

"I'm so sorry. What did that girl say when you left?"

"I couldn't tell her about any of that," Jordan said, shaking her head. "She was totally straight, dating the star quarterback, no less. I was ashamed, and more than anything, I didn't want her to hate me. So I took the coward's way out and disappeared without an explanation. I didn't think she'd understand."

"So she didn't know you were in love with her? And you haven't seen or talked to her in all these years?"

"Nope. Not a word. Aside from the fact that I thought she'd hate me, I couldn't be friends with her anymore. It'd become too painful to be in love and not be able to act on my feelings. Unrequited love sucks." Jordan's shoulders slumped as she inhaled a shaky breath. She felt empty inside, like a hollowed-out log, as memories of that time flooded back.

"Huh. I've never heard you use the L-word before. That's so sad. Are you still in love with her?"

Jordan shot her gaze upward to Doug. "No! Of course not." That came out a little stronger than Jordan had intended, so she softened her tone. "We were teenagers. And like I said, it was a long time ago. No one could stay in love with someone for a decade when they're not even together."

They couldn't, right? Admittedly, Jordan had compared every woman she'd dated to Sophie, and no one came remotely close to the Disney Princess, but she couldn't still be in love with her.

"Is that part of the reason you don't want to go back? You're afraid of running into her again?"

"I doubt she lives in Monarch. She's probably married with two point five kids and living in Utah. That's where we were planning to go to college."

"If she is there, would you tell her the truth? I mean, would you tell her you were in love with her?"

Jordan shook her head. "No. What would be the point? It'd just make us both uncomfortable."

"What was her name?"

"Sophie. Her name was Sophie."

CHAPTER FOUR

Welcome to Monarch

"Would you slow down a sec? You're running around like a mad-woman," Doug said.

"If I slow down I might change my mind." Jordan frantically stuffed clothes into a suitcase as Doug lounged on her bed. She rummaged through a box of sweaters, wondering if she'd need them. December along the central coast was usually cool, so she grabbed a few.

Was she seriously going to go to Monarch for two months? See her father again and maybe Sophie? Jordan was torn between desperately wanting to see her and praying that she wouldn't. She didn't revel in the idea of dredging up her painful first love. It'd taken years for the gut-wrenching agony of unrequited love and separation to fade. Sometimes, late at night, she wondered if the loss had actually dissipated or if she'd just slapped a Band-Aid on it in the form of work and fleeting relationships. She certainly didn't want to rip that sucker off to reveal a fresh wound.

It's two million dollars. It's two million dollars. That became her mantra, the only thing that kept her moving. With that much money, she and Doug could accomplish everything they wanted with SOS. She could do this. She *had* to do this. No way in hell would she pass up that much money.

"Are you going to be okay here by yourself?" Jordan stopped packing long enough to study Doug. "I won't be back until February, and I don't know how much help I'll be working remotely. A leopard-person works at the sanctuary. I'll just sit back and let him do all the work, but I'm sure I'll have to do something."

"I'll be fine. We might have to cut back on clients, but it'll be worth it in the long run." Doug shifted on the bed and suddenly looked uncomfortable. "What if you go and decide not to sell?"

"Are you kidding?" Jordan laughed. "I don't want anything to do with Monarch. And I could care less about a butterfly sanctuary. Mr. Simms, that lawyer, has already set up a meeting with a real-estate agent. I'm selling. You can count on that."

Doug sighed in relief. "That's what I thought, but it's good to hear you say it."

Jordan looked at her cell phone as it rang. "Ugh. It's Bibi. She's been calling me at the office. Let me grab this and get rid of her."

Jordan walked into the living room for some privacy as she answered the phone. "Bibi, why are you calling me? We broke up."

"Mon chéri, finally we speak. I've missed you so. And correction. You broke up with moi. I did not break up with you. Can't we talk about this?"

"Look, I'm sorry the way things ended. I'm sure I could have handled it better. Maybe we can get together and talk when I get back." Jordan didn't intend to ever see Bibi again. By the time she got back from Monarch, she'd have surely moved on and forgotten they'd even dated.

"Where are you going?"

"It's a long story, but I'll be away for a couple of months."

"Months?! Why so long? Where will you be?"

"I have to go to Monarch. It's something to do with my family."

"I didn't even know you had family. Where is this Monarch?"

"It's along the central coast. I really need to get on the road. I'll call you when I get back."

"Maybe I could come with you. I have a month off before we start shooting another commercial."

"No! It's a ridiculously small town with no decent restaurants. You'd be bored stiff. I really have to go now. Good-bye, Bibi." Jordan disconnected and wondered if maybe she'd just made a huge mistake by telling Bibi where she'd be.

❖

It took Jordan longer than necessary to drive the two hundred and fifty miles from Los Angeles to Monarch. She stopped at least ten times along the way in an attempt to delay the inevitable. Her stomach clenched as the mileage signs progressed…twenty…ten…five. At the two-mile marker, she gripped the steering wheel, dread weighing her down like a brick in the pit of her stomach.

Are you happy now, Grandma? Your little bribe worked.

"That's new," Jordan said to herself as she passed a massive WELCOME TO MONARCH butterfly-shaped sign at the city limits. In fact, as she drove through town she didn't recognize much. All the stores on Main Street were painted in orange and black and had been renamed, such as the Butterfly Beauty Parlor, Caterpillar Car Wash, and Monarch Messenger.

"They're a little butterfly obsessed, wouldn't you say?" she mumbled.

Actually, Jordan liked that everything looked so different. This way, maybe she could pretend she wasn't in Monarch after all. As she cruised through town, she grumbled obscenities under her breath. She'd forgotten how small the place was. How would she survive two months without the Beverly Center, Saks, and dining at the Ivy? She might go insane from boredom. This was bound to be the longest two months of her life.

It's two million dollars…it's two million dollars…

Jordan slammed on her brakes to avoid rear-ending a blue Ford. Could this person be driving any slower!? She glared at the I ♥ BUTTERFLIES bumper sticker on the car going fifteen miles per hour in a thirty-five zone. From what she could tell, the driver didn't need medical attention, so she sat on her horn, hoping that'd wake the woman up. It was like no one had ever honked in town before. Pedestrians stopped on the sidewalk, drivers screeched to a halt, and a police officer sprang into action like a bank robbery had just occurred. Jordan hunkered down in the seat and floored it, passing the slowpoke when the coast was clear.

Now where the hell were the condos? Jordan had leased a furnished place along the beach and close to the butterfly sanctuary. Google Maps was no help since she couldn't get a cell signal, so she drove down Main Street several times and took a few side streets, which all resulted in dead ends. How could she be lost in such a small town where she'd spent most of her teen years? It wasn't her fault, though, since everything looked different and there weren't even any street signs.

Jordan hated asking for directions, but she had no choice. Under the ruse of needing coffee, she claimed a parking spot on Main Street, right in front of Madame Butterfly's Psychic Parlor. Great. They didn't have street signs, but they had a psychic. Seagulls squawked overhead, and the musty scent of salt and fish filled the air when Jordan opened her car door. She stood on the sidewalk and frowned at her cell phone. Still no bars. A flicker of light from the supernatural house of horrors caught her eye. Out of curiosity, she inched closer and peeked into the window. The place looked completely dark except for dozens of flaming candles. Talk about a fire hazard. Jordan squinted, half expecting to see a séance in progress, but all she spotted was a huge crystal ball and wild-looking tapestry hanging on the walls. The place gave her the creeps, so she backed away and walked down the sidewalk holding her phone high in an attempt to catch a signal. As Jordan turned the corner, past the Butterfly Bookstore, she ran smack-dab into a short, busty woman who was as solid as a rock. Jordan stumbled backward and stared into piercing ebony eyes accentuated by thick black eyeliner and false eyelashes an inch long. The woman had bloodred hair piled at least a foot high and wore a flowing indigo gown with gold swirls. She looked like a carnival fortune-teller.

"What's your rush, my dear?" The fortune-teller spoke in a thick Russian accent.

"I'm sorry. I was trying to get cell service." Jordan held up her phone.

"Are you new in town?"

"Sorta. Is your cell working? Is there bad reception here or something?"

"I wouldn't know. I don't have a cellular device. Where are you visiting from?"

Jordan had no intention of telling a stranger her life story. "The south. Well, I should get going. Sorry about running into you."

The fortune-teller matched Jordan's stride as she followed her down the street. "You seem familiar. Do I know you?"

Jordan peered at the woman sideways. "I'm pretty sure we've never met."

"What brings you to town?"

"I'm sorry, but I'm really late." Jordan quickened her pace, relieved that the woman's short, stubby legs couldn't keep up. When Jordan was in the clear, she glanced back and saw the tail end of the sparkly indigo gown disappear into the psychic parlor.

Butterfly wind chimes clanged as Jordan opened the door to Bertha's Coffee Shop. A woman behind the counter looked up, inhaled sharply, and placed both hands on her cheeks. The smattering of patrons turned toward the door, all eyes on Jordan.

Do they know I'm the honker? Is that what this is about?

"Oh, my heavens, a real, live celebrity in my restaurant!" The woman flew out from behind the counter and was inches away from Jordan within seconds. She'd never seen anyone move so fast. Jordan took a step back, the woman clearly invading her personal space.

"Welcome to Monarch, Ms…Ms…well now, I never forget a face, but I'm not so good with names." The woman's bright, shining face looked up at her questioningly. She had plump, rosy cheeks, sparkly blue eyes, and wore a ruffled flower apron. She reminded Jordan of Mrs. Claus.

"Jordan. Jordan Lee."

"That's it! I'm Bertha." The woman inched forward and studied Jordan closely. "Why, you're prettier than a mess of fried catfish. I saw you on *Ophelia*. I can't believe you're actually standing right here in my coffee shop." The woman talked fast and couldn't have been more excited if she'd just won the lottery.

"So tell me," Bertha whispered. "Is it true what the tabloids say? Is Ophelia having an affair with her bodyguard?"

"Well…um…I wouldn't know," Jordan said.

"Oh my, listen to me. I'm just going on and on. Come on in and have a seat."

Jordan followed the woman to the counter and sat on a barstool. She saw a flash of something blue out the corner of both eyes. Looking to the left and then the right, she wondered if she wasn't seeing double. Two identical women sat on either side of her. They looked to be in their sixties, both wearing blue dresses and with blue tinted hair, which was probably the result of a dye job gone wrong. Their spindly legs dangled from the barstools, which made Jordan wonder if they were even five feet tall. They reminded her of elves. Had she stumbled upon the North Pole?

"This is Molly and Mabel," Bertha said. "They own the used bookstore just down the street."

"Let me guess. You two are sisters."

Both women giggled and covered their mouths with a hand. "Identical twins," one of them said.

"What can I get you?" Bertha asked.

"Just coffee. Black is fine."

"I have some cherry pie. Baked it myself. How about a slice?"

"No thanks," Jordan said.

"Are you really a celebrity?" blue-haired woman number one asked.

"Don't you remember we saw her on *Ophelia*?" blue-haired woman number two said.

"I can't even remember what I had for breakfast, much less what was on TV. Are you an actress?"

"No. I own Soul Mate Outreach Solutions in Beverly Hills."

"Beverly Hills, ooh la la," both women said in unison.

"Ms. Lee is a matchmaker to the *stars*," Bertha said. "How long will you be in town?"

"Please call me Jordan. And I should be here for a few months."

"Oh, how wonderful! I know you work with celebrities, but I have a friend who could really use your expertise. I was just telling her about you the other day."

"Well, if I have time I'd be happy to help her out." Jordan looked at her cell phone. Still no bars.

"Did you come for the Monarch Festival?" one of the twins asked.

"Not exactly." Jordan glanced around, hoping this was an Internet café. No such luck.

"Now, now, girls. Let's not hound Ms. Lee." Bertha leaned across the bar and whispered, "But really, though, what brings you to Monarch?"

Jordan smirked. These women were cute. Nosy, but cute in an old-fashioned, Mayberry sort of way.

"Actually, you might be able to help me. Do you know where Moonshadow Beach Drive is? I'm looking for the condominiums." Jordan took a sip of quite possibly the best coffee she'd ever tasted, but then again, after that instant crap, anything would be good.

"Of course, Ms...I mean Jordan." Bertha smiled and grabbed a napkin and pen. "Go up yonder to Main Street and take a left in front of the Larva Laundry." Bertha sketched out a map as she spoke. "Then follow that road until you get to the first stop sign, then take another left. That'll be Moonshadow Beach Drive. Go straight, along the ocean, and the condominiums will be on your right. You can't miss 'em."

"This is great. Thank you." Jordan stuffed the napkin into her bag.

"It'd be wonderful if you came to the festival." Bertha produced a butterfly-shaped flyer like a skilled magician. These people did love their butterflies. They must have a cut-out factory somewhere.

Jordan read the flyer to herself: HELP SAVE THE MONARCHS. BUTTERFLY DAZE FESTIVAL—SATURDAY DECEMBER 8TH.

"Yeah, great. I'll be sure and do that." Scary how convincingly she could lie. Sometimes she even fooled herself.

❖

Sophie didn't normally work at the sanctuary on Sundays, but she suspected the monarch eggs would hatch and didn't want to miss that. A video camera perched on a tripod in front of two cups, which each held a tiny white egg. She'd spent the afternoon working on her computer and checking the eggs, which sat on her desk. Upon the fifteenth examination, both pearls vibrated at the same time, and Sophie's heart pounded in excitement. They'd be hatching any minute now.

Sophie clicked on the video camera and zoomed in on the two eggs. She'd captured the birth of one caterpillar before, but never two at the same time. Satisfied that everything was in frame and focused, she took her eyes off of the video screen. She wanted to see the process live, not through a camera lens.

Both eggs cracked open at the same time as two miniscule black heads poked out from their respective shells. It took several seconds for each caterpillar to begin wiggling through the hole. Sophie was amazed how they were mirroring each other every step of the way. They were both struggling so hard to free themselves that she resisted the urge to help, reminding herself that nature didn't need assistance. After several minutes, the tiny caterpillars hatched at the same time. Sophie looked around, elated and wishing someone were here to share the excitement. At times like this, being single felt lonely.

She watched as the white creatures moved their black heads back and forth and stretched their segmented bodies. Their first meal would be the eggshell, loaded with protein. Later, though, Sophie would put milkweed in the cups, and they'd munch on that as they grew. She watched the birth over and over, each time even more amazing than the last. She loved every stage of the monarch lifecycle but found something special about the birth. It was new life, a new beginning. It gave her hope.

After locking up the sanctuary for the night, Sophie headed to the beach. The ocean was almost as awesome as butterflies. It didn't get much better than walking barefoot along the shore with a vibrant red-and-orange sunset as a backdrop. Sophie edged closer to the water's edge but jumped back as it washed toward her. She stopped suddenly and bent down to pick something up, then shook her head and stuffed a Snickers wrapper into her pocket until she found a trash can. Litter was one of her pet peeves. *Tourists*. Of course she wasn't sure it came from a tourist, but she couldn't believe a Monarch resident would be so disrespectful.

Continuing her stroll, Sophie sneered when she passed the condominiums. Just another symbol of how money-hungry corporations were destroying nature. Several years ago, trees had been uprooted and the land leveled to build the monstrosity complex, which was a little too close to the sanctuary for her taste. Thank goodness Frances had refused to sell; otherwise, the condos could be sitting where the sanctuary now stood. Sophie shuddered at the thought of the eucalyptus trees and milkweed field being destroyed. Hopefully Charles, or whoever inherited the land, would protect it as Frances had.

Sophie flinched as something flew toward her and landed on her shoulder. It was a super-cute ladybug with an oval red body and black polka dots. According to Madame Butterfly, ladybugs were a sign of good luck and signaled that wishes would be fulfilled. After a few minutes, the ladybug flew away. Sophie gazed at it in flight until she saw a breathtaking sight. A beautiful woman leaned against the railing of her deck, looking out into the ocean. She was wearing a flowing ivory robe that billowed in the breeze as she ran her hand through wind-tousled hair. Sophie's chest tightened. Something about the woman reminded her of Jordan.

Sophie would never forget the first time she saw Jordan in Mrs. Conner's fifth-grade math class. Jordan and her father had just moved to town after her parents' divorce. It couldn't have been easy being the new kid in school, which was something Sophie never had to experience since she was born in Monarch. With downcast eyes and drooping shoulders, Jordan had stood by the teacher's desk. When her gaze lifted to hunt for an empty chair, their eyes had locked. Everything else in the room disappeared except for Jordan. Sophie had felt like Jordan reached into her chest and squeezed her heart. She was breathtakingly beautiful, with blazing hazel eyes, rosy lips, and the face of an angel. Hands down, she was the prettiest girl Sophie had ever seen.

For weeks after that, Sophie had tried to befriend Jordan, attempting to strike up a conversation in the hall or at lunch, but Jordan had been shy and distant. It wasn't until Sophie's mom landed in jail that they'd become friends. Sophie was sitting under the large eucalyptus tree, crying, when Jordan approached. Sophie had tensed when Jordan sat beside her, expecting an onslaught of questions about her jailbird mom.

Instead, though, Jordan asked, "Do you like butterflies, Princess?"

"Why'd you call me Princess?" Sophie asked through a sob. Jordan responded with a shrug. "Yes. I love them."

"I'd never seen a monarch until I moved here. Do you know anything about them?"

They spent the next hour with Sophie teaching Jordan everything she knew about butterflies. Jordan sat attentively and asked endless questions. Sophie was shocked, and felt a little guilty, to realize she actually had a smile on her face. It was the first time she hadn't thought about her mom in days.

The sound of a seagull squawking overhead brought Sophie back to the present. Tears sprang to her eyes, whether because of memories of her mother…or Jordan, she wasn't sure.

CHAPTER FIVE

Butterflies in the Mist

Jordan woke early after only a few hours' sleep. The condo was nice, but the fact that she was actually in Monarch had kept her awake half the night. And thinking she'd seen Sophie walking on the beach hadn't helped. Crazy. Would every blonde in Monarch remind her of Sophie?

Leaning against the kitchen counter, Jordan sipped a cup of strong coffee and grabbed her cell phone as it vibrated. "Hey, Doug."

"Hey. Just making sure you made it safely. How are you doing?"

"Honestly? I don't know how I'll survive for two months. Monarch is the size of Mayberry and filled with Aunt Bea types."

"You went to school there. Weren't you prepared for that?"

"Yeah, well, I forgot how small it is, and it's changed quite a bit. It looks like a butterfly threw up in the town square."

"Ew, that's gross. And I don't think butterflies throw up. Are you okay? I'm going to worry about you."

"I'm fine. Just take care of things there."

"Don't worry about anything here, and call me if you need to talk. I'll check in with you soon."

"Thanks. Talk to you later."

Jordan grabbed a pen and circled the date, December third, on a butterfly calendar hanging on the wall. That was the start of her two-month jail sentence. She'd mark off the days with an X until her release on February third, when she'd not only be free, but rich as well.

Since Jordan wasn't scheduled to meet Mr. Simms at the sanctuary until that afternoon, she headed for the beach. If she had to be stuck someplace for two months, at least she had a luxury condo by the ocean. Jordan couldn't even remember the last time she'd been to the beach, even though she lived only thirty minutes away. She spent all her time at work, entertaining clients, or schmoozing at parties, which didn't leave much time for nature activities.

Jordan walked to the water's edge and stretched her arms high overhead, breathing in the scent of damp salt and seaweed. The waves were gentle, almost like being at a lake on a windy day. It was a foggy, gray morning with the sun straining to break through an overcast sky. Jordan zipped her fleece jacket as a cool wind blew her way. Aside from one lone figure barely visible through the haze, she was completely alone. The central coast was different from LA, fewer crowds and cleaner beaches—except maybe for this one.

As Jordan kicked a plastic bottle down the shoreline, her thoughts drifted to her father. Ever since she could remember, she'd craved his acceptance and praise, which she never received. He kept his emotions buried deep within and was never one to be affectionate. She couldn't remember a time when he hugged her or said "I love you." He'd always been distant and strict, which seemed to get worse after the divorce. Even so, Jordan had loved her father. In many ways, he was her sole parent since her mother traveled so much. Maybe he'd changed over the years and regretted his actions. Jordan wasn't sure, though, if she wanted to reconcile with him. Hurt and bitterness still burned in her soul. How could he have been cruel enough to disown her?

As she strolled down the beach, a trail that climbed to the bluff overlooking the ocean caught her eye. She was certain it led to the eucalyptus grove that housed her and Sophie's tree. Jordan's stomach clenched. Seeing the tree again, which was the last place she and Sophie were together, would be painful. Jordan wasn't sure if she was ready to walk down memory lane, but before she knew it, she was heading for the trail.

Once she reached the top of the bluff, she stopped to catch her breath. It was a steep climb, and flip-flops weren't the best hiking attire. After resting for a bit, she headed down the path into the forest. As the early morning fog rolled in, a thick, gray mist hung in the trees, which made the place seem eerie in a *Friday the 13th* horror-movie sort of way. She felt like Little Red Riding Hood, half expecting the big bad wolf, or something worse, to jump from behind a tree. The farther she walked, the hazier things became. Maybe this wasn't such a great idea. She considered turning back, but her desire to see the tree again urged her on. When Jordan turned a corner in the trail, she stopped. Several yards ahead stood the largest eucalyptus tree in the forest. Her heart ached as thoughts of that New Year's Eve emerged. She didn't want to relive that night.

Jordan sneezed twice as the scent of eucalyptus tickled her nose. Great. She was allergic to nature. She took a few steps forward before she heard a rustle in the bushes and stopped abruptly. Her heart raced. It could be anything, a squirrel, deer…Bigfoot. Jordan broke out in a cold sweat, hoping she wouldn't faint. The sound was growing louder, the monster edging closer. Was this where she'd die? In the middle of nowhere? They'd never find her body out here. As much as she wanted to run, she was too petrified to move. Jordan flinched as something stepped into the clearing, and her heart leapt into her throat.

It wasn't Bigfoot. It was Sophie. She was sure of it.

Jordan ducked behind a tree so as not to been seen. Sophie extended her arms in a wide circle, stretching them high overhead before ending with both palms together at her chest. A ray of sunlight peeked through the haze and shined a beam of light, which illuminated her in golden hues. She looked stunning. Jordan's heart fluttered, amazed she was actually a few yards away from Sophie. So many times she'd thought she'd seen Sophie walking down Rodeo Drive or at a party. Her heart would skip a beat and the world would stop spinning, until she realized it wasn't her. But this wasn't a mirage. It was the real, live Sophie.

Jordan crept closer to get a better look. Sophie's eyes popped open when Jordan stepped on a thorn and released a muffled cry, which sounded like a wounded animal. Damn flip-flops. She froze, hidden behind the tree, as Sophie glanced around the forest. Seemingly deciding she wasn't in danger, Sophie approached the eucalyptus tree. She walked around the circumference three times while looking up into the branches. When she stopped and held out her hand, two butterflies landed in her palm. She smiled at the winged creatures, which were inches away from her nose. Jordan could see Sophie's lips moving but couldn't make out what she was saying. After a couple of minutes the butterflies flew back into the tree, carrying the whispered messages with them. Sophie walked around the trunk of the tree and repeated the process, except this time only one butterfly landed in her palm.

As Jordan tiptoed around the tree to get a better view she ran into an overhanging branch. Her nose itched, tickled, and she sneezed hard three times in a row.

"Who's there?" Sophie asked.

Jordan wanted to run, but she'd surely be seen. Instead, she stepped from behind the tree and sneezed twice more. Sophie put one hand over her mouth and the other over her heart. They stared at each other for several long, tense moments.

"I'm…I'm sorry if I scared you," Jordan finally said.

Sophie gaped at Jordan like she'd just risen from the dead.

"Are you okay? It's me. Jordan."

"Jordan?" Sophie spoke in barely a whisper.

"Yeah." Jordan stuck trembling hands into her pockets.

"Oh my God. What…I mean…I just…I never expected…"

Jordan took several steps forward, on shaky limbs. "I didn't mean to scare you. Apparently, I'm allergic to eucalyptus trees." When Sophie didn't respond, she said, "I didn't use to be. I guess living in the city will do that to a person. I'm allergic to cats, too. I learned that one the hard way. And maybe strawberries." *God, why am I listing all my allergies like I'm in a doctor's office?* Jordan willed herself to shut up and waited for Sophie to respond, which seemed to take an eternity.

"What are you doing here?" Sophie's voice quivered.

"It's kind of complicated." Jordan gazed at Sophie. She still looked like a Disney Princess, with shoulder-length blond hair and the biggest, most beautiful blue eyes Jordan had ever seen. "Do you live here? In Monarch?"

"Yes."

"Ah. I didn't know."

Sophie visibly stiffened. "How could you? You've been gone almost ten years. What are you doing here?" Sophie put her hands on her hips, the shock apparently wearing off, as evidenced by her sharp tone.

"I'm here for some family business."

"Your father said you don't keep in touch with family."

A sickening dread washed over Jordan. It was quite possible her father had told Sophie about all the romantic, erotic feelings she'd written in her diary.

"I don't."

"So, why are you back after all this time?"

"It's a long story." Actually, it wasn't a long story, but Jordan's modus operandi was to be evasive. Doug said she'd have made an excellent FBI agent, being so secretive, but Jordan preferred to think of herself as careful. It sounded less inhospitable.

Sophie cocked her head and raised an eyebrow, silently urging her on.

"My grandmother passed away, and it seems she left me some property."

Sophie's jaw dropped and her mouth opened wide. "*You* own the butterfly sanctuary?"

"Crazy, huh? I figured I'd be the last person on earth my grandmother would leave it to. It's around here somewhere. Do you know where?"

"I should. I've been running the place since it opened five years ago."

Jordan pointed at Sophie. "*You're* the leopard—"

"Lepidopterist."

"Yeah, that. Wow, I had no idea."

They were silent for several moments as the news sank in.

"Sophie—"

"So I guess I'll see you later? At the sanctuary."

"I'll be there this afternoon. I think—"

Sophie turned and bolted down the trail. Jordan watched as she disappeared into the forest. She felt nauseous. The last person she expected to see was Sophie, and least of all at their tree. Fearing her knees would buckle, she walked to the eucalyptus and plopped down with her back against the trunk. She closed her eyes and rested her head against the smooth bark.

She shouldn't feel weak. Her heart shouldn't ache. She shouldn't want to cry. And most of all, it shouldn't feel like no time had passed since they were last together.

Remembering their initials engraved in the tree, Jordan opened her eyes and ran her fingertips over the SOS...over and over again. Why did Sophie have to live in Monarch? And why did she have to run the sanctuary? Well, Jordan would gladly help her find another job and give her the best reference possible. Surely Sophie would understand why she had to sell the place. It was a whopping two million dollars, for Christ's sake. Who wouldn't understand *that*?

❖

Sophie's heart hammered as she ran out of the forest to the bluff overlooking the ocean. When she was out of sight and far enough away from Jordan, she took a deep breath. For years, Sophie had dreamt of the moment she might actually see her again. She had hoped and prayed this day would come. So why wasn't she happy? Why hadn't she run into her arms? Because she was angry. Damn angry. Best friends didn't disappear without a trace, ignore phone messages, and show up out of the blue ten years later.

Jordan was the last person Sophie had ever expected to abandon her. It had hurt when Cindy left, but Jordan's leaving had been ten times worse. Maybe because she'd loved Jordan ten times more. Sophie had never been as close to anyone as she had Jordan. She shared her deepest thoughts, secrets, and feelings…well, all except one. Jordan didn't have a clue as to how Sophie had felt about her, that she pretended it was Jordan holding her close as she danced with her prom date, and that she wanted to die when Jordan left. She didn't know any of that because Sophie had barely been able to admit it to herself at the time. Falling in love with a girl wasn't something she'd planned or even wanted. In fact, it wasn't until Sophie was crying in her aunt's arms after the earthquake that she'd realized how much she loved Jordan, and by then it was too late. She was gone.

Sophie wiped away an angry tear. This still shouldn't hurt so much.

Three dolphins jumping in the distance caught Sophie's eye. They were a reminder to be lighthearted, playful. She took a deep breath and willed the anger to subside, without much success. She knew negative energy was bad for her aura, and who needed that?

Don't give away your power. Jordan can't hurt you again if you don't let her. Focus on the future of the sanctuary. The butterflies are all that matter.

CHAPTER SIX

Got Milkweed?

Jordan sat under the eucalyptus tree probably longer than she should have. When she finally got back to the condo, she took a quick shower, since she wanted to arrive at the sanctuary before Mr. Simms did. After scarfing down a sandwich, she grabbed the directions and headed out the door. Even though the sanctuary was only a mile from the condo, Jordan drove, not wanting to get lost on the intertwining hiking trails. As the building came into view, her heart pounded. She was nervous about seeing Sophie again.

The sanctuary sat on the outskirts of the forest and looked strikingly small from the outside. Large, shady oak trees and a field of weeds, which Jordan was pleased to see, surrounded it. A hotel would fit nicely there, and minimal trees would have to be destroyed. Unfortunately, the sanctuary would be torn down, but if it was as shabby on the inside as it was on the outside, no one should put up too much of a fuss. She hoped.

When Jordan entered, she noticed how crowded and disorganized the place was. Books were stacked to the ceiling, equipment was strewn about, butterfly nets were everywhere, and unpacked boxes took up most of the floor space. When she gazed at Sophie, her stomach fluttered. She was sitting at a desk staring intently at a computer screen while slightly biting her lower lip. Big blue eyes peered out of wire-framed glasses that made her look intelligent, in a sexy-librarian sort of way. Yellow had always been her color, and still was, since the shirt she wore complemented her complexion perfectly. She looked cute enough to squeeze, like a stuffed animal you wanted to cuddle with all night.

Jordan zigzagged around boxes and stood in front of the desk. "Hi."

Sophie nodded once without taking her eyes off the computer

screen. Jordan couldn't blame her for the cold shoulder. Ironic that she'd been evasive when she left so Sophie wouldn't hate her, but that's exactly what had happened anyway. If Jordan could break through Sophie's icy exterior, maybe they could be friends again. After all, Jordan's life had never felt complete without Sophie.

"I'm sure it's a shock to see me again," Jordan said.

Sophie looked at Jordan and raised an eyebrow. "You could say that."

"I missed you."

Sophie's eyes narrowed. "Don't even go there. You disappeared without any explanation. I had no way of reaching you. You left me alone in the forest after a major earthquake. Don't you dare say you missed me."

They both turned toward the door when a man entered. Business suit. Briefcase. Bald. Serious expression. He must be the lawyer. The guy had bad timing, or maybe good, considering where the conversation was heading.

"Are you Ms. Jordana Lee? I'm Mr. Simms." The man raised his spindly legs to step over a box and held out his hand.

Jordan could have sworn she heard Sophie giggle at the use of her given name, which she knew Jordan despised.

"Please, call me Jordan. It's nice to meet you." Jordan grasped his thin, clammy hand. "Do you know Zophia Opal Sanders?" Jordan glanced at Sophie, who had a slight grin. Maybe the ice was melting?

"Zophia? I thought you were—"

"Zophia is my birth name, but I go by Sophie, as Jordana very well knows." Sophie pushed up her sleeves like she was getting ready for a fistfight. Okay, maybe the ice wasn't melting after all.

"I see," Mr. Simms said. "Well, I thought perhaps I could show you around the property, Ms. Lee."

"Yes. That'd be great."

Sophie pushed her chair back and stood up. "Care if I join you? I know this land better than anyone."

Jordan glared at Mr. Simms in an attempt to telepathically relay that she'd rather Sophie not tag along. She was afraid he might reveal her plans to sell, and Jordan would rather break the news slowly, over time.

"If Ms. Lee isn't opposed…" Mr. Simms looked questioningly at Jordan.

Great. A lawyer who couldn't read minds. She had no choice but to agree. As Sophie saved her computer document, Jordan whisked Mr. Simms into a corner to let him know she wanted to keep her plans for the sanctuary a secret.

Once outside, they walked down a path through the large open field, which was where Jordan suspected the hotel would be built. Mr. Simms stopped midway down the trail, with overgrown weeds on either side of them.

"As you know, you have two acres of land." Mr. Simms pointed at the horizon. "The property starts here and includes this field, the sanctuary, and well into the forest, which I'll show you next."

"Why wasn't something ever done with this land instead of letting weeds and wildflowers take it over?" Jordan asked.

Sophie shot her an incredulous glare. "This is milkweed."

"Okay. So?"

"God, Jordan, you lived here eight years. Didn't you learn anything? Monarch butterflies lay their eggs on milkweed, and it's the only food source for caterpillars."

"Wait a second. I know for a fact that caterpillars eat leaves, tree sap, pollen, and even fruit."

"We're talking about *monarchs*." Sophie sighed loudly.

"How do you know all this?"

"I have a master's in wildlife biology from Utah State University with a specialty in conservation." Sophie paused and looked Jordan directly in the eye. "If you had stuck around you'd know that."

And there it was.

Mr. Simms looked nervously from Jordan to Sophie. He was a little skittish to be a lawyer. Jordan didn't think he'd fare well in an LA courtroom.

"Um…shall we continue the tour?" He cleared his throat and walked down the trail, not seeming to care if they followed.

They walked in silence as Mr. Simms led them through the forest and right next to their eucalyptus tree. It was a chilly afternoon, so most of the monarchs were huddled on the branches, with a few rebels flying around. Jordan couldn't help but smile when one landed on top of Sophie's head.

"The butterflies seem to know you. One just landed on your head," Mr. Simms said.

Sophie froze as she looked at Jordan. Was she remembering the last time they were together? From the sadness in her eyes, Jordan was certain she was.

"So this is all part of my grandmother's property? Including this tree?" Jordan asked.

"Yes. It includes the majority of the grove. You now own two acres of quite valuable land."

Sophie's head jerked toward Jordan, the sorrow in her eyes replaced with apprehension.

"I see," Jordan said, like she was hearing that for the first time. She walked around the tree, Sophie's eyes following her every move.

"Well, if you don't have any other questions I need to head back to the office. I'll check up on you every few days, as discussed in the stipulations."

"Yes. Thank you for your time," Jordan said.

Mr. Simms trotted down the trail, leaving Jordan and Sophie alone in the forest.

"What stipulations? What did he mean?" When Sophie held out her hand, the butterfly on top of her head flew down and rested in her palm.

"How do you do that? I've never once had a butterfly land anywhere on me."

"Jordan?" The unmistakable look on Sophie's face said she wanted an answer…and now.

She had no reason not to open up to Sophie about her grandmother's will so she told her everything. Well, almost everything. She left the part out about selling the land.

Sophie crept closer to Jordan, the butterfly still resting in her palm. "I don't understand. Why does your grandmother want you to work at the sanctuary?"

"Now, that I don't know."

Sophie peered at Jordan. "Why does she want you to reconcile with your father? Did you have an argument?"

"You could say that. He threw me out."

"Is that why you left? Because of your father?" Compassionate eyes gazed at Jordan. God, she'd missed the Disney Princess.

"Yeah. We had a disagreement."

Jordan braced for the onslaught of questions about what the argument was about and why she'd disappeared, but that never came. Instead, Sophie asked an even more difficult question.

"What are your plans for the sanctuary? What will you do when the two months are up?"

So much for trying to keep a secret. Jordan couldn't lie to Sophie.

"Well, I did get an offer from a hotel chain. And get this, it's for two million dollars."

"Oh my God, Jordan. You can't sell! They would destroy the milkweed field and chop down the trees." The shrill tone of Sophie's voice caused the butterfly in her palm to fly into the tree.

"Did you hear me when I said it's for—"

"I don't care how much it is. Eucalyptus trees used to be where the condos are right now. The monarchs are dying off. We have to stop this." Sophie's face turned bright red, and her eyes were practically popping out of her head.

"Look, I understand where you're coming from, but I don't think it's my responsibility to save the butterflies, and I'd be crazy not to take this offer. It's a boatload of money, which I need more than a butterfly sanctuary. I'd use it to expand my company, which is everything to me."

"Well, this"—Sophie motioned around the forest—"this is everything to me. I won't allow you to sell."

"*You* won't allow me to sell? The last I heard, my grandmother left the property to me, not you."

"You would actually harm innocent creatures!?"

"God, Sophie, you make me sound like a serial killer. It's butterflies, for Christ's sake. This isn't the only eucalyptus grove around."

"I'll fight you every step of the way. I won't let the sanctuary be destroyed." Sophie shook her head in disgust and stormed away.

Jordan clenched her jaw. Sophie had some nerve. She was an employee, not an owner. Jordan wasn't about to let anyone stand in her way of selling the land, least of all Sophie.

CHAPTER SEVEN

Shake On It

Jordan wasn't driving her Jaguar; it was driving her. She had no idea how she ended up on Forest Lane, but there she was, right in front of her father's house. At least she thought it was still his place. Jordan parked across the street and hunkered down in the seat. The house looked smaller than she remembered, even though it was one of the largest in Monarch. It was a two-story white house with a wide porch that wrapped around. The lawn and bushes were expertly manicured, and a silver Lexus sat in the driveway. When the front door opened, Jordan slipped farther into her seat. It was Rebecca, her dad's wife. She'd recognize that bleached blonde anywhere. Rebecca stopped in the doorway and yelled something into the house. A few moments later, a long-haired boy came out, throwing his hands up in the air. Rebecca yanked the headphones out of his ears and screamed something that was almost audible. The kid stomped to the car with Rebecca following in ridiculously high heels and an oversized gold bag draped on her shoulder. Jordan watched as they sped away.

Wow, that was quite possibly her half brother. Her dad and Rebecca had married when Jordan was fifteen, and considering Rebecca was only twenty-five at the time, they could have had a kid after they threw her out. He looked about seven years old. Sadness washed over Jordan. Her father finally had the son he'd always wanted. She'd been replaced.

When Jordan arrived at the sanctuary, she parked next to Sophie's Jeep and gazed at her reflection in the rearview mirror. She looked sleepy but not too bad, considering it was a God-awful eight a.m. Sophie had said she usually got in at seven, and even though Jordan was the boss, she didn't want to look like a slacker.

Popping open the glove compartment, she rummaged for a tube

of red lipstick. She snapped off the cap, smeared the tip over her lips, and looked in the mirror to check out the results. *I look like a tired hooker.* Frantically, she searched for a napkin, map, anything she could use to wipe some of the stuff off. Mentally, she thanked Bertha when she found the directions to the condo she'd written on a napkin. Jordan blotted her lips and combed fingers through her hair. She wasn't sure why she bothered to fix herself. It wasn't like Sophie cared how she looked.

When Jordan entered the sanctuary, Sophie was standing behind a long table spreading seeds on a wet paper towel, which was rolled and placed inside a plastic bag.

"What's that?" Jordan asked.

"*Asclepias cordifolia.*"

"Excuse me?"

"Heartleaf milkweed seeds." Sophie wrote the date on the bag and stuck it in a small refrigerator.

"I'm assuming that's not a snack for later?"

Sophie glared at Jordan, expressionless, and continued rolling seeds in paper towels.

"Why do you put them in the fridge?"

"They have to be refrigerated for ten to twelve weeks. Before we plant the seeds, we soak them in warm water for twenty-four hours." Sophie continued working as she spoke, avoiding eye contact.

Jordan walked to a side table stacked with packets of seeds, mailing labels, envelopes, and flyers.

"What's all this for?" Jordan asked.

"That's *Asclepias eriocarpa.* Woolly pod milkweed seeds."

"Are you going to roll them like a joint, too?" Sophie shot her a nasty glare. Obviously, seeds were nothing to joke about. "I'm bugging you, aren't I?"

"I'm sorry. I don't mean to be rude. I'm just not used to company." Sophie looked at Jordan, her eyes quickly moving up and down her body.

"And I'm probably the last person you ever expected to see here."

Sophie visibly tensed. "Well, you *are* the boss, so I guess I should give you a tour." Sophie stepped from behind the table and stood by Jordan. She looked adorable in faded jeans, hiking boots, and a fitted purple T-shirt. Jordan caught a whiff of the sweet scent of yellow buttercup roses. *Geez, she even smells like a Disney Princess.*

"This is for a mass mailing to schools up and down the coast,"

Sophie said as she motioned to the items. "The flyer encourages kids to plant milkweed. Like I said before, without it the monarchs would die off, which is exactly what's happening with companies destroying milkweed fields to build condos, malls, and hotels." Sophie peered directly at Jordan. "That's why you can't sell the land."

"Can't? You're forbidding me?" Jordan suddenly felt five years old and resisted the urge to stomp her feet. "We're talking about a lot of money. Don't get me wrong. It's not that I'm greedy—"

"Oh?" Sophie raised an eyebrow. "I saw the car you drive. It must have cost you at least fifty grand."

"Now you're just being judgmental. I've worked tirelessly to build my company from scratch. If I can afford to buy a few luxuries, then so be it." Jordan gritted her teeth.

"Well, I've worked tirelessly to save the butterflies."

"What makes you think that's more important than my company?"

Sophie laughed. Not a nice ha-ha laugh, but one of those you-must-be-kidding laughs. "You're seriously comparing nature conservation to a company in a high-rise on Rodeo Drive?!"

How'd she know we're on Rodeo Drive? "We're not in a high-rise. We're on the fourth floor, Ms. Smarty-Pants!" Jordan inwardly groaned. She couldn't come up with a better comeback than smarty-pants?

"You're incorrigible! Money is more important to you than wildlife." Passion burned in Sophie's eyes. Even though she was being close-minded and difficult, Jordan couldn't help but be a little turned on by angry Sophie. She looked downright sexy all flush-faced and chest-heaving. Jordan blinked a few times and averted her eyes. It was easier to think clearly when she wasn't looking directly at sexy Sophie.

"I'll have you know I make a donation every year to the California National Wildlife Association, and I volunteer at the Los Angeles Zoo. You don't know anything about me. You haven't even seen me in ten years."

"And whose fault is that?" Sophie crossed her arms and tapped her foot wildly.

Jordan paused, took a deep breath, and let it out slowly. "Look, we're getting nowhere here. Like it or not, you're stuck with me for two months. It's going to be hell for both of us if we don't reach some sort of agreement."

Sophie leered at Jordan, her jaw muscles visibly tensing. After a few moments, she pursed her lips and stared at the ceiling long enough for Jordan to glance upward to see what she was observing. Finally, Sophie looked at Jordan and said, "I know it's not my place to order you around."

"Really? Because you could've fooled me."

Sophie clenched her fists and looked like she was about to deck Jordan, but then obviously changed her mind. Instead, she stared at the space above Jordan's head as though to avoid eye contact. "Can you find it in your heart to do me one favor?"

Jordan cocked her head. "Maybe. What is it?"

"Promise me you won't sell before February. That's all I ask. Just give me two months to show you how important my work here is. Please?"

In a matter of seconds, angry Sophie had morphed into someone who looked terribly vulnerable and afraid. Her body relaxed, her expression softened, and her beautiful blue eyes were practically pleading. Jordan had to struggle not to wrap Sophie in her arms. Maybe it wouldn't kill her to wait two months. She'd be rich soon enough.

"All right," she said. "But in return you have to promise to spare me any more save-the-butterfly speeches. And no more dictating what I can do with my property. Do we have a deal?"

Jordan extended her hand to Sophie, who stared at it for several seconds, seemingly mulling over the proposition. Finally, she nodded and slipped her hand into Jordan's. It was the first time they'd touched since seeing each other again. Jordan loved the feel of Sophie's hand, so soft and delicate. No wonder butterflies landed in her palm. When their eyes met, Jordan's heart pounded. She was well aware that several seconds had passed and neither was letting go. They had long since stopped shaking and were now basically just holding hands, which was fine with Jordan. She could have stood there all day. When Sophie's eyes dropped to their clasped hands, she abruptly pulled back like she'd touched a snapping turtle.

Sophie glanced at Jordan before averting her eyes to the floor. "So, uh…I believe I was giving you a tour." Sophie walked to a shelf that held two clear containers.

Jordan followed and peered into the cups. "Are those caterpillars? They're so tiny. Why are they white?"

"They hatched a couple of days ago. They'll grow fast and change colors."

"Are they alive? They aren't moving." Jordan poked one of the cups as Sophie slapped her hand away.

"Don't touch!…Please. They shouldn't be moved. Yes, they're alive. In two weeks they'll evolve from larva to chrysalis."

"What to what?"

"Larva is the caterpillar stage, and chrysalis is when they form a cocoon. What's so special about these two is that they were born at exactly the same time."

"Like twins," Jordan said.

"Yeah. Exactly." Sophie's eyes twinkled as a slow smile crept across her lips. Jordan hadn't realized until that moment how much she'd missed that smile. "I filmed their birth. Would you like to watch it? I can play it on my computer."

"Sure, why not?" Watching the birth of anything wasn't on the top of Jordan's bucket list, but considering it was caterpillars, it couldn't have been too much of a bloody mess.

Jordan sat at the desk as Sophie clicked through hundreds of video files. Finding one entitled "twin birth," she pressed play and stood behind Jordan as they watched. Even Jordan had to admit it was an amazing sight. She couldn't believe how those long caterpillars were crammed into that tiny egg. It took them at least five minutes to wiggle out. Once they did, it was pretty cute when they elongated their bodies and twisted their heads around like they were checking out their new home. And, best of all, there wasn't one drop of blood in sight.

"That was incredible," Jordan said when the video ended.

"Did you really think so?" There was that beautiful smile again.

"Totally. I just wish I could have seen it in person, Soph." Jordan wasn't sure if it was the use of her shortened name, but Sophie's smile dropped and her expression hardened. She turned off the computer, walked in front of the desk, and crossed her arms over her chest.

"Why didn't you have contact with me? We were best friends. How could you leave so abruptly and stay away for ten years?" Sophie's voice was strained and she looked near tears.

Jordan wanted to puke. She knew this conversation would happen sooner or later, but she'd hoped it'd be later. "I'm so, so sorry. I was young and stupid. I felt hurt and abandoned by my father. I wanted to get away from everything."

"From me, too? I don't understand."

I was so in love with you I couldn't see straight. I thought you'd be disgusted. I couldn't bear the thought of you hating me. And I couldn't be near you one more moment without kissing you. You weren't just a friend to me.

But Jordan didn't say any of that. She couldn't.

"I didn't mean to hurt you, Sophie. And then so much time passed that I didn't think you'd ever want to hear from me again."

"But I contacted you several times a few years ago, and you never responded."

Jordan frowned. "What? Where?"

"At your office. When I found out about your company, I called and left several messages with your receptionist."

"Tiffany," Jordan whispered and closed her eyes. "Tiffany is the most inept receptionist in the universe. I never received your messages. I would have called you back."

Sophie paused, as though considering the validity of the information. "I never would have done that to you. Never." She spun around and walked out the sanctuary.

Jordan's heart ached. She hated that she'd hurt Sophie, and it was obviously a hurt that still lingered even after all these years.

CHAPTER EIGHT

Blind Date

They didn't make napkins like they used to. Sophie had easily torn three into shreds within five minutes. She glanced around Bertha's Coffee Shop from her booth, searching for a place to discard the pile of shavings. She didn't want her Internet date to know how nervous she was. Gathering a handful of tattered napkins, she briefly thought about stuffing them in her bra. Kill two birds with one stone. Get rid of the evidence while enhancing her assets, but that would be deceiving, and Sophie was all about honesty. Especially after Cindy.

Sophie tensed as the front-door wind chimes jingled. She clutched the napkin tight in her fist, letting her eyes dart to the entering figure. Phew, it was just Molly and Mabel. They were probably here for lunch or, more likely, to check out Sophie's blind date. Why she'd picked Bertha's she'd never know. She loved the townspeople, but they were nosy as hell. Molly gave Sophie two thumbs up from the counter, as Bertha beamed behind her. Sophie wished she could be as confident as they were. Having a blind date was the last thing she wanted to do, but she had to at least take the first step in meeting someone if she wanted to find her soul mate.

Sophie looked at her watch. Ten minutes late. Well, she'd cut the woman some slack. She was driving from Tallon, which was forty miles away. Sophie had offered to drive there, but the woman had insisted on meeting in Monarch, which immediately raised suspicions. Did she not want to be seen in her own town? Did she have a girlfriend or was she a curious straight woman? Red flag number one.

Sophie held her breath as the door opened. It wasn't her date. It was Jordan. She slipped low into the booth, not wanting to be seen. She'd told Jordan she was working offsite, whatever that meant. Actually, she was shell-shocked about seeing her again and wanted a day to get her head on straight. Jordan walked to the counter and sat on a barstool beside the twins. Sophie let her gaze travel down Jordan's body. She wore a white button-up shirt tucked into well-worn jeans, which hung just below the waist and had strategically placed rips in the right thigh, showing hints of creamy skin. They were the kind of tattered jeans found in an expensive shop on Rodeo Drive as opposed to a Monarch thrift store. The woman could pull off casual and classy all in one blow.

As Jordan and Bertha chatted, Molly crossed her fingers and shook both hands in the air. Sophie had a sneaking suspicion they were talking about her. She hunkered down farther in the seat. It'd be just like them to point her out. Instead, Bertha handed Jordan a bag, and she was out the door without even a glance, Sophie surprisingly disappointed to see her go.

"Excuse me, are you Sophie?" A woman standing beside the booth looked vaguely like her date's photo, except a much older version, by at least twenty years. Had she posted her junior high school picture? Red flag number two.

"Yes. Are you…" Sophie blanked. What was the woman's name? It started with a C and was sorta long.

"Candace. But my friends call me Candy."

Wait…wasn't her last name Kane? Candy Kane? Seriously? Sophie stood and held out her hand, not realizing she still clutched the shredded napkin in her fist, which she shoved into her pocket.

"It's nice to meet you, Candace." Sophie refused to call her Candy.

"Sorry I'm late," Candace said, as they both slid into the booth. "Traffic was really backed up."

Really? Traffic from Tallon to Monarch was never backed up.

"No problem. Have you eaten? Bertha makes the best Italian subs around."

"Actually, just coffee for me."

Sophie motioned to Bertha, who was standing beside their booth in record time with a pad and pen.

"What can I get for you two gals?" Bertha asked cheerfully.

"Just two coffees, thanks," Sophie said.

"Coming right up." Bertha winked at Sophie. Was that supposed to mean she approved of her date? Obviously, she didn't know the woman already had two strikes against her.

"So, Candace—" A hand in midair interrupted.

"Candy. All my friends call me Candy."

"So…uh…what did you say you do for a living?"

"I'm a landscaper. Most of my clients are individuals, but I do have some businesses as well."

"Thanks, Bertha," Sophie said, as two steaming cups were placed on the table.

"I love being in nature and getting my hands dirty," Candace said. "There's no way I could be cooped up in an office all day."

Sophie could relate. She liked nothing better than being in the eucalyptus grove with the butterflies. Maybe Candace wasn't so bad after all. And she did have gorgeous green eyes.

"I just have to say, you are one beautiful woman, Sophie."

"Oh, thank you. That's very sweet of you." Yes, Candace had potential. "If we're giving out compliments, you have the most striking eyes I've ever seen."

Candace leaned across the table and whispered, "Can I let you in on a little secret?"

"What's that?" Sophie leaned closer, matching her whisper. She flinched as Candace poked herself in the eye, pinched out a contact lens, and balanced it on the tip of her finger.

"Chroma contacts."

"Oh, my. Chroma what?" Sophie drew her head back. Candace looked freakish with one brown eye and one green.

"Colored contact lenses. They change your eye color. Actually, I figured you wore them, too. Your eyes are so blue. Is that your natural color?"

"Of course!" How insulting. She'd never be that deceiving.

Red flag number three. Good-bye, Candy Kane.

❖

Jordan really needed to learn how to cook. But then again, it was a great excuse to get an Italian sub at Bertha's. It was possibly the best sandwich she'd ever eaten. The crisp bread was fried in butter and olive oil and filled with grilled onions, salami, prosciutto, melted provolone cheese, and various spices she couldn't identify.

"Ms. Lee…I mean, Jordan, it's so nice to see you again." Bertha wiped her hands on a butterfly-print apron.

"You as well. I'm here to pick up my order."

"That'll be ready in two shakes of a butterfly's wings."

Jordan wasn't sure if that meant soon or if it'd be a while. She sat on a barstool and nodded to Molly and Mabel, who were seated beside her.

"Go on. Ask her," Molly said as she nudged Mabel.

Jordan looked back and forth between the twins. "Ask me what?"

"Well, I'm the Monarch festival president and…well…we wondered if you'd be the festival's guest of honor."

Molly swiveled on her stool to face Jordan. "It's this Saturday. It would be such an honor to have a celebrity there."

Think fast. Say something to get out of this butterfly soiree. "I…uh…I appreciate the invitation, ladies. Really. But I'm hardly a celebrity, and I have some family business to attend to so I'm not sure I'll have time."

"You are so a celebrity. You've been on *Ophelia*," Mabel said. "You wouldn't have to do much. Just ride in the parade, judge the Tiny Tot King and Queen Pageant, and maybe call out a few numbers during butterfly bingo."

Bertha nodded vigorously. "And it's for a good cause. We'll be raising money for the sanctuary. Well, actually, *your* sanctuary now."

Jordan could have cared less about raising money for a building she was about to destroy.

"Have you met Sophie yet?" Molly asked.

Before Jordan could respond, Bertha leaned across the bar and whispered, "Don't look now, but she's sitting in a booth in the corner waiting for a blind date." Instinctively, Jordan started to turn her head. "No! Don't look. She'd kill us for pointing her out."

"Sophie is the sweetest woman you'll ever meet. Her last relationship was a disaster, and it just crushed her," Molly said. The three women frowned and shook their heads in unison. "She deserves someone who will treat her right. And we're keeping our fingers crossed that this date will be the one."

"Sweet as a peach," Bertha said. "Remember that friend I was telling you about when you first arrived? Well, that was Sophie. It'd be so great if you could help her find her soul mate."

A bell from the kitchen dinged, signaling Jordan's order was up. Bertha grabbed the bag and placed it on the counter.

"No, no," Bertha said, as Jordan reached for her wallet. "It's on the house."

"You can't keep treating me. You have a business to run."

Bertha smiled and placed a warm hand on Jordan's arm. "Your money is no good here. But do think about the festival."

As Jordan walked toward the door, she had an urgent desire to turn her head and see Sophie's date, but she resisted. The thought of seeing Sophie flirting with some guy turned her stomach sour. She did feel bad about her last relationship being such a bomb. Jordan hated the thought of anyone hurting her. Maybe she'd get the scoop if they had a chance to actually talk about anything other than butterflies.

Jordan sat in her car, opened the bag, and inhaled the heavenly aroma. She should really wait until she got back to the condo to eat. How gluttonous was she? Obviously quite a bit since she ripped open the sandwich and took a generous bite.

"Mmmm…God, that's good." Jordan closed her eyes and moaned. She took another bite and wished she'd gotten something to drink. For a second she considered going back inside, but didn't want to run into the lovebirds.

As Jordan took the last bite of her sandwich Sophie exited the coffee shop. Alone. Maybe the guy was a dud? Or maybe Sophie was waiting on him since she'd sat on a bench, which was directly in front of Jordan's car. Jordan gave her a weak wave when their eyes met. They stared at each other until Jordan opened the car door. It seemed rude not to at least say hello.

"Care if I sit?" Jordan motioned toward the bench.

Sophie slid over, as far away from Jordan as possible.

"Sooo," Jordan said, catching sideways glances of Sophie, who was staring straight ahead. "Nice day. Cooler than I'm used to. I wonder if it'll rain much while I'm here. We haven't had much rain in LA." *Seriously? You're discussing the weather?* "So, how was the date?"

Sophie's head jerked toward Jordan. "I should have figured Bertha and the girls would fill you in."

"All they said was that you had a blind date."

"Yeah, well, it's a date I wish I'd skipped."

"Sorry about that." *Well, maybe not so sorry.* "You know I own Soul Mate Outreach Solutions."

Sophie looked directly at Jordan. "Yes. SOS. Just like my initials."

Jordan swallowed hard and nodded. "So, if you'd like, I could help you out while I'm here. You know, take you on as a client. At no charge, of course. If you'd like."

Jordan had no idea why she'd offered to find Mr. Right for Sophie.

That would not be an enjoyable task. She'd never admit this to anyone, but she still had feelings for Sophie, as evidenced by the thumping of her heart, which sounded like an overzealous kid banging a bass drum. Jordan scooted a little farther away on the bench. If she could hear the pounding, surely Sophie could as well.

Sophie seemed to consider the idea and then shrugged. "How'd you end up in LA? I thought you were in New York."

"I was. After I got my GED and took some business courses, Doug and I moved to Beverly Hills to start SOS."

"Doug? Is that your boyfriend or husband?" Sophie shot Jordan a quick glance before staring straight ahead, stiff as a cardboard box.

Jordan chuckled. "No. He's my best friend and business partner."

"You never married?"

"No. You?"

Sophie shook her head. "You've made quite a name for yourself. I didn't mean to put your company down yesterday. I'm sure you're very successful."

"You've done well, too. A master's in wildlife biology. That's impressive. When did you move back to Monarch?"

"About five years ago. Your grandmother offered me a job running the sanctuary. I'm not sure why she even opened it, but I'm glad she did. We've made great strides in monarch conservation."

Jordan didn't want to talk about butterflies. "How are your aunt and uncle?"

"They're great. My uncle retired several years ago, and they travel all over. I bought their cabin."

"That's on the outskirts of the eucalyptus forest, isn't it? Is it—"

"No," Sophie said, reading her mind. "It's not on the land you own."

Thank God for that. At least she wouldn't have to kick Sophie out of her house.

Sophie bolted to her feet. "I should get going."

"I'll walk you to your car." Jordan stood, not ready for their time together to end.

"That's okay. By the way, I'll be out of town tomorrow and Friday visiting schools to conduct monarch-conservation classes."

Jordan suspected that Sophie's trip wasn't so much about teaching classes as getting away from her. "Can I do anything while you're gone?"

"Don't touch anything."

Bertha walked out of the coffee shop, and they both turned toward the door. "I'm glad I caught you two. Sophie, maybe you can convince Jordan to be the festival guest of honor."

Sophie looked at Jordan questioningly. "The girls asked that I be in the festival," Jordan explained. "But I'm not sure I can make it."

"Don't bother, Bertha. She'll never do it." Sophie snickered and shook her head.

Jordan frowned. "What's that supposed to mean?"

"There's no way in hell you'll be the guest of honor at a small-town butterfly festival."

Jordan threw her shoulders back and puffed out her chest. "Is that so?"

"I know you. You'll never do it." Sophie rolled her eyes.

Jordan glared at Sophie for several seconds before turning to Bertha. "I'd be happy to take part in the festival."

Bertha clasped her hands and whooped loudly. Then she handed Jordan a flyer that read: BUTTERFLY DAZE. FEATURING JORDAN LEE, RENOWNED BEVERLY HILLS SOUL MATE OUTREACH SOLUTIONS OWNER.

Jordan furrowed her brow. "That was fast. I just now accepted, and it's already on a flyer?"

"We work quick around here." Bertha winked at Sophie as they both grinned like the Cheshire cat.

"Wait a second. Why do I feel like I've just been duped?" Jordan asked. "Oh my God. I walked right into that, didn't I?"

"You'll have a wonderful time. I'll fill you in on your duties later," Bertha said as she disappeared into the cafe.

"Duties? What duties?"

"Don't worry," Sophie said. "Worst case, they'll dress you up like a butterfly and prance you up and down Main Street."

"You're kidding, right? Please tell me you're kidding." She wouldn't put it past these butterfly maniacs to do just that.

CHAPTER NINE

Home Alone

Jordan's gaydar pinged wildly. She'd just arrived at the sanctuary when Mr. Simms and a woman walked in. The lady's hair was pulled back tightly, she wore no makeup, and she looked like she'd just come from a golf tournament. She was attractive but could do with a little eye shadow and lip gloss. In fact, she looked more masculine than Mr. Simms, which wasn't saying much since he was a bit on the wimpy side.

"Ms. Lee, I'd like you to meet Nanci Roberts from Chrysalis Realtors."

The woman strode forward with stilted movements that made Jordan wonder if she hadn't put too much starch in her Dockers.

"That's Nanci, with an *i*." She spoke in a deep baritone and grasped Jordan's hand so hard she almost heard a bone crack.

"Hello. It's nice to meet you. I'm Jordan…with an *n*. Chrysalis? Isn't that the cocoon stage of the butterfly lifecycle?"

"I'm impressed. Are you a butterfly aficionado?"

"Not at all. In fact, I just learned that the other day."

"And a good memory to boot. Color me captivated."

Something about Nanci bugged Jordan. She couldn't put her finger on it…until she smiled, and then there it was, that fake smirk she'd seen hundreds of times on Bibi. This woman belonged in Beverly Hills.

"I chose the name Chrysalis for my company because, like the cocoon," Nanci said, holding her arms out in a wide circle, "I'm about helping people find their own residential nest."

Seriously? Did she just say that?

Mr. Simms looked around nervously and whispered, "I understand Ms. Sanders is away on business. Is that correct?"

"Yeah. She's visiting schools."

"That's good. I didn't want to compromise your wishes." Mr. Simms wiped a bead of sweat from his forehead. "Ms. Lee would like to keep her plans to sell private for now."

"Not a problem. I can be trusted." Nanci smirked.

Jordan's skin crawled. She wasn't sure if that was because of the nervous lawyer or the creepy real-estate agent. Regardless, this was a small town so she'd have to work with what she had. Jordan led them to a flimsy card table, where they took a seat in folding chairs.

"Have you been in touch with your father?" Mr. Simms asked as he placed a worn black briefcase on the table.

"Not yet." Jordan squirmed. She didn't want to discuss her father. "Before we get started there's something I need to make clear. I promised not to sell the land for the next two months."

Mr. Simms's thin eyebrow shot up. "You've changed your mind about selling?"

"No, no…not at all. I just can't make any deals until after February first."

"That shouldn't be a problem since your grandmother's estate will be in probate for at least that long." Mr. Simms opened his briefcase and fumbled papers with his bony fingers. Several pieces escaped and floated to the floor. Nanci displayed another phony grin as he scrambled to recapture the documents.

"So how does all this work? What's the big picture?" Excitement bubbled within Jordan. This was really happening. She was going to be rich and SOS would reap the benefits.

"I'll issue a deed transferring ownership of the land and sanctuary to you after the estate is settled. You can sell after that time."

"And that's where I come in," Nanci said. "I'm new to Monarch but have many years as a successful real-estate agent, I assure you."

"How long have you lived here?" Jordan asked.

"About a month now. I understand that Kelstrom, who owns the Grand View Hotel and Spa, has made an offer."

"Yes, but that was to my grandmother. Are they still interested in purchasing the land?"

"Very. We should have no problem striking a deal."

"That's great. Do you think they'll cut down any trees?" Jordan hated the thought of her and Sophie's tree getting chopped to pieces.

Nanci looked at Mr. Simms, who shrugged. "Well, most of the land contains overgrown weeds, so maybe some of the trees can be spared," Nanci said.

"Actually, it's milkweed," Jordan said.

"Excuse me?"

"It's not weeds. It's milkweed plants, which is what monarch caterpillars eat and lay their eggs on."

"Why, you *are* a butterfly aficionado!" Nanci with an *i*'s overuse of the word "aficionado" annoyed Jordan.

"Here are some documents for you to look over," Mr. Simms said. "Specifics about the land and sanctuary." He handed Jordan a heap of disheveled papers. "Do you have any questions?"

Jordan thumbed through the stack. "Not right now, but I'm sure I'll have a lot later. I just want to get through the next two months."

"Understandable, Ms. Lee," Mr. Simms said, as he closed his briefcase. "Well, we'll be on our way. I just wanted to give you a quick overview and introduce you to Ms. Roberts."

They all stood and walked to the front door.

"Just one more thing, Mr. Simms. Do you have any idea why my grandmother wanted me to work at the sanctuary? It's one thing insisting that I live here to try to make amends with my father, but she didn't seem to care about this place."

Mr. Simms pursed his lips and thought for several long seconds. "I'm not completely sure. Your grandmother was an odd bird. She seemed...different the last several months of her life."

"Different how?"

"Just...not herself." Mr. Simms looked deep in thought, then shook his head vigorously, as though erasing an Etch-a-Sketch.

"Call me if you have any questions," Nanci said. "I left my card on the table."

Jordan winced when Nanci jabbed her on the arm. It was probably a move to indicate that they were beyond the hand-shaking stage and already buddies.

With Mr. Simms and Nanci out of the way, Jordan sat at Sophie's desk and glanced around the sanctuary. It was empty and quiet. What was she going to do for the next two days alone? In fact, what was she going to do for two months? Jordan leaned back in the chair and sighed, reminding herself to be grateful. Anyone else in her position would be ecstatic to inherit valuable land. All she had to do was endure two months in butterfly hell. Well, that, and see her father again.

Jordan pushed the chair back forcefully and walked to the twin caterpillars. They were already changing colors, a hint of orange and black tinting their white bodies. They certainly didn't stay caterpillars very long. Sophie had said they'd be cocoons in less than two weeks. It really was an amazing process, how something went from a miniature pearl egg to a caterpillar to a butterfly. It was like morphing from one creature to a completely different one, and one that could fly, no less. Jordan had a sudden urge to watch their birth again. She didn't think Sophie would mind, so she powered up the computer and found the video.

After viewing it a couple of times, Jordan looked at her watch with a fright. It was only eleven a.m. This day was going to drag. She opened the Internet browser on Sophie's computer, checked the weather, and then caught up on some LA news. When she couldn't decide what else to surf, she clicked on Sophie's favorites. There were lots of nature and butterfly sites and, surprisingly, Jordan's company website, as well as the YouTube video of the *Ophelia* interview. Interesting.

Jordan stared into space for God knows how long before she realized she'd been twiddling her thumbs. Did people actually do that? The boredom must be getting to her. She'd never twiddled before in her life. Sophie had told her not to touch anything, but no way would she survive two days without touching something—anything.

❖

It was around six p.m. Friday when Sophie rolled into town. She'd spent the last two days distributing milkweed seeds and teaching classes. The kids had seemed excited to learn about monarchs, which always made her happy. It'd been a successful trip, albeit a tiring one. She just wanted to go home, take a hot shower, and go to bed. And she would have, except that she wanted to check on the caterpillars and make sure Jordan had locked up for the weekend.

"What's she still doing here?" Sophie grumbled when she saw Jordan's Jaguar. Her stomach clenched with the uncertain fate of the sanctuary. Quickly, though, she squelched the fear and reminded herself to think positively. She had two months to convince Jordan not to sell.

It took Sophie a moment to comprehend what she was seeing when she opened the door. The sanctuary looked completely different. It was…organized. She walked to the center of the room in a daze. Books, which had been scattered everywhere, now sat on a bookshelf—a bookshelf that hadn't existed before. Butterfly nets hung from the ceiling, which freed up quite a bit of floor space, and mounds of milkweed seeds were separated and in labeled compartments.

Sophie eyed the printed labels. Wow, they were even spelled correctly. *Asclepias curassavica, Asclepias speciose.* Amazing. As great as all that was, though, the best thing was that the hundred milkweed seed packets and planting directions were in addressed envelopes ready to be mailed. Sophie was speechless.

She looked at her computer desk and saw Jordan hunched over, asleep. How cute was that? She tiptoed, careful not to wake her with the creaking wood floors. Sophie gazed down at Jordan's radiant, peaceful face and couldn't deny the tender feelings that filled her heart. As much as she disliked that fact, she still cared deeply for Jordan. Life was terribly unfair sometimes. Her first, and greatest, love had disappeared before she was ready to admit her feelings, not that Jordan would have been receptive.

Carefully, Sophie moved a strand of hair out of Jordan's eyes. Her fingertips itched with the desire to touch her: one caress of her velvet skin, one stroke of her lips, maybe even a kiss on her forehead. It might be her only opportunity to ever have physical contact. Instead, she lightly touched the ends of Jordan's silky hair. It was best not to get too close, not to let Jordan into her heart again. In two months she'd be gone.

As Jordan stirred, Sophie stepped back quickly. With half-closed eyes, Jordan looked up and blinked several times before speaking, her voice husky and sexy as hell. "Did I die and go to heaven? You look like an angel."

Not sure how to respond, Sophie just stared. After a few moments Jordan raised her head and looked around as though unaware of her surroundings. She sat up straight and shook her head a few times.

"What did I just say?"

"You said I look like an angel," Sophie whispered.

"I must have been dreaming. What are you doing here? What time is it?"

"A little after six. Did you do all this?" Sophie motioned around the room.

"Yeah. I hope you don't mind. I was bored out of my mind. I had to do something."

"Mind? It's incredible. Where'd you get the bookshelves?"

"I went to Target in Tallon. I also got that organizer, which worked great for all the seeds."

"And you even packaged the school project. I don't know how to thank you."

"I was afraid you'd be angry. I mean, you did tell me not to touch anything."

"Sorry about that. Obviously, I was mistaken."

Jordan stretched her arms overhead and yawned. "Well, I'm glad you approve. How was your trip?"

Sophie smiled. "Great. I love working with kids. I almost became a teacher."

"Really? What stopped you?"

"I wanted to have more of an impact on monarch conservation. Plus, this way I can do both."

As Sophie looked at Jordan, she couldn't help but marvel at what a beautiful woman she'd grown into. She was the entire package—smart, successful, and drop-dead gorgeous. She probably had guys falling all over her. *Lucky bastards.* With that thought, Sophie turned and walked to the caterpillars on a table.

"How are the twins?" she asked, peering into the containers.

"They're growing like milkweed. I think they missed you. They were asking me a bunch of technical questions about how to spin a cocoon, but I didn't have a clue." Jordan joined Sophie, standing close behind.

"They talk now?" Sophie smirked.

"Uh-huh. I said they'd have to wait until their mom gets home."

Sophie glanced at Jordan over her shoulder and was met with sparkling hazel eyes and a playful smile. Her gaze dropped to Jordan's full lips, surprised that she wondered if they were soft, what they tasted like, if Jordan was a sensual kisser. Sophie jerked her head back to the caterpillars and reminded herself that Jordan was her straight boss who had the power to destroy all her hard work.

As Sophie reached to grab milkweed to feed the caterpillars, she gasped when her hand grazed the wood table. "Ow," she said, a sharp stab in her finger.

Jordan grabbed Sophie's hand and examined it. "You have a splinter. Do you have tweezers?"

"I can take care of it." Sophie tried to pull away, but Jordan held firm.

"You're in pain. I can see it in your face. Just tell me where the tweezers are…Please."

Sophie's insides turned into a mushy swamp when she gazed into compassionate, pleading eyes. "In the top desk drawer."

Moving at lightning speed, Jordan grabbed the operating instrument and was standing beside Sophie in record time. Jordan licked her lips, appeared nervous, and looked at Sophie as though she requested permission to proceed. When Sophie nodded, Jordan carefully took her hand, which fit perfectly in Jordan's palm.

"This might hurt a little. It's in pretty deep, but I think I can grab the end." Jordan glanced at Sophie before getting to work.

There was probably pain, but Sophie didn't feel anything with Jordan two centimeters away, smelling like a fresh field of flowers. She inhaled deeply, trying to place the fragrance. It was milkweed, but which one? Asclepius syriaca? No, more like *Asclepius tuberosa.* Sophie inhaled again. Yes, that was it. Jordan wafted of the scent of bright-orange, nectar-rich flowers commonly known as butterfly weed. Actually, it had fourteen other names, including Canada root, fluxroot, butterfly flower, Indian posy, and butterfly love. Sophie tried to remember any other facts about the milkweed, *anything* that would take her mind off Jordan's soft locks that grazed her skin. Jesus, she was so close if Sophie puckered her lips she'd plant a kiss on Jordan's cheek.

Jordan raised her head and looked at Sophie. "Are you okay? Did it hurt?"

Pain, right. She should have felt pain. It shouldn't have been an enjoyable experience. Sophie dropped her gaze to their clasped hands, Jordan's thumb lightly caressing her skin. She slipped out of Jordan's grasp and took two steps back. "It's fine. Thanks for your help."

Sophie walked to her desk, a safe distance away. She wrapped her arms around her body and glared at Jordan. "Have you thought any more about what you're going to do with the sanctuary? Since you cleaned things up around here, does that mean you're keeping the place?"

Jordan squished her eyebrows together, a blank expression on her face. "I thought we weren't going to talk about that. Didn't we make a pact?"

Sophie raised an eyebrow. "That means you're selling?"

"What?...I...huh?"

"You can't do it, Jordan. You'd kill thousands of monarchs by displacing their home and destroying their food source. I forbid you to sell." Sophie knew she was being unreasonable, but she had a sudden desire to pick a fight.

Jordan stepped back, her face as red as a radish. "Are we back to that again? Where do you get off telling me what I can do? I did you a favor by promising not to make any decisions until February."

"Ohhh, yes. You're just a saint."

"I'm the boss! That's who I am. You have no right to order me around. You…You…" Jordan swayed and her eyes glazed over right before they rolled back in her head. When she fell face forward, Sophie lunged and tried to break her fall. Luckily, she prevented Jordan from cracking her head on the hardwood floor. Adrenaline coursed through Sophie's body, her heart beating wildly. Jordan had collapsed and was out cold.

"Oh my God, Jordan. Are you okay?" Sophie's hand shook as she touched Jordan's clammy forehead. "Jordan, can you hear me?" She lightly shook her shoulders but got no response. Fear welled within her. She wasn't sure what had happened or why. Had Jordan fainted, or something worse? Maybe she'd had a stroke or an aneurism. Sophie felt for a pulse, relieved to feel thumping. She ran to the desk and picked up the phone to call 911. Before she dialed, Jordan moaned and thrashed her head back and forth. Sophie put the phone down and ran back to her side.

"Can you hear me? Jordan?"

Jordan's eyes fluttered open. She looked afraid and confused. "What…why am I on the floor?"

"I think you fainted." Sophie's voice quivered.

"Oh God, I'm such an idiot." Jordan covered her face with her hands.

"What's going on? Are you all right?"

Jordan peeked at Sophie through her fingers. Sophie could only imagine the horrified look on her face. She'd never been so scared before.

"I'm fine. Really." Jordan sat upright with Sophie's assistance, taking a few moments to steady herself. "It's just something I do. I pass out sometimes when I get upset. It's no big deal." Jordan looked embarrassed.

"No big deal? You were unconscious. Have you been to a doctor? Maybe it's something serious."

"No, no. Trust me. I've had a million tests and seen hundreds of doctors. I need to learn how to handle stress. I've tried meditation, tai chi, visualization, yoga. Nothing's helped."

Sophie put a hand on Jordan's arm, still not convinced she was okay. "Are you sure? I mean, people don't just faint."

Jordan shrugged. "I'm not most people. Really, I'm fine."

Sophie studied Jordan closely. "So you only do it when you get upset?" Jordan nodded. "Maybe I could help."

"How?"

"Have you ever tried meridian tapping? It's a form of Chinese acupressure."

Jordan thought for a moment, then said, "I can safely say that's one thing I haven't tried."

"Maybe I could teach you sometime."

"I'm up for anything that might help. This is one thing I've never been able to control."

"Oh, my. This is all my fault. I'm the one who upset you. I was being such an ass." Sophie buried her face in her hands.

Jordan pulled Sophie's hands down and looked into her eyes. "It's okay. Really."

"So when did your fainting spells start?"

"Well, actually…the first time was…um…ten years ago. I followed you home after the earthquake and fainted in the forest."

Sophie's eyes narrowed. "You followed me home that night? I didn't see you."

"I kept my distance. I wanted to make sure you got home safely. I fainted when you were on the porch with your aunt."

Sophie laid her hand over her heart "Really? You watched out for me? I'd always thought you left me there."

"I'd never do that."

The sincerity in Jordan's eyes touched Sophie's heart. Talk about feeling like a grade-A, first-class loser. Not only had she ragged on Jordan until she passed out, but now she found out Jordan didn't leave her alone after the earthquake after all. Was there anything else she didn't know about that night?

Chapter Ten

Butterfly Daze

How in the world had Jordan gotten herself into this? As she sat on an outdoor stage facing hundreds of people, she managed to keep a smile plastered on her face during the mayor's God-awful long speech, but by the time Mabel spoke she was dozing off.

"...Jordan, the Monarch Festival guest of honor."

Jordan. That's me. Jordan rose as Mabel motioned her toward the podium and jabbed a gigantic key to the city in the shape of a butterfly in her hand. Horrifyingly, Mabel then handed her the microphone, leaving her stranded alone onstage. It had never occurred to Jordan that she'd actually have to speak. She thought the most she'd have to do was smile until her face cracked.

She blew a few times into the mic, discouraged that it was working, and looked at hundreds of expectant faces staring back at her. A few people flinched when she cleared her throat, which reverberated over the loudspeaker. "Uh...thank you all for coming...um..." Jordan didn't have a clue what to say. She could BS her way through just about any topic except butterflies. She glanced back at Mabel, who had a slightly worried expression. "Um...it's an honor to be here today to celebrate the kickoff of monarch season. Butterflies are beautiful creatures... and...and as Confucius said, 'Everything has beauty, but not everyone sees it.'" *Oh my God. What am I even saying?*

Jordan felt someone tap her shoulder, relieved to see that it was Sophie.

"Do you need some help?" Sophie whispered.

Jordan nodded enthusiastically. "Everyone, I'd like to introduce you to Sophie Sanders, who runs the monarch sanctuary." The crowd applauded and whistled. Jordan shoved the microphone into Sophie's hand.

"Thank you. As Jordan was saying, monarchs are amazing…"

Mesmerized by the beauty of her savior, Jordan didn't hear one word she said. It must have been good, though, because people laughed and clapped. She loved the way Sophie's eyes sparkled and her face lit up when she talked about butterflies. Jordan could stare at that face all day.

When Sophie concluded her remarks, Jordan said "thank you" about a million times. She really wanted to give Sophie a humongous hug, but the most they'd done was shake hands so she didn't want to make things feel awkward.

Mabel grabbed Jordan's arm. "Now, let's skedaddle. We need to get you on that horse."

"Horse?" Jordan asked, suspicious.

"For the parade!"

Oh God. There's a parade?

"Sophie, you should join, too. Everyone loved your speech. You can ride with Jordan."

Sophie shook her head and backed away. "No, no—"

"Hey, you got me into this. You can't miss out on all the fun." Jordan grabbed her arm before she could get away. "There's just one thing," she whispered to Mabel. "I've never ridden a horse before."

"Actually, neither have I," Sophie said.

Mabel looked momentarily concerned, which made Jordan think they were in the clear, before her face lit up. "We have just the one you two can ride. She's as gentle as a puppy. Now let's get going. We still need to put the sash and crown on you."

Oh God. There's a sash and crown?

Dixie May. That was the horse's name. She was huge but did look relatively docile. Actually, she was quite beautiful, with shiny, reddish-brown—or maybe that should be sangria—hair and snow-white hooves, if that's what they were called.

Mabel placed an orange-and-black satin ribbon across Jordan's torso and stuck a bedazzled crown on her head. Sophie did a double take and suppressed a giggle.

Jordan held up a finger in warning. "No laughing. I look like a Ms. America reject. Do you have any idea how much I hate this?"

"What would your LA friends think if they could see you now?"

Jordan burst out laughing. She was pretty sure they'd have plenty of snooty remarks. "I'm just glad the paparazzi aren't here. TMZ would have a field day with this look."

Sophie bit her cheek, probably to keep from laughing. "You're being a good sport. It's nice of you to do this."

"Well, I never go back on a promise."

Sophie's smile dropped and she looked suddenly serious. "That's good to know."

Jordan wondered if she was referring to her agreement not to make any decisions to sell before February.

Sophie ran a hand across the horse's stomach, ending in a couple of pats. "So, this is Dixie May? To be honest, I'm really nervous. I mean, she's a very large animal."

"I know. Isn't there a fire truck or float we could ride on?" Jordan glanced around.

"What if she bucks us off? Like…like…Rhett and Scarlett's daughter in *Gone With The Wind*." Sophie's voice cracked with emotion.

"*That's* your only horse reference?"

"She died in that movie!"

Jordan's tone softened when Sophie genuinely looked frightened. "We'll be okay. It's not like we're galloping around a racetrack. We'll be barely moving." Jordan wasn't sure who she was trying to convince more—Sophie or herself.

A John Wayne look-alike approached them from behind. "I hear you city folk have never been on a horse before." He walked around to the front of Dixie May and stroked her mane. "Which one of you gals will be driving?"

Jordan raised her hand. "Um, I guess that's me."

"All right. The beauty queen goes first."

Jordan rolled her eyes at the "beauty queen" remark.

John Wayne asked that she face the back of the horse and put the reins in her left hand, her left foot in the stirrup. She placed her right hand on the cantle—whatever the hell that was—took a few hops so she was facing the horse, then bounced twice before pushing up and swinging her right leg over until she was sitting in the saddle. That wasn't so bad, except now she felt like she was on top of a sixty-story building. She hoped they didn't meet with the same fate as Scarlett's daughter because it would be a long, hard fall to the ground.

Sophie had a tougher time mounting than Jordan did. It took several attempts, and once in the saddle, she immediately wrapped her arms around Jordan. It was actually kind of nice, like getting a hug, which was something she never thought they'd ever do.

"Can you cluck?" John Wayne asked. "You know, with your tongue. To make the horse move, cluck your tongue and squeeze her sides with both legs. And when you want to stop, lean back slightly, say 'whoa,' and pull back on the reins."

"Cluck, go. Whoa, stop. Got it."

"You're not leaving us, are you?" Sophie asked, sounding fearful.

"Don't you fret, little lady. I'll walk right beside you the entire way."

Jordan didn't appreciate Sophie's lack of confidence in her. She clucked and squeezed, and Dixie May began trotting. This wasn't so scary after all. In fact, it was kind of fun. They made their way into the line of marching bands, floats, and decorated cars, stopping behind a gang of twirlers wearing butterfly wings.

Jordan glanced back at Sophie. "You okay?"

"Yeah, it just feels so…high. Don't you dare go fast."

"I won't. I'll take good care of you." Jordan laid her hand on Sophie's knee, hoping to reassure her. Ever since they were kids, something about Sophie had made Jordan want to take care of her, keep her safe. She'd never felt that way about anyone else.

It seemed like hours before the parade participants started moving. Jordan's butt was numb from sitting in the saddle for so long, but finally, they were scurrying down Main Street with scads of people lined up along the sidewalks. Thankfully, Dixie May was the first horse in line so they didn't have to deal with smelly horse droppings. Jordan chuckled to herself. She still couldn't believe she was in a butterfly festival wearing a crown and riding a horse. This was a first. Sophie could probably talk her into anything. Well, almost anything. Jordan had to admit, though, it was hard to be a sourpuss. She couldn't really frown at people waving and smiling at her, especially the little kids. So, she plastered on a happy face and made the best of it.

Once they were through the parade route, John Wayne helped them both dismount Dixie May. They petted her soft, slick hair and thanked her for not bucking them off.

Within seconds, Mabel was by their side. "Good job, girls. Now, Jordan, we need to get you to butterfly bingo, where you'll call out the numbers."

Jordan shot Sophie a pained look. Sophie cocked her head, grinned, and shrugged. With everything going on, Jordan hadn't noticed how adorable Sophie looked today. Her hair was pulled back in a ponytail, and she wore dark-blue jeans and a black-and-white striped T-shirt. Before Jordan had time to fully appreciate the view, Mabel whisked her away.

After bingo, Jordan had a couple of hours free—before she had to pin a medal on the chili-cook-off winner—so she wandered down Main Street. It was closed to traffic and packed with arts-and-crafts booths. As she passed a display of framed monarch prints she ran smack-dab into Rebecca, her stepmother, who mouthed the word "fuck." Next to Rebecca stood her father, who did a double take. The long-haired kid she'd seen the other day kept walking, oblivious to what was happening.

"Chuck!" Rebecca yelled.

Probably short for Charles Junior. Not only a son, but also a namesake.

The boy stopped and yelled, "What?"

"Here!" Rebecca pointed to the ground in front of her.

Jordan studied Chuck as he approached. He was a carbon copy of her when she was a kid. Light-brown hair, hazel eyes, and long eyelashes.

Tentatively, Jordan met her father's eyes. He looked a bit older, gray around the temples and with a few wrinkles. Rebecca, on the other hand, hadn't changed a bit. She was still blond out of a bottle, dressed like a hooker on Sunset Boulevard, and had a waist as thick as a pencil. Jordan squinted as the sparkles from her flashy costume jewelry practically blinded her.

"Let's gooo," Chuck said, pulling on Rebecca's arm. When no one made a move, he looked up at Jordan. "Who's this?"

After a dreadfully long pause, Rebecca said, "That's Jordan."

Chuck squished his eyebrows together and stared up at the sky. After a few moments his face lit up. "My sister!? The lesb—"

"Don't you dare say that word, young man." Rebecca scowled. Looking slightly embarrassed, she added, "It's just that we like to watch his vocabulary."

And the word "lesbian" shouldn't be allowed in anyone's vocabulary?

"Hi. I'm Chuck, but you can call me Chucky. Like that doll in the horror movie. Do you like scary movies?"

"Not particularly," Jordan said. The kid was a lot friendlier than his parents, even with the Chucky reference.

"We're going to get a hot dog. Wanna come?"

"Probably not, but thanks anyway." Jordan looked at her father. "I was sorry to hear about Grandmother."

Charles glared, stone-faced. "I heard you were back in town."

"Yes, well, I didn't have much of a choice." Jordan wasn't sure how much, if anything, he knew about her grandmother's letter.

"Hey, Jordan, I have a basketball game Friday. You wanna come?" Chuck asked.

"I'll think about that." She resisted the urge to pat him on the head. He was a cute kid.

"Dad's been helping me with my free-throw shooting. I'm getting really good."

Jordan felt a stab of jealousy. Her father had never helped her with anything when she was young. She pushed the feeling aside, reminding herself she wasn't in competition with a seven-year-old.

"We need to get going. Nice seeing you again." Rebecca grabbed Chuck's arm and pulled him down the street.

Chuck looked over his shoulder and yelled, "Bye, Jordan. Don't forget about my game Friday."

Jordan looked at her father. "I have a brother?"

He nodded once in response. "How long are you in town?"

"Longer than I'd probably like. Um, could we meet for coffee sometime?"

"Why?"

"Just…I can explain when we meet."

Charles paused for what seemed like an eternity. "All right. When?"

Jordan tried not to show how shocked she was that he'd agreed. "How about Tuesday at nine? Bertha's Coffee Shop?"

"See you then."

Jordan sat on a bench and stared at her father long after he'd disappeared into the crowd.

Sophie approached and sat beside her. "Was that your dad?"

"Yeah. He actually agreed to have coffee with me."

Sophie put her hand on Jordan's arm. "Are you okay?"

"I'm not going to faint, if that's what you mean." Jordan halfheartedly grinned.

"You know, if you ever want to talk about it. I'm a great listener." Jordan lowered her gaze, completely silent. "You didn't say why he sent you to live with your mother." More silence. "Well, whatever the reason I can't imagine you could have done anything to deserve that. Do you think you'll ever forgive him?"

Jordan jerked her head toward Sophie. "Why should I?"

"To free yourself. Forgiveness isn't something you do for him. It's something you do for yourself."

"If you knew the whole story you wouldn't say that. And anyway, I'd think if anyone would understand, it'd be you. With your mom and all." Jordan didn't want to bring up a painful memory for Sophie, but their situations were similar. They'd both been abandoned by a parent.

"My mom did the best she could."

Jordan gaped at Sophie. "How can you say that? She robbed a bank and then completely disappeared after she got out of jail."

Sophie shrugged. "You don't know what her childhood was like, how her parents treated her. At the time, I didn't understand, of course, but later as I got older I forgave her. Sometimes we don't know everything that's going on with someone."

Jordan stared at the ground and shook her head. "I'm not sure I could ever let it go."

"What your dad did was horrible. No question. I'm not saying you should excuse his actions. It's about letting go of the resentment and hurt for yourself, not him, so you can be at peace."

Jordan looked into Sophie's clear blue eyes, which were filled with kindness. It was incredible how amazing she'd turned out, considering her difficult childhood. She was the most loving, giving woman Jordan had ever known.

"Let's not talk about my dad anymore." Jordan forced a smile.

"All right," Sophie said quietly and nodded. "So, what's on your festival agenda now?"

Jordan hunkered down and glanced around for Mabel. "Hopefully nothing."

"Good, 'cause I'm on my way to say hello to Madame Butterfly. You should come with me."

"The psychic? No, thanks. That's not really my thing." Jordan chuckled.

Sophie stood and grabbed Jordan's arm, pulling her to her feet. "Still the skeptical type, I see. Come on. Live dangerously for once." In a surprising move, Sophie linked arms with Jordan and tugged her down the sidewalk.

"I don't know about this." Jordan protested, but with Sophie attached to her arm she was likely to follow her anywhere.

❖

When Sophie opened the door to the psychic parlor, the scent of sage filled the air as candles flickered in the near darkness. Jordan squinted and placed a hand on Sophie's shoulder, afraid she'd trip over a Buddha statue or something. As her vision adjusted to the lighting, she saw a humongous quartz crystal ball in the center of the room. Two chairs were placed around it, along with a fancy, high-back throne fit for a queen, which Jordan assumed was for Madame Butterfly.

"Madame? Are you here?" Sophie glanced around the room. She turned to Jordan and started to say something but stopped. They were standing so close their noses almost touched. Jordan stared into sea-blue eyes until she dropped her gaze to Sophie's sensuous lips. They were bright crimson, like maybe she'd just guzzled a Big Red soda pop or sucked on a strawberry Popsicle. *Geez, could I be any less romantic? I should be comparing her lips to a rose petal.* Sophie cleared her throat, which prompted Jordan to look back to her eyes.

"Um, sometimes she's in the back," Sophie whispered.

Jordan took an inordinately long time to respond, her mind a scramble of alphabet soup with Sophie so close. "What?"

"Madame."

"Oh. Yeah. There's a back?"

"Behind the curtain. The one over there." Sophie pointed but never took her eyes off Jordan.

"Yeah. There's usually always a back. I mean, our SOS office has a back. It's…um…where we keep staplers and paper and…lots of stuff. Actually, it's a closet, but it's in the back."

"Sophie? Is that you?" A purple curtain swooshed open, just like in the *Wizard of Oz*, except that this wizard was a short, rotund woman. In fact, it was the same woman Jordan had run into on the street when she'd first arrived in Monarch. She wore the same indigo gown with gold swirls and had a scowl on her face that scared the crap out of Jordan. Within seconds, when she saw Sophie, the frown transformed into a wide smile.

"My dear, it's so good to see you." As Madame embraced Sophie, she stared Jordan up and down suspiciously. Jordan averted her gaze, looking anywhere except at the wizard.

"It's been far too long since you've been to see me. How have you been?"

"Just fine. I'd like you to meet Jordan. She's in town for a couple of months."

Madame perched glasses on the tip of her nose and regarded Jordan closely. "It's nice to see you again."

Jordan turned to Sophie since she had a what-the-hell look on her face. "We ran into each other, literally, when I first arrived, but we haven't been formally introduced."

Jordan wasn't sure if she should shake hands or curtsey, considering the queen's throne and all. Madame made the decision for her when she pulled Jordan into an embrace so tight it felt like she was squeezing the soul out of her. After what felt like a thirty-minute hug, Madame finally released her, allowing her to breathe again.

"I knew your grandmother," Madame Butterfly said.

"*My* grandmother? As in Frances Lee?" Jordan found it hard to believe her grandmother associated with psychics.

"She said you'd be coming to town."

"When did she—"

"I give you a reading, yes?"

"No! I mean, no thanks."

"I do." Madame grabbed Jordan's arm, pulled her to the crystal ball, and practically shoved her into one of the chairs. Sophie followed and sat beside Jordan as Madame perched on her throne.

"Give me your hand," Madame said.

Jordan did as commanded, embarrassed that her fingers quivered. Madame lightly traced several lines in her palm. If Jordan hadn't been so nervous, she would have giggled from the tickle. After grunting a few times, Madame closed her eyes and took a deep breath. Someone should really tell her that glittery green eye shadow had gone out in the 70s, along with that Aqua Net–drenched beehive hairdo. She wasn't even a hip psychic. Jordan glanced at Sophie, who was staring intently into Jordan's hand.

Finally, Madame spoke without opening her eyes. "I see a brick wall that hides many secrets. There's much isolation. Loneliness." *What? She can't be reading me. I'm not isolated or lonely.* "You're homeless. You feel like an outcast, like you don't belong. You pine for someone that you love but—"

Jordan abruptly stood and pulled her hand away. "Wait a minute… wait a minute. I'm not homeless. I have an expensive condo in Beverly Hills. And I'm not lonely. I'm surrounded by people. Lots of *famous* people. And as for the love stuff, that's just insanity." Jordan knew she was coming on strong, but this woman was way off and needed to know it.

"It's what I see," Madame said calmly.

"Well, I'm sorry, but your crystal ball needs polishing. There's no brick wall in my aura or energy or whatever you call it." Jordan motioned around her as though knocking down an invisible wall.

"I'm sorry if I offended you."

"You didn't offend me. You're just wrong." Jordan's nostrils flared as heat rushed to her cheeks.

Madame Butterfly paused before she turned her attention to Sophie. "Would you like a reading, dear?"

Sophie looked at Jordan with confusion and uncertainty. "I think that might be enough for today. Maybe we should get going."

Jordan lowered her eyes, embarrassed by her outburst.

Madame Butterfly rose and walked them to the door. "Come back soon. And it was a pleasure meeting you, Jordan."

"Yeah, likewise." That didn't sound convincing even to Jordan's ears.

Jordan and Sophie shielded their eyes as they stepped outside. The sun was a blinding spotlight after being in the candlelit room.

"Sorry about my outburst," Jordan said. "I wasn't expecting a reading."

"Madame can be a little forceful sometimes, but her intentions are pure. I always find her insights to be accurate."

"Well, anyone can have an off day. That's so weird that she knew my grandmother. Did you know they were friends?"

"I had no idea. I didn't think Frances was the sociable type."

They walked down Main Street, Jordan glad to see that the festival was winding down. The crowd had dispersed and booths were being dismantled. This was a day she'd rather forget.

Sophie peered at Jordan out the corner of her eye. "Do you remember when you offered your SOS services? Well, I was thinking maybe I could take you up on that."

Jordan stopped. She couldn't have been more surprised if Sophie had sprouted butterfly wings and flown away. "Really? Sure. Just let me know when you want to get together."

"Are you free tomorrow? Say around one o'clock at my cabin?"

"That'd be great!" Jordan smiled widely, feeling lighter than she had in years. This day hadn't turned out to be so bad after all.

CHAPTER ELEVEN

Soul-Mate Sunday

Sophie studied her reflection in the mirror. Why, she wasn't sure, because her makeup and hair looked exactly as it did fifteen minutes ago. She glanced at the clock. Maybe she had time to change. After trying on six outfits she'd settled on low-riding jeans, a turquoise T-shirt, and sandals. Was she too casual? Maybe she should wear that yellow sundress everyone said made her look so pretty. Jordan was from LA, land of the beautiful people. A bright sundress wouldn't turn her head. Not that she wanted to impress her, of course, but she didn't want to look like a slob either.

Okay, Sophie could admit it. She was nervous. Why she'd invited Jordan over was beyond her. Seeing her again had caused a nonstop ache in the center of her chest, and she frequently wanted to cry for no apparent reason. Maybe she'd suggested they get together because of Madame Butterfly's reading. As angry as Sophie was, she hated to think that Jordan was isolated and lonely. Plus, Madame had said that Jordan had secrets, which was intriguing. So, it wasn't completely insane to invite her over, but it was totally insane to be tearing her closet apart looking for that sundress. Finally, Sophie gave up the search, deciding it made her look like a gigantic lemon anyway, and headed into the living room.

"Hey, Mr. Limpet. How about I read our forecast for today?" Sophie grabbed the *Monarch Messenger* and thumbed to the love horoscopes. "You will be provided with an interesting opportunity to get to know someone in a new and different way. Everyone has sides of themselves that are hidden or rarely surface. If you keep an open mind, love could be just around the corner."

Sensing she was being watched, Sophie jerked her head up to see Jordan standing in the doorway with a grin and a mischievous twinkle in her eyes. Sophie had forgotten she'd opened the front door earlier to let a cool breeze into the cabin. Jordan leaned against the door frame, looking like a sexy Calvin Klein ad. Her blue-jean shirt was tucked into faded jeans, which hugged her hips perfectly. Jordan ran fingers through thick, wind-tossed hair, her sultry gaze never leaving Sophie. Good thing she hadn't found that yellow sundress. It wouldn't have been nearly hip enough.

"I see you still read your horoscope," Jordan said.

"Didn't anyone ever teach you to knock? Or is that how it's done in LA? You just burst into someone's home without announcing yourself?"

Jordan's sexy grin didn't falter. "First, there was no bursting, and second, your door was open. Is that how it's done in the boondocks?"

Sophie bit the inside of her cheek. "You can come in now, you know."

Jordan pushed off the door frame and strutted into the living room. This was a Jordan Sophie hadn't experienced yet, the self-assured Jordan. The nervous, rambling one was easier to handle. This Jordan seemed...dangerous.

"Did I hear that right? This little fellow's name is Mr. Limpet?" Jordan tapped on the aquarium, which caused the betta fish to flare out his gills. Sophie wondered if Jordan would remember, and she didn't have to wait long to find out. "From your favorite movie, right? *The Incredible Mr. Limpet.*"

"Yeah. The one you never would watch with me. You really missed out, you know. It's a Don Knotts classic."

"I almost rented it once. I had it in my hand, but...I dunno..." Jordan glanced around the cabin. "You've changed the place."

"I wanted to make it my own after I bought it from my aunt and uncle. I'll give you a tour if you'd like."

Jordan followed Sophie as she led them through the cozy two-bedroom cabin. Sophie's spiritual side shone through in every room, with crystals, incense, Buddha statues, and chakra paintings.

"What's this used for?" Jordan popped her head into a room that housed an altar, candles, an orange Himalayan salt lamp, and a colorful mandala painting on the wall.

"I come in here to meditate or just relax. I didn't need an extra bedroom since I don't get many overnight guests."

"It's nice. Feels calming." Jordan walked to the center of the room and took a deep breath. "What's that scent?"

"Amber and lavender incense."

"I always did like that about you." When Sophie looked at her questioningly, Jordan continued. "That you're into spiritual stuff. It's... cute."

"Cute?" Sophie asked.

"That's probably the wrong word. More like interesting, or maybe different, but in a good way."

As they walked down the hall, Sophie skipped her bedroom, but Jordan stopped and walked into it, with Sophie reluctantly following. It felt uncomfortable to have Jordan in her personal, intimate space. This was where she slept and had sex—occasionally. Jordan approached the bed and ran her fingertips across the light-gray silk comforter. Shivers cascaded from Sophie's head straight to her groin as her pulse quickened. *Geez, Sophie, you have to get laid, and soon. You're getting turned on by a straight woman touching your bed. How pathetic is that?*

Jordan flinched as a black spider ran across the floor and stopped directly in front of her. She lifted her foot like she was about to stomp it with her shoe.

"Don't you dare!" Sophie darted toward Jordan and grabbed her arm, pulling her back. "I can't believe you were going to kill him." Sophie ran out the room and returned with a cup, then bent down and scooped the thing up. "Spiders are ancient symbols of power and growth. They remind us to be mindful of the choices we make in life."

"I'm sorry. I figured everyone thought spiders were icky." Jordan's shoulders slumped, embarrassment etched on her face.

"It's okay. I get a little passionate about these things. How about we set this little guy free?"

Jordan followed Sophie to the front door and watched as she put the cup on the ground and allowed the bug to escape when he was ready.

"Well, I guess we just have one more room, and that's the kitchen," Sophie said.

It was a happy place, painted in bright yellow and with a large bay window that provided lots of light. Jordan immediately zeroed in on Sophie's favorite item as she approached the dining table.

"This wood is gorgeous. What is it?" Jordan swept her hand across the smooth, shiny surface.

"Brazilian cherrywood," Sophie said proudly. "I found the table and chairs in an antique store and fell in love with it. It's far bigger than I need, but I couldn't pass it up. Don't you love the texture and the intricate patterns of the darker colors mixed with crimson?"

Jordan stared at Sophie's hand as she traced a spiral pattern with her fingertip. "It's beautiful."

"Do you want something to drink?" Sophie asked.

"Sure. Is coffee too much trouble?"

"Well, I don't actually have a coffeepot, but I do have something up here." Sophie stretched to reach the top shelf.

"Here, let me help. I'm taller than you."

Jordan stood close behind and reached into the cabinet. Sophie inhaled sharply, heat rising to her cheeks, when Jordan's breasts brushed against her back. Yes, she needed to get laid…and soon. Jordan grabbed the box and stared at it with a frown.

"I'm sorry it's instant, but it's all I have. This Frenchwoman on the commercials makes it look better than it really is. I can make some tea instead."

Jordan sneered and put the box on the counter. "Actually, that would be great. Can I help?"

"Thanks, but I've got it. Why don't you have a seat?" *As far away from me as possible, please.*

As Sophie busied herself brewing tea, she felt Jordan's eyes follow her every move. Feeling self-conscious about being watched, she spilled water and fumbled with the tea bags, dropping several on the floor. Luckily, Jordan didn't comment on what a klutz she was being, which would have embarrassed her even more. Sophie placed two cups on the table and sat across from Jordan. They both blew into the steaming liquid as an uncomfortable silence settled between them.

Finally, Sophie looked over the rim of her cup and said, "You've changed. You seem…different."

"What do you mean?" Jordan's hazel eyes were a striking green. When they were kids Sophie had teased that her eyes were like mood rings. They changed color depending on her emotional state. Hazel was relaxed, green was nervous, and brown mixed with gold was excited.

"You seem more reserved, guarded. Just different than when we were teenagers."

"Hmm. You seem the same. You're still sweet, caring, and trying to save the world. Or I guess, in this case, the butterflies. And you still look like a Disney Princess."

Sophie smiled. "I remember you used to call me that."

"So," Jordan said, sitting up straighter in her chair. "Let's see how SOS can help you. First, tell me what you're looking for in a mate."

"Well, first and foremost I want someone I can trust. That's a biggie. My last relationship didn't end well and involved infidelity."

Jordan frowned. "I'm so sorry, Sophie. You of all people don't deserve that. You're someone who should be worshipped. Anyone would be lucky to have you as their girlfriend." Jordan blushed and stared into her tea.

"Do you believe in soul mates? I mean, your company is called Soul Mate Outreach Solutions. Do you think there really is such a thing?"

Jordan answered without hesitation. "Of course. I think there are many people someone could date, commit to, and be happy with, but to me there's that one person who surpasses all. It's a connection that goes beyond love. It's a true meeting of hearts, souls, and minds. It's a relationship unlike any other. That's what I think, anyway."

Who knew Jordan was such a romantic?

"I think so, too."

"So, what else are you looking for?"

"I want someone who gets me. She should respect my values, my—"

"She?" Jordan furrowed her brow, confusion etched on her face.

"Yes. I'm a lesbian."

Jordan was as stiff as a wax figurine. "You're gay?"

"I thought you knew. Didn't Bertha tell you?"

Jordan paused, staring into her tea, as though absorbing the information. "No, not at all."

"Is that a problem?"

"No, of course not. Wow, you're a lesbian. I had no idea." Jordan rubbed hands up and down her pants legs. "So, you're out? I mean, people in Monarch know?"

"Most certainly. I'd never be in the closet. Don't they have lesbians in LA?" Sophie smirked.

"Yeah, but most of them aren't out. At least not the ones I know." Jordan's eyes darted from her tea to Sophie. "So, when did you know you were gay?"

"I came out to myself in college." That wasn't a lie, but it wasn't the complete truth either. From the look on Jordan's face, though, Sophie didn't think she'd be able to handle the whole story.

"How did your aunt and uncle react?"

"They were shocked at first, and honestly, it did take them a while to accept it. Are you sure you're okay with this?"

"Of course. I'm sorry. I just need to adjust my thinking and look for a Miss instead of a Mister." Jordan halfheartedly smiled.

An unexpected sorrow covered Sophie like a prickly wool blanket. What was it about Jordan that made her so sad sometimes? Maybe the loss of their friendship, or maybe—in this case—because Jordan wasn't a lesbian as well.

CHAPTER TWELVE

Rainy Nights and Mondays

God wasn't funny. Just when Jordan had decided to swear off women, she found out her first love was a lesbian. And not only that, but a beautiful, amazing, single lesbian. Maybe this was a test. The big guy was making sure she was serious about that celibacy vow. Well, fine. Jordan could take anything he could dish out. Discovering Sophie played for her team was a shock. Sophie said she came out in college, but Jordan wondered if she knew when they were teenagers. She hadn't said anything, but then again, neither had Jordan. She didn't want to consider the possibility that they'd both been in love with each other but hadn't acted on it. That would just be tragic.

Jordan opened her car door and put a white sack containing two Italian subs in the passenger seat. She'd texted Sophie earlier saying that she'd be in around noon and would bring lunch. Sophie had responded, *Hurry up, I'm already hungry and it's only 9 a.m.* She was so cute. But not cute enough to break her pledge, of course. Jordan would be happy if they were just friends again. Anything more would never work. They lived in separate worlds, with different priorities, plus Jordan was about to destroy everything Sophie had worked for the past five years.

Jordan did wonder why she hadn't told Sophie she was a lesbian, too. She settled on the fact that it was because she was a private person, and really, it was no one's business. Being completely honest, though, it was because the longer she stayed in the closet, the easier it was to keep Sophie at arm's length.

Jordan inhaled deeply and held her breath, like she was taking a hit. The scent of fried butter, olive oil, onions, and spices filled her Jaguar. Her stomach grumbled loudly as she sat at a red light staring at the white bag. Instinctively, she licked her lips, then shifted her gaze to the rearview mirror, where someone in the car behind her waved wildly. It was no one she recognized, but she raised her hand anyway. Whoever it was had a big smile plastered on his face as he went from waving to pointing straight ahead. Jordan looked in front of her and saw that the light was green, so she stepped on the gas. She chuckled to herself. If she'd been in LA, the person would have honked and given her the finger.

It seemed to take forever to drive the two miles. Jordan couldn't wait to sink her teeth into a sandwich, but she was also looking forward to seeing Sophie again.

"Lunch has arrived," Jordan said as she walked into the sanctuary.

"Thank God. I'm starving." Sophie was sitting at her desk with her nose buried in a book. She had little makeup on—which she didn't need with her beautiful complexion—and wore a faded Utah University sweatshirt. The laid-back-Monday Sophie looked adorable. Well, okay, all the Sophies were adorable.

"Whatcha reading?" Jordan placed a take-out bag on the desk. Sophie held up the book as Jordan said, "*The Mating Habits of the Monarch Butterfly*. Now that's hot stuff. Sexier than a Harlequin romance, I'm sure."

Sophie's cheeks tinted pink, which made her look even prettier, if that was possible. She opened the bag and peeked inside. "Mmm. That smells amazing."

"Tell me about it. I had to drive all the way here with that in the front seat." Jordan grabbed a couple of bottled waters out of the mini-fridge as Sophie unpacked the sandwiches. "I need to start jogging again. My pants are getting tight from eating so many of these."

"You look great to me." Sophie's eyes roamed up and down Jordan's body. More blushing, more cuteness.

They sat at Sophie's desk, moaning in unison as they ate without conversing. The sound of strings and piano seeped through the speakers when Sophie clicked something on her computer. Jordan frowned when a guy started singing in Italian. She was about to protest, but it was surprisingly soothing.

"What's that?" Jordan asked.

Sophie paused to swallow a mouthful. "Andrea Bocelli. Have you heard him before?"

"I think I saw him on TV once. Opera dude, right?"

"He does sing opera, but I like his crossover stuff."

After polishing off lunch, Sophie reclined in her chair and patted her stomach. She reached to turn off the music, but Jordan stopped her. She couldn't understand a word the guy was singing, but it was romantic. She liked it.

"So what do you do for fun besides read butterfly books and play midwife to caterpillars?" Jordan asked as she took a swig of water.

Sophie paused. "I like hiking, biking, antiquing. Guess I'm pretty boring compared to LA women, huh?"

"Not at all. You're the most interesting, amazing woman I know." *Not to mention the most beautiful.*

Sophie held Jordan's gaze for several seconds. "You're a jogger?"

"I used to be, but I've been so busy with SOS I haven't done it in a while."

"Why do I get the feeling you're a workaholic?"

"Because you're psychic?" Jordan grinned. "Hey. Let's go running on the beach later."

"Me? I can barely walk in the sand, much less run. Anyway, I heard it's supposed to rain."

"Aw, come on. It'll be fun. We can close up shop early and get a run in before sunset. Pretty please, with milkweed on top?"

Sophie smiled widely with a twinkle in her eye.

"What?" Jordan asked.

"I see you still beg like when we were kids, which—if I remember correctly—always seemed to work in your favor."

Jordan smiled. "So that's a yes?"

"On one condition. Let me teach you how to do meridian tapping so no more fainting spells."

Jordan puckered her lips and stared into space, mulling over the idea. "Ohhh, all right. Deal." Jordan felt downright giddy. Sophie was warming up to her and seemed to have forgiven the past. It was like a hundred-pound weight had been lifted off her shoulders.

Sophie straightened her posture and faced Jordan. "Okay, this is super easy to learn."

"What...you mean *now*?" Jordan had Googled "tapping" after Sophie mentioned it before, and what she saw had made her chuckle. How could thumping various parts of your body relieve stress? The things some people came up with were crazy. Jordan didn't want to hurt Sophie's feelings, though, so she played along.

"No time like the present. Okay. Tapping is similar to acupuncture since it stimulates the meridians and energy flow, but without the needles."

That was one positive, at least. "What do I do?" Jordan asked.

"Focus on the negative emotion, which in your case would be anxiety, and use your fingertips to tap five times on each of the twelve meridian points. Tapping, while concentrating on accepting and resolving the issue, will access your body's energy and restore it to a balanced state."

Sophie demonstrated, with Jordan mimicking her every move. After several times she had the hang of it. It was simple enough and surprisingly she did feel calmer, but that could have been because she was having so much fun with Sophie. She didn't care if they were drumming body parts, just as long as they weren't arguing about butterflies.

After the lesson, Sophie worked on the computer as Jordan took photos and videos of the caterpillars for the research files. They left early to go home and change, with Jordan arriving at Sophie's cabin around five.

Jordan's eyes practically popped out of her head when Sophie opened the door. Talk about sexy. She had on tight black yoga pants and a baby-blue fitted knit shirt that brought out her eyes, not to mention her voluptuous figure. Why couldn't she have worn baggy sweats? It was so much easier to be pals with someone who didn't make you drool. Jordan stood awkwardly in the center of the living room while Sophie stretched her calf muscles in a lunge that nearly had Jordan hyperventilating. Sophie's ex-girlfriend must have been insane to cheat on her.

"Just need to stretch out a bit. Then we can go," Sophie said.

Stretch all you want. In fact, we can skip the run and I can watch you contort your body every which way. Geez, get a grip and stop lusting over your friend.

The breeze off the ocean was chilly, but it didn't take long to warm up when they started moving. Jordan reveled in the way her muscles stretched and loosened as she ran. It felt divine to move limbs that were usually stiff from her sitting at a desk all day. After about fifteen minutes, though, Jordan was already huffing and puffing. She really needed to work out more. This was embarrassing, especially when Sophie wasn't even breathing hard. Jordan ate healthy and kept her weight down, but she was obviously out of shape. Thankfully, when she suggested they switch to a power walk, Sophie didn't give her a hard time about it.

After she caught her breath, Jordan asked, "So, what happened with the blind date you had the other day?"

"She got three strikes. All for being dishonest."

"Ah, well, that'll do it. Was she at least attractive?"

"She had beautiful eyes…until she popped out color contact lenses."

Jordan laughed. "Are there many lesbians around here?"

"More than you'd think. Tallon is a fairly large city that has a gay-and-lesbian center. Actually, Bertha is setting me up with someone. I haven't met her yet. She's only been here a month or so."

"Hmm. You and Bertha seem close."

Sophie shook her head. "My aunt and uncle were great, but I never felt like I had a real family until I met Bertha, Mabel, and Molly." Sophie paused and looked at Jordan. "And you. You were family." Sophie jabbed Jordan hard on the arm. "I'll race you. Last person to the pier makes the hot chocolate." And then she took off in a blur.

"Hey, no fair! You got a head start!" Jordan ran but stayed several yards behind Sophie the entire way, not that she minded since the view was so nice.

Once they reached the pier, Jordan bent over with her hands on her knees, trying to catch her breath. "You cheated."

"You're just a sore loser." Sophie propped her foot on a railing and stretched out her hamstring. Impressively flexible, she bent over her leg, her knee perfectly straight.

"I think you lied to me," Jordan said.

Sophie stopped mid-stretch. "What do you mean?"

"You're faster than a cheetah. I thought you said you couldn't run."

"Maybe you're just slow," Sophie said, playfully. "I'm freezing, and you owe me a hot chocolate. Let's go home."

Jordan resisted the urge to analyze why her heart swelled at the thought of them going home…together.

Sophie had been right about the rain. It started pouring before they reached the cabin. They rushed inside and stood by the door, dripping wet. Sophie suggested they shed their soggy clothes and get into a hot shower, which kicked Jordan's imagination into overdrive. She wasn't sure what had gotten into her. She was surrounded by beautiful women, actresses and models, so why was she thinking like a horny teenager around Sophie?

Jordan apologized for dripping on the hardwood floor as she squished to the bathroom in her Nikes. In horror, she stared at her reflection in the mirror. She looked like a wet raccoon, hair plastered to her scalp and smeared mascara. Not the impression she wanted to make. Sophie gathered towels and a pair of gray sweats, which she put on the counter before leaving Jordan alone. The spray of warm water felt heavenly on her chilled skin. She would have stayed in the steamy shower for hours if Sophie hadn't been waiting her turn. She quickly washed, blow-dried her hair, and dressed in Sophie's sweats. They were about the same size, except Jordan was a few inches taller, which resulted in crop sweats—not that she cared. At least they were dry.

When Jordan emerged from the bathroom, Sophie stood in the kitchen wearing a pink chiffon robe, her hair still dripping wet. She glanced at Jordan before continuing to take items out of the cupboard.

"You look good in my clothes."

"Thanks. The shower felt wonderful. What's all this?" Jordan eyed milk, sugar, chocolate powder, salt, vanilla extract, and a saucepan on the counter.

"Hot chocolate. Remember?"

"Yeah...but...don't I just nuke some water and scoop in chocolate?"

"Au contraire. In the country, this is how we make proper hot chocolate." Sophie handed Jordan a notecard.

"A recipe?"

"Okay. I'm outta here. Just don't burn the place down."

Jordan watched as Sophie sashayed to the bathroom, but not before giving Mr. Limpet a couple of food pellets. She stared at the items on the counter, a little nervous about the task ahead since she rarely cooked—if hot chocolate was considered cooking. At least it took her mind off wet, naked Sophie in the shower. Jordan studied the notecard before combining cocoa, sugar, water, and salt in the saucepan. The mixture boiled as she stirred vigorously for several minutes. Reducing the heat, she then added milk and vanilla. Finally, Jordan tasted a spoonful of the drink, pleased with the outcome. She turned the heat down further to keep it warm until Sophie finished in the bathroom. Jordan didn't want to dig, but hot chocolate required marshmallows, so she scavenged through the cabinets until she found a bag in the cupboard.

Sophie emerged wearing red sweat pants and a white T-shirt, her hair in a ponytail. She looked comfortable and amazingly adorable.

"Mmm…that smells great." Sophie peered into the saucepan.

"I hope you don't mind but I found some marshmallows."

"That's perfect." Sophie looked at the clock, which made Jordan worry she'd overstayed her welcome. "I didn't realize it's already seven. Are you hungry?"

"No. Surprisingly I'm not."

"Me either. So, I was thinking we could be unhealthy and have cookies and hot chocolate, and maybe I could put a movie on. What do you think?"

"Sounds great." Jordan couldn't stop grinning at what sounded like the best idea she'd heard…ever.

Jordan poured the drinks while Sophie arranged chocolate-chip cookies on a plate. They carried everything into the living room and set it on the coffee table. Jordan made herself comfortable on the couch while Sophie rummaged through DVDs.

"What movies do you have?" Jordan asked.

Sophie slyly grinned as she popped in a disc. She turned off the lamp, so the only light was coming from the flickering TV screen, and sat next to Jordan.

"Seriously? This is what we're gonna watch?" Jordan laughed.

"It's about time you see *The Incredible Mr. Limpet*. I can't believe it's taken over ten years for you to finally watch it with me." Sophie grabbed a pillow and hugged it.

"Shouldn't we move the aquarium over so Mr. Limpet can watch it with us?"

"He's already seen it at least a dozen times."

When Sophie reached to grab the hot chocolate, her leg grazed Jordan's thigh. It was a simple, innocent thing, yet Jordan couldn't think about anything except the point where their skin met. Heat surged through her body as her pulse raced. Slowly, Jordan inched away. She'd never be able to concentrate on the movie with Sophie so close.

Jordan settled into the couch and leaned her head back, her eyelids heavy. It had been a long day, and she hadn't realized how tired she was until she allowed herself to relax. Maybe she could just shut her eyes for a second. Sophie was so engrossed in the movie she probably wouldn't even notice. The next thing Jordan knew, Sophie was jabbing her arm, hard.

"You're sleeping!"

Jordan bolted upright and opened her eyes wide. "Am not. Well, okay, maybe a little." She yawned and rubbed her eyes. "But it's a cartoon. What happened to the real people? Don Knotts turned into a fish, for Christ's sake. And there's no way his glasses would stay on underwater. That's not even realistic."

"It's not supposed to be realistic, you killjoy." Sophie peered at Jordan sideways. "What? Why are you looking at me that way?"

"Nothing. It's just…I'm having fun. With you."

Sophie's eyes softened, a slight grin on her lips. "I'm having fun, too."

"So, I guess we're becoming friends again?"

"Mmm…maybe." Sophie smiled widely.

They finished watching the movie in silence. When Sophie clicked off the TV, they heard rain pummel the rooftop like a machine gun. Thunder rumbled in the distance as lightning flashed through the window.

"It's really storming," Sophie said. "It's probably not safe for you to drive. If you want…you can stay the night. My couch folds out into a bed."

It took Jordan longer than necessary to politely decline the offer. The thought of sleeping a few feet away from Sophie made her tingle from head to toe. She needed to keep her emotions in check. It was great to be friends again, but she was in Monarch for one reason only: to do her time so she could sell the land and get the hell out of there.

CHAPTER THIRTEEN

Family Reunion

This was about the silliest thing Jordan had ever done. She was sitting in her car on Main Street, tapping her forehead with her fingertips. Sophie had said to tap five times, but being an overachiever she was going for ten. With her luck, she'd probably have little bruises on various body parts since she was thumping with vigor. About halfway through the meridian tapping, her cell phone rang. Normally she'd ignore it, but it was Doug.

"Hey, boss. How was your first week in butterfly hell?"

"Has it only been a week? God, it feels like I've been here forever. Remember that girl I told you about? Sophie? Well, she not only lives here but runs the Monarch Butterfly Sanctuary."

"Whoa. Seriously!? When did you find out? Why didn't you call me? Am I not your best friend?"

"Yes, Dougie. You're my best bud," Jordan said with a chuckle.

"So what did she say? What happened?"

"Well, she's understandably angry at me, but I think she's warming up. And get this…she's a lesbian."

"What?! The love of your life is a lesbo? I'm getting chills here. Did you ask her out? What did she say when you told her you play for the same team?"

"Well, actually…I haven't told her yet."

"Wait a sec. I must have a bad connection. You didn't tell her you're gay? Why not? Does she have a girlfriend?"

"No. It's complicated."

"Complicated, my ass. You're fucking scared."

Jordan groaned. "No psychoanalysis, please."

"You're going to have to open your heart to someone, sweetie. And this girl sounds like the perfect one."

"Perfect, huh? Sure, aside from the fact that I'm about to put her out of a job and sell the land she loves. Can we not talk about this right now? I'm having a mini-panic attack. I'm about to meet with my dad." Jordan looked at her watch. "In fact, I need to go. He'll be here any minute."

"All right, but promise to call me afterward. Good luck."

"I will. Talk to you later."

She needed luck, and lots of it. Jordan had no idea what she'd say to her father or how he'd react. At least he'd agreed to meet, which must be a good sign. Either that or he wanted the opportunity to spit in her face. She was glad she'd suggested Bertha's. It was a warm, homey place. Maybe it'd help her relax. Jordan continued to stimulate her meridian points, and after she was done, she actually felt calmer. Maybe there was something to this stuff after all.

Jordan sat upright in the driver's seat. She didn't have any reason to be so nervous. She had the upper hand here. Her father had thrown her out, and despite what he thought, she'd done nothing wrong. She was a strong, successful, independent woman. *I am woman, hear me roar!* Jordan pumped her fist in the air, but her resolve quickly melted like butter on a hot skillet when her father entered the cafe. In thirty seconds, she'd gone from a lion to a cub.

Jordan took a shaky breath, opened her car door, and walked to the coffee shop. The moment she entered, she spotted her father sitting in a corner booth. He looked nervous, which gave her an ounce of satisfaction. Bertha shot her a sympathetic look as she walked to the bar.

"Can I get two coffees?" Jordan asked.

"Coming right up." Bertha poured two cups and placed them in front of Jordan. "Nervous?"

Jordan stuck her hands in her pockets. "You could say that. I haven't talked to my father in ten years."

"I can't imagine you could have done anything so horrible that would make him throw you out." At first Jordan was surprised Bertha knew about her past, but then she remembered that the coffee shop was the center of the gossip mill. "You're a wonderful, intelligent, nice, beautiful woman. Anyone would be honored to have you as their daughter. Anyone with a right mind, anyway." Bertha shot Jordan's father a dirty look.

The center of Jordan's chest warmed, and a hard lump formed in her throat. If she didn't know better, she'd think she was about to cry.

She'd spent most of her life not feeling good enough. To have someone say, with such honest conviction, that she was worthy of her father's love, meant everything.

Jordan cleared her throat. "Thank you. You're a good friend, Bertha."

"I just tell it like it is." Bertha patted her arm and winked.

Jordan glanced at her father. "Guess I should get this over with."

"I'm here if you need me."

Jordan smiled, hoping Bertha knew how much her words meant to her. They barely knew each other, but she'd been more hospitable than her own family had. Jordan took a deep breath and walked across the cafe.

"Hi, Dad." She put the cups on the table and slid into the booth.

"Jordan." He blew into the steaming coffee, avoiding eye contact.

"Did you want cream and sugar, because I can get—"

"No, this is fine."

Jordan took a sip and snuck peeks at her father over the rim of the cup. Her breath caught when he looked directly at her. She'd forgotten how intense his dark eyes could be, like two cold cast-iron skillets. She looked down, needing to break the contact.

"Why did you want to see me?" Charles asked.

Okay, right to the point. No small talk.

"Honestly, I'm here for one reason only. And that's because of Grandmother." Charles was stone-faced, aside from a twitch in his left eye. "She wrote me a letter demanding that I live in Monarch for two months, have contact with you twice, and try to make amends before I'm allowed to take over the land and the sanctuary."

"I should've figured she'd try something like this. Haunting me from the grave." Charles shook his head.

"Personally, I didn't think she'd care one way or the other if we reconciled. And I don't understand why she'd leave me anything. We weren't close."

"She's doing it to get back at me."

"Why?"

Charles paused, as though choosing his words carefully. "So, you only wanted to see me because of the will?"

"Yes. But…maybe Grandmother is right. Maybe we should at least talk about what happened."

"There's nothing to talk about. You went to live with your mother."

Jordan glared at her father. "Yes, because I *had* to. It wasn't exactly my choice."

"You didn't put up a fight."

Heat rose to Jordan's face as a pulse pounded in her ears. "I was eighteen! You threw me out! You bought me a plane ticket, shoved it into my hand, and told me to leave. Where else was I supposed to go? I didn't have any money, no other family except for you and Grandmother. I told you I didn't want to leave, but you were irate. I'm not sure if you know this, Dad, but you're not the easiest person to talk to."

Anger flashed in Charles's ebony eyes. "You had a good life. I took care of you for eighteen years, and this is the thanks I get?"

"Yes, Dad. You took good care of me until I disgraced you by having feelings for my best friend. Then you took college away from me. You took my home away from me. You took *her* away from me."

"We're done here." Charles slid out the booth and threw a five-dollar bill on the table. Before Jordan could utter another word he was gone.

Well, that was about as much fun as a vanilla ice cream in the dirt. And she'd probably have more luck winning the lottery than getting him to meet her again. Sophie was insane if she expected Jordan to forgive her father. Why would she want to forgive a man like that?

"I don't mean to be nosy, but are you okay?" Mabel asked as she approached Jordan's table.

"I'm fine. My dad and I have a…challenging relationship, but I guess you probably already know that."

Mabel sat opposite Jordan in the booth. "I don't know Charles very well, but he does always seem to have a scowl on his face. Nothing like Frances."

"You knew my grandmother?"

"Not very well, but I saw her a few times with Madame Butterfly." Mabel grinned widely. "Hey, you know what you need? Happy hour!"

Jordan raised her coffee cup high in the air. "Actually, Mabel, I think you might be onto something there."

Mabel grabbed a napkin, jotted something down, and handed it to Jordan. "It's this Thursday at the library. Well, I better get back to the bookstore before Molly sends out a search party. See you Thursday!"

Jordan studied the directions on the napkin. The Library must be a new bar in town. Molly and Mabel probably weren't the girls-gone-wild type, but a heavy dose of cheap booze sounded pretty good about now.

Jordan glared at her cell phone on the table as it dinged with a text from Bibi.

I miss you and am sending a gift your way soon.

Jordan didn't respond, mostly because she couldn't think of anything nice to say.

❖

Sophie looked at her watch and frowned. It was almost eleven and Jordan wasn't in yet. How long could it take to drink coffee? Maybe things hadn't gone well with her father and she was playing hooky. Disappointment bubbled within Sophie. She didn't want to admit it, but after only a week she'd gotten used to having Jordan around. She gazed at the caterpillars, hoping they'd take her mind off the hazel-eyed beauty. Excitement shot through her solar plexus when Jordan opened the door.

"Hey," Jordan said as she plopped her backpack on a table and shuffled toward Sophie. "Wow, the kids are really growing. Why'd you put them in the same container?"

"I figured since they're practically twins they shouldn't be separated. It's okay to keep a few caterpillars in one enclosure as long as it isn't crowded."

"What are they eating?"

"Their skin." Sophie laughed at the disgust on Jordan's face. "They're molting. It's normal."

"Guys, you should really try the Italian sub from Bertha's. It's sooo much better than what you're munching on. Is that one trying to escape?" Jordan pointed to a caterpillar crawling up the side.

"No. They do that when they're getting ready to spin a cocoon, which should be by the end of this week."

"Really? So we'll get to see them do that?" Jordan's eyes sparkled with excitement. "When do they become butterflies?"

"After they enter the chrysalis stage, it'll be about ten to fourteen days, so around the end of December."

"Now that's something I'd really love to see. It's kinda sad, though. They won't be caterpillars anymore. I've gotten used to having them around. It's like a death."

"Actually, that's the metaphor for the cocoon stage. But then look at what they'll become. Beautiful butterflies."

"But we'll have to let them go then." Jordan walked to a chair, plopped down, and slid low into the seat, looking like she was about to face the guillotine.

"It's not *that* depressing, is it?"

"It's not the butterflies."

"Did things not go well with your dad?"

Jordan responded with a grunt, sadness simmering in her eyes.

"How about we get out of here and take a walk on the beach?" Sophie grabbed Jordan's hand, pulled her up, and practically pushed her out the door.

Even though the sun was shining, the wind was gusty and brisk. Sophie stuffed her hands into her pockets and pulled her jacket tighter around herself. She peered at Jordan, who seemed lost in her own world. As they walked along the shore in silence, they occasionally jumped back as the waves washed toward them.

Sophie stopped abruptly and picked up a sliver of paper in the sand. "Look, it's from a fortune cookie. Now if this isn't a sign, I don't know what is."

A slow smile crept on Jordan's face.

"What's so funny?" Sophie asked.

"You, but in a cute way. So, what's your fortune say?"

Sophie looked at the paper and read, "Exciting times are coming your way."

"In bed," Jordan said.

"What?"

"You're supposed to say *in bed* after reading a fortune."

"You just made that up." Sophie nudged Jordan's shoulder.

"No, seriously. You've never heard that before?"

"That must be an LA thing."

"It's an everybody thing." Jordan grabbed the paper and read, "Exciting times are coming your way…in bed."

"It does sound better your way," Sophie said, surprised by her sultry tone.

"Well, exciting in bed isn't something I'd know about."

"What do you mean?"

"The last person I dated said I was a cold fish." Jordan closed her eyes and groaned loudly. "Oh, my God. Why did I just say that?"

"No way. That can't be true. You're…sexy."

Jordan kept her eyes closed and shook her head. "Please forget I said that." She squinted one eye open. "Please?"

Sophie smiled. "Okay, but I still don't buy it."

They walked a bit farther down the beach until Sophie suggested they sit in the sand and enjoy the view. The water was blue-green, with calm waves cascading onto the shore. As beautiful as the surroundings were, Sophie couldn't take her eyes off Jordan. She marveled at her long eyelashes, perfect nose, and sensuous lips. Jordan's mood-ring eyes were the exact color of the ocean, which for her meant she was nervous.

After a few moments, Sophie asked, "What was it like seeing your father again?"

Jordan paused and turned to Sophie, her eyes a dark teal now. "Awkward. Uncomfortable."

"You never did tell me what your argument was about. Why did he throw you out?"

Jordan studied the point where the ocean met the sky. "It's a long story."

"We have time. You can trust me, whatever it is." Sophie bit her lower lip and patiently waited as Jordan seemingly mulled over the idea of opening up.

"You know my father. It wouldn't have taken much for him to disown me. He was pretty strict."

The overwhelming sadness in Jordan's eyes made Sophie want to wrap her arms around her and protect her from any more pain. She wanted to kiss Jordan tenderly and tell her that no matter what had happened, she didn't deserve such treatment and that she was perfect. Instead, Sophie laid her hand on Jordan's knee, hoping that one day soon she'd feel comfortable enough to open up.

CHAPTER FOURTEEN

Not-So-Happy Hour

This couldn't be right. As Jordan cruised through town, she grabbed the napkin Mabel had given her and checked the address. She was on the right street, but this didn't look like an area that would have a bar. She rolled to a stop at the address and read a sign: MONARCH PUBLIC LIBRARY. The Library is an *actual* library? What a weird place to have a happy hour. She would have sped away, but Sophie's Jeep was there, so she decided to check it out.

Jordan heard boisterous laughter as she opened the door to the building, so she followed the sound down a hall until she reached the main library. About twenty-five women were drinking from wineglasses and munching snacks. To the right stretched a long table covered with an array of scrumptious-looking dishes that made Jordan's stomach growl.

"Jordan! You made it!" Mabel, who smelled like grape juice and apple pie, embraced her. "Let me introduce you to everyone." Mabel linked arms with her and walked her to a group of women.

Jordan spotted Nanci and Sophie huddled in a corner, looking cozy. A twinge of jealousy gripped her. That was weird. She wasn't the jealous type, and certainly not with someone she wasn't even dating. As though sensing she was being watched, Sophie locked eyes with Jordan. She raised her wineglass, sending her a telepathic hello.

"…and this is Mrs. Holmstead. Her husband is the county sheriff." Jordan peeled her eyes away from Sophie as Mabel introduced her to various women.

"It's so exciting to meet a celebrity," one of the women said. "I saw you on TV and had no idea your grandmother was Frances and that your father is Charles. Imagine that."

Jordan smiled and nodded. She stole a glance at Sophie, who was still staring right at her as Nanci chatted nonstop.

Molly walked to the group and stood by Mabel, making it hard for Jordan to tell them apart in their matching red dresses with white lace around the collar. "Were you here when the turn-of-the-century earthquake hit?" Molly asked.

"I was. In fact, it was my last night in town."

"You have to come to Bertha's shake, rattle, and roll bash," Mabel said. "I know it's silly to commemorate an earthquake, but it was the biggest one that's hit the central coast in over thirty years. And on New Year's Eve, no less."

"Speaking of Bertha," Molly said. "I wonder where she is? She's supposed to bring her Italian cream pie. I've been waiting for that all day."

As the women surveyed the crowd looking for Bertha, Jordan excused herself and made a beeline for Sophie when Nanci left to raid the buffet. Jordan kept her gaze on Sophie as she walked toward her. She looked particularly radiant, so much so that Jordan couldn't get the lyrics to the song "You Are So Beautiful" out of her head.

"Come here often?" Jordan asked.

"Is that your best pickup line?" Sophie's clear blue eyes sparkled with delight. "Are you going to ask what my sign is next?"

"I already know you're a Pisces. You're devoted, sensitive, and intuitive. Your symbol is two fish swimming in opposite directions. You live both in the physical world as well as the spiritual."

"I'm impressed."

Jordan smiled proudly. "You should be."

"And modest, too. So what are you doing here? I didn't think this would be your scene."

"I think I was tricked. When Mabel invited me to happy hour, this wasn't exactly what I envisioned. And I thought the Library was a bar in town."

Sophie put a hand over her mouth and suppressed a giggle. "Don't make me choke on my grape juice."

"Grape juice? You mean it's not even wine? Is there *any* liquor here?"

"Not a drop. This is an alcohol-free zone. I guess Mabel neglected to explain that fact."

"Must have slipped her mind. So how do you know Nanci with an *i*?"

Sophie cocked her head and studied Jordan. "How'd you know that's how she introduced herself?"

"I...uh...met her in town once." Jordan hoped Nanci remembered to keep the sanctuary plans a secret. Sophie didn't need to know she'd already decided to sell.

"Actually, this is sort of a blind date. Bertha set us up. We just met tonight."

"Oh. Well, I don't want to intrude."

Sophie grabbed Jordan's arm as she inched away. "Don't go. I don't even know her. I want you to stay." The sincerity in Sophie's eyes convinced her.

"So," Jordan said, looking around the room. "Does everyone here know you and Nanci are lesbians?"

"Sure. Why do you ask?"

"They all seem so accepting. I figured it'd be difficult to be gay in such a small town."

"Most Monarch residents are supportive, but I'm sure not everyone...like your father."

Jordan jerked her head toward Sophie. "My father? Why? What did he say?"

"It's nothing he said, but when I moved back from college he seemed to take a particular dislike to me. I approached him several times to ask about you, and he practically slammed the door in my face. I got the feeling he was disgusted by me, and I couldn't figure out why until it dawned on me that the only thing different was that I came out of the closet."

"God, Sophie. I'm so sorry he treated you like that. What an ass."

"It's okay. Really. I could have cared less what he thought of me. All I wanted was information about you." Sophie placed her hand on Jordan's lower back, leaned close, and whispered, "I still don't know what made you stay away so long, but I do plan to find out. One of these days you'll open up to me, Jordan Lee, and you'll see you can trust me."

Shivers cascaded up and down Jordan's spine as goose bumps appeared on her arms. She wasn't sure if Sophie's touch or the softness in her voice as she whispered her name had caused such a reaction.

Sophie removed her hand and inched back, appearing suddenly nervous. "Actually, I wanted to ask you something."

Before Jordan could respond, someone placed a hand on her shoulder. She turned around, face-to-face with the intense, dark eyes of Madame Butterfly.

"It's nice to see you again, Jordan."

"Ah, yes. How are you tonight?"

"I'm well, my dear. I'll be conducting psychic readings later for the ladies if you'd like to join."

"Nooo, thanks. I'm good."

"Well, if you change your mind, let me know." Madame smiled at Sophie before walking away.

"That woman scares the crap outta me," Jordan said.

"Madame? Why? She's harmless."

"She smiles at you but gives me those intense I-know-what-you're-thinking stares."

"Did any of Madame Butterfly's reading ring true? Like…are you pining for someone you love but can't be with?"

Jordan glanced at Sophie before averting her eyes downward. "No. Not at all."

"So you're not in a relationship in LA? You're not in love?"

Jordan's heart hammered. "Weren't you going to ask me something? Before Madame interrupted us?"

"Oh, yes…well, I'm driving up the coast Monday for a couple of days and…well, would you like to join me? It's for work. I'll stay in Big Sur and visit a couple of schools conducting educational classes. You don't have to, of course, but you got so bored last time I was away. Not that you didn't do an awesome job organizing everything, but I just thought maybe…possibly…you know…"

"Sophie, you can stop explaining. I'd love to go. I've never been to Big Sur."

"Really? I—"

"Did someone say Big Sur?" Nanci asked. "It's beautiful there. Hello, Jordan. It's nice to see you again. Watching you two from across the room, I'd swear you were old friends. But didn't you just meet a few weeks ago?"

"Actually, Jordan and I went to school together for eight years."

"Really? Small world. Sophie, did you hear about the new art museum in Tallon? Maybe we could check it out sometime."

"Sure. That sounds great."

"I think I'll check out the food spread," Jordan said, feeling like a third wheel. Even though Sophie gave her a you-don't-have-to-leave look, Jordan walked away, wishing she had something stronger than grape juice to drink.

Jordan was filling a plate when Bertha walked in carrying a pie in each hand and looking out of breath and excited.

"There's that Italian cream pie." Molly grabbed the desserts from Bertha. "Where have you been?"

Bertha rapidly patted her chest, attempting to catch her breath. Had it not been for her ginormous smile, Jordan would have thought she was having a heart attack.

"You won't believe who's right outside the door," Bertha said breathlessly.

"Who?" everyone asked in unison.

"Is Jordan here? Please say she's here." Bertha looked around until she spotted Jordan and ran toward her. Everyone circled them, obviously curious as to what the ruckus was about. Sophie and Nanci even cut their cuddle time short.

"Girls, we not only have one celebrity in our midst, but two!"

"Who's here?" Molly asked, excitedly.

Jordan had a bad feeling about this new development.

"Wait here. Don't move a muscle." Bertha ran out of the room.

Jordan shrugged as all the women looked at her questioningly. Within a few seconds, Bertha emerged with the international instant-coffee queen herself.

"Bibi?! What the…" Jordan's mouth fell open, and she had a sudden urge to duck under the buffet table.

"Darling, it's so good to see you." Bibi grabbed Jordan's shoulders and gave her a kiss on each cheek.

Jordan stared, completely stunned. "What are you doing here?"

"I texted that I was sending a gift. Well, here it is!" Bibi swung out her arms like she expected Jordan to dive into her embrace. Instead, Jordan stared and blinked rapidly.

"How'd you find me?"

"I stopped at the coffee shop to ask for directions, and this nice lady said you'd be here. Why didn't you tell me you're a landowner? Surely you're not staying in this…place." Bibi sneered at the women around them.

Jordan winced. Bertha must have told Bibi that she owned the sanctuary. She couldn't blame her, though. It wasn't exactly a secret.

"But *why* are you here?" Jordan suddenly realized they were in the company of others and this probably wasn't the best line of questioning, especially with Sophie two feet away. This wasn't the way she wanted to be outed. Jordan glanced at Sophie, who had a concerned expression.

"Are you who I think you are?" Mabel peered closely at Bibi.

"You're the Frenchwoman on those coffee commercials, aren't you?" Molly asked.

"Oh, my, am I seeing double?" Bibi looked from Molly to Mabel.

"They're twins." Jordan felt suddenly protective of the women. She didn't want Bibi saying anything to belittle them.

Bertha linked arms with Bibi and pulled her to the buffet table. "You must try a piece of my pie. You're so thin. You need more than just coffee, dear."

Jordan jumped at the sound of Sophie's voice behind her. "Why didn't you tell me you knew her?"

"What do you mean? I know a lot of famous people I haven't told you about."

"When you were at my place and saw her picture on the coffee box, you didn't say anything." Anger flashed in Sophie's eyes.

"Oh. Well, Bibi and I aren't exactly friends. I didn't want to get into our history then."

"You have a lot of secrets, don't you? I'm beginning to think Madame's reading was right."

Bibi whisked Jordan around, shot Sophie a dirty look, and whispered, "Why don't we cut out of this honky-tonk party and have our own special celebration at your condo?"

Jordan peered at Sophie out the corner of her eye. She needed to get Bibi out of there before she said anything more.

"Sure, yeah, let's go." As everyone bid their good-byes, Jordan watched Sophie and Nanci head back to their cozy corner.

❖

Jordan fumbled in the dark for her keyhole with Bibi hanging around her neck. As they stumbled into the condo she pinned Jordan against the wall and kissed her forcefully. Before Jordan knew what was happening, Bibi slipped her hands inside Jordan's shirt and unhooked her bra. Jordan put her hands on Bibi's shoulders and pushed back, which caused a momentary flash of anger in Bibi's eyes.

"What are you doing?" Jordan kept her hands firmly on Bibi's shoulders.

"Darling, if you don't know what I'm doing, then it's been much too long since you've been with a woman." Bibi leaned in for another kiss as Jordan turned her head.

"We broke up. We're not dating."

Bibi's lower lip jutted out in a pout. "You said we could talk."

"This isn't exactly talking. Look, you're a beautiful woman. I know there are hundreds of women in LA who would love to be with you. But you and I...we don't fit." Jordan dropped her hands and rubbed the back of her neck.

"Is it that blonde you were looking at? Are you sleeping with her? Is that why you came here?"

"What? Who are you talking about?"

"That vanilla cream puff who couldn't take her eyes off you."

"Sophie? We're just friends."

"Then why are you here? That woman said you own land. Surely you're selling."

"That's really none of your business."

"Come back to LA with me." Bibi grabbed Jordan's hands as she pulled away.

"No. Look, I'm sorry—"

"I drove two hundred and fifty fucking miles to surprise you, and this is what I get!? And just what am I supposed to do now that I'm stuck in the middle of nowhere?" Bibi stormed into the condo with Jordan following.

"There's a motel in town if—"

"Motel!? You want Bibi to stay at a *motel*?"

The expression on Bibi's face was straight out of a horror movie. She really should branch out into starring in scary flicks.

"Right. No. Of course not. It's late, so you can sleep in my bed and I'll crash on the sofa, and you can leave in the morning. Is your bag in the car? I'll grab it for you."

Bibi slumped into a chair. "Be careful with it. It's Armani."

Jordan wasn't surprised to see five bags in Bibi's trunk. The woman never could pack light. After getting Bibi settled in her room, Jordan gathered some blankets and laid them on the sofa. When she went into the kitchen for a glass of water, she contemplated hiding the large, sharp knives on the counter but resisted. Bibi was annoying but not dangerous.

Jordan stretched out on the couch and closed her eyes. Just as she was drifting off to sleep, an image of Sophie and Nanci popped into her mind. Not that anything was wrong with the real-estate agent, but Jordan's intuition told her she wasn't right for Sophie.

No, Sophie needs someone more...like me. Jordan bolted upright, suddenly wide-awake. *Where'd that come from?*

CHAPTER FIFTEEN

Candy Canes and Kisses

Who'd be texting at six a.m.? Sophie yawned, turned over in bed, and grabbed her cell phone. Tingles coursed through her body when she saw Jordan's name. Her excitement plummeted, though, when she read the note.

Won't be in today. What time should I be there Monday to leave for Big Sur? Have a good weekend.

Sophie responded: *8 a.m.*

She wasn't sure why the phrase "Have a good weekend" ticked her off so much. She guessed that meant Jordan would be busy with her guest and wouldn't be at work. Sophie reclined in bed and thought about Jordan and the coffee queen. There was something strange about that woman. Jordan had said they weren't friends, nor did she look happy to see her, so who was she? An enemy? And why didn't Jordan tell Sophie that she knew her? The whole thing felt off.

Sophie took a deep breath and attempted to clear her mind. Jordan occupied her thoughts far more than she'd like. She needed a girlfriend. It'd been a month since she'd done the soul-mate ceremony. Shouldn't she have met someone by now? All Sophie wanted was a woman lying next to her. Correction: a naked woman. Actually, make that a hot, naked woman. Was that too much to ask? An image of Jordan flashed through Sophie's mind. Not just any image, but a hot, nude image where she was lying on her back, with one arm behind her head and the other draped across Sophie's stomach. The sight of her, even though it was a daydream, was arousing. Sophie imagined covering Jordan's breast with her mouth, sucking, licking, until she cried out in pleasure.

Sophie slipped a hand underneath her T-shirt and caressed her breast. Her nipple hardened as she lightly pinched and squeezed. The thought of Jordan's tongue mimicking her touch left her breathless and with a pulsation down below. Instinctively, Sophie squeezed her thighs together in an attempt to relieve the throbbing ache. As she continued fondling her breast, she let her other hand creep inside her shorts, not surprised to find that she was wet. Craving immediate release, she pressed hard against her clit but stopped abruptly when she pictured Jordan planting kisses down her stomach.

Why do I keep thinking about her?

Determined to come hard and quick, Sophie slipped off her shorts and underwear and stroked herself. When was the last time she'd had an orgasm? Three months? Six months? God, had it been that long? After Cindy dumped her, Sophie's sex drive had plummeted. She hadn't had a sensual thought since...well, until Jordan had arrived. For some reason that woman had an effect on her.

"Come on, concentrate," Sophie scolded herself as she rubbed faster. "Ugh! This isn't working." Exasperated, she gave up and sprawled out on the bed. After a few moments, a thought popped into her mind. Hadn't Cindy given her a stocking stuffer that might help in this particular situation? Sophie bolted out of bed, opened her closet, and rummaged through a cardboard box. She pulled out tools, extension cords, and photo albums, until she finally saw what she was hunting: an unopened candy-cane vibrator. Sophie read the package and chuckled at the one-liner, "Santa isn't the only one coming tonight." At the time, she thought it was a cute gag gift but never had the gumption to actually use it. Something about pleasuring herself with a candy cane seemed anti-Christmas. Sophie studied the woman on the package, who wore a revealing crimson velvet miniskirt and low-cut blouse, with the striped red-and-white vibrator strategically placed between her legs. From the look of rapture on her face it must have been doing the trick, which was enough to convince Sophie to rip open the package.

She sat on the bed, installed the batteries, and lay down, willing herself to relax and not think about Jordan, since masturbating while fantasizing about your straight friend was downright creepy. Sophie pressed the button on the vibrator and froze when nothing happened. She pressed it again, with no response. Thinking she must have the batteries in backward, she switched them around. Repeatedly, she punched the button and then resorted to shaking the thing when it didn't turn on. Finally, it started working. She felt a little guilty saying a silent prayer that it'd stay on long enough to provide release. God probably didn't take kindly to vibrator pleas.

The pulsations felt good, but Sophie couldn't get past the fact that she had a candy cane between her legs. *Forget about the striped vibrator, Sophie. And God, don't think about that blind date who insisted you call her Candy Kane. Think about Jordan if you have to, but just come already.*

Sophie pictured Jordan hovering above her, beautiful hazel eyes filled with desire, full lips waiting to be kissed. The longing to feel Jordan's mouth, taste her lips, her tongue, became unbearable. Sophie slipped a hand around Jordan's neck and pulled her down for a searing kiss. The moment their lips met, the vibration abruptly stopped.

"You have got to be kidding me." Sophie shook the thing and even banged it against the headboard. Figured Cindy would have given her a crappy present.

Sophie threw the vibrator across the room and released a frustrated growl. Instead of touching herself, she should have just taken a cold shower. That way she wouldn't be left frustrated, with steamy thoughts of naked Jordan, and with an odd, intense craving for a candy cane.

A run on the beach was a sad replacement for an orgasm, but it was the only thing Sophie could think of to release pent-up energy. She donned Nikes, sweat pants, and a sweatshirt. It was cool outside, but she passed on the fleece jacket, knowing it wouldn't take long to break a sweat, since she planned on an intense run.

Sophie sped through the eucalyptus forest on the way to the beach, not even slowing down to visit the butterflies. Once she reached the ocean's edge, she stopped to catch her breath. It was an overcast morning, the sun nowhere in sight. Only a small portion of the water was visible until it melted into a haze. Foggy mornings were the norm along the central coast and something Sophie didn't mind today since it matched her mood.

The tide was low, which made running easier. She jogged close to the water on wet, firmly packed sand. She flew down the shoreline, disappointed to see the quickly approaching condos. Great. All she needed was another reminder of Jordan. She was glad they were friends again, but some of her daydreams hadn't been of the friendly nature. As Sophie ran past the condos she tried not to look at Jordan's deck, but a magnetic force turned her head.

What Sophie saw caused her to stop abruptly. It took several seconds for the image to register. She squinted, thinking the fog had distorted her vision, but no, the scene was undeniable. Jordan and the French coffee queen were standing on the patio kissing. Like majorly kissing. Not just a friendly peck on the cheek, but a full-force, all-out, lip-locking, probably even tongue-touching kiss. Sophie looked down and then back up again. Nope, she hadn't imagined it. It was like their lips were adhered together with superglue.

What the hell? Was Jordan bi? Or experimenting? Or a lesbian? She couldn't be gay. She'd have told Sophie by now. Or would she? Sophie had a feeling Jordan was hiding something. Maybe this was it. But why would she conceal her sexuality knowing Sophie was out? Sophie stumbled backward before sprinting down the beach.

CHAPTER SIXTEEN

Out of the Closet

Jordan sat on her deck and wondered why she'd told Sophie she wouldn't be in today. Granted, it'd taken most of the morning to get rid of Bibi, but now she was bored. Jordan grimaced at Bibi's last-ditch effort to stay. She'd latched onto Jordan like a blood-sucking tick and given her a searing good-bye kiss. It'd taken all Jordan's strength to push her away. The woman obviously couldn't take rejection.

It was one o'clock. Jordan could still go to the sanctuary, see the caterpillars...and Sophie. With that thought, she bolted out of the lounger and grabbed her keys.

Sophie was hanging a large net when Jordan opened the door. Her head jerked toward the entrance. "What are you doing here?"

"Thought I'd come by and see how the guys are doing." Jordan walked to the caterpillars and peered into the enclosure. They were both hanging upside down in a *J* shape. "Are they shedding their skin again?"

"Yes."

"What's that weird greenish color underneath?"

Sophie joined Jordan and looked at the caterpillars. "That's the cocoon. So how does your guest like Monarch?"

"What?" Jordan looked at Sophie questioningly.

"The French actress."

"Oh, Bibi. I don't think this is her kind of town. She headed back to LA this morning. What are the nets for?"

"Monday morning I'll move the cocoons in there. So who is she exactly? You said she wasn't a friend."

"Just someone I know in LA. What happens when they're in the cocoon?"

"The caterpillar's organs and other body parts dissolve and re-form into new limbs and wings. Is there anything you want to tell me?"

Jordan looked at Sophie. "What do you mean?"

Sophie started to say something but then retreated, returning her attention to the hanging net.

"Is something wrong?" Jordan asked. No response. *Okay, guess she doesn't want to talk about it.* "What's the temp in Big Sur this time of the year? What should I pack?"

Sophie kept her back to Jordan as she spoke. "You don't have to go with me, you know."

"I want to. If you still want me, that is."

"You're the boss."

Something was definitely up, but Jordan didn't have a clue as to what it was. They'd been getting along so well, but now it felt like when she'd first arrived, with Sophie angry and distant. Jordan looked at the caterpillars, silently wishing she had a cocoon to disappear into.

After a few minutes, Sophie faced Jordan. "I saw you."

"What?" Jordan asked.

"I was running on the beach, and I saw you kissing that woman on your deck."

Jordan closed her eyes, rolled her head back, and groaned.

"What's going on? Are you bi?"

Jordan took a deep breath and let it out slowly. "I'm a lesbian."

"Why didn't you tell me!?" A mixture of hurt and anger flared in Sophie's eyes.

"I don't know. It just never came up." Okay, maybe that was a little white lie.

"What are you talking about? There were dozens of times you could have told me. Oh…wait…are you in the closet? You're not out?"

Jordan walked across the room and sat on the edge of Sophie's desk. "I'm not in the closet, but I don't scream it from the rooftops either. Look, I'm sorry I didn't tell you. I'm just a very private person. Doug tells me I'm too secretive, and maybe he's right. But I honestly didn't mean to be deceiving."

"I have a real problem with dishonesty, Jordan. After my last relationship, trust is a big issue for me. If we're going to be friends we need to have complete honesty."

"I would never lie to you. I just…omitted a fact about myself."

"That's the same thing as lying."

"I don't agree. I never told you I was straight. You just assumed I was."

Sophie clenched her jaw and squinted her eyes. "It feels deceptive. I wish you'd trusted me enough to tell me. I thought we were friends."

"We are. I'm sorry. It's not that I don't trust you. I'm just private. It's something I need to work on, I know."

Sophie paused for several long seconds and glared at Jordan. "All right. So, that…Bibi woman…she's your girlfriend?"

"God, no. Well, we did date a few months, but I ended it before coming here. Her showing up was a complete surprise. And she forced that kiss you saw on me. I guess you didn't see me push her off?"

"No. I missed that. All I saw was a major lip-lock." Sophie raised an eyebrow and looked like she'd just tasted something disgusting.

"So, we're okay? I'm forgiven?"

Sophie pressed her lips together and looked like she was about to ask another question—probably a lot of questions—but refrained, to Jordan's relief. "I suppose, but no more secrets, all right?"

Jordan held up two fingers. "Scout's honor." She felt a pang of guilt about hiding the fact that she planned to sell the sanctuary. She did, though, intend to keep her promise not to do so until after February, so that wasn't like lying. Was it?

Sophie sat at her desk and stared at the computer screen, the tension in the air still palpable. They needed to change the subject, maybe something to lighten the mood.

"Call me crazy," Jordan said, "but I was thinking about going to my brother's basketball game tonight. Would you like to go with me?"

"Aren't you worried your father will be there?"

"Actually, that might be a good thing. We didn't end on a good note, and I'm not sure how to ask him to get together again."

"Well, I'd go, but I'm attending a gallery opening with Nanci tonight."

"Ah. A hot date, huh?"

"It's just a friendly outing, which I suppose technically could be deciphered as a date."

"I don't think she's right for you." *Did I just say that out loud?*

Sophie studied her. "Oh?"

"I'm a professional matchmaker. I know these things. And I've totally been slacking. I'm supposed to be helping you find Mrs. Right."

"And that isn't Nanci?"

"Definitely not."

"She seems nice, but I don't know her very well." Sophie shrugged. "I'll see how it goes."

"Okay, but don't say I didn't warn you," Jordan said, hoping she sounded lighthearted. "So, Big Sur on Monday, right? How many days are we staying?"

"Two nights. We'll drive back Wednesday. Pack something warm since it gets cold there at night. There aren't many lodging options, so hopefully you don't mind sharing a room."

It hadn't dawned on Jordan that she'd be bunking with Sophie on this little road trip. And from the sudden blush on Sophie's cheeks, it had just now occurred to her as well.

❖

If it weren't for Bertha knocking on her windshield, Jordan probably would have driven away. She'd been sitting in her car outside the school gym for at least fifteen minutes trying to muster up the courage to go inside. Bertha jabbed a butterfly cookie into her hand when she rolled down the window.

"Are you here for the game?" Bertha asked.

"I was thinking about it." Jordan waved the cookie in the air. "Thanks."

"I make those for the kids. They like a little treat afterward. Well, what are you doing sitting there? Come on in!" Bertha opened the car door and pulled Jordan out of the driver's seat.

"I'm not so sure I should be here."

"Whyever not?" Bertha linked arms with Jordan and walked them briskly toward the gymnasium. "Isn't your little brother playing tonight?"

For a second, Jordan wondered how she knew about Chuck but then remembered who she was talking to. In fact, Jordan wouldn't be surprised if Bertha knew she was a lesbian, even though she'd just come out to Sophie a few hours ago.

"Yeah, but I don't really know him. I'm not sure he'd want me here."

"That's nonsense. Any kid would be happier than a tornado in a trailer park to have a famous sister like you."

Jordan snorted a laugh. "You do have a way with words, Bertha."

"I'm just speaking the truth. Where's your actress friend? Is she coming tonight?"

"No. She had to head back to LA this morning."

Thanks to Bertha, Jordan's nerves had subsided a bit by the time they entered the gym. Obviously, this was the place to be on a Friday night in Monarch. The bleachers were packed.

Bertha grabbed Jordan's hand and pulled her along. "Coach Bryant always saves me a courtside seat. You can sit with me."

They walked around the gym and squeezed onto the bench behind the home team. Bertha gave the coach a quick wave, which garnered a wink that had her giggling like a schoolgirl. Jordan smiled to herself. Bertha had the hots for the coach, and from all appearances it seemed to be mutual.

"So, Bertha, have you ever been married?"

"Once, for a few wonderful years. Wilbur didn't come back from the Vietnam War, like so many others." Bertha got a faraway look in her eyes.

"Oh, I'm sorry. And you never met anyone after that?"

"No. He was the love of my life, and now I'm far too old at sixty-five to find a husband."

"Sixty-five isn't old! You're one happening chick. You own a successful business, you're a great cook, you're attractive. Sooo…is the coach single?"

Bertha shot Jordan a curious look. "He's a widow. His wife died of cancer about five years ago."

"Hmmm…looks like a nice guy."

"Now, Jordan Lee, I'm not one of your fancy Beverly Hills clients. Soul mates can't be replaced."

Jordan couldn't argue with that, but the matchmaker in her wanted to make a love connection. Bertha deserved to be with someone who would put a smile on her face. The coach looked like a nice, jovial sort of fellow, who reminded her of a Buddha with his big belly and infectious smile. Most of all, Jordan liked the way his eyes sparkled when he looked at Bertha. She had a good feeling about him.

"Jordan!"

Someone called her name, but she wasn't sure where it was coming from.

"Jordan! Over here!"

She looked down the line of incredibly short basketball players until she spotted Chuck waving both arms high in the air. She held up her hand before glancing in the stands to see Rebecca staring right at her. Her father, though, was nowhere in sight.

Jordan eyed the opposing team, the Baskerville Bees, across the court. Even though Monarch Butterflies didn't sound terribly threatening, she was pretty sure they could kick some Bees ass.

"Where's the scoreboard?" Jordan asked, looking around the gymnasium.

"They don't keep score," Bertha said.

Jordan stared at her, dumbfounded. "How do they know who wins?"

"They play for fun."

For fun? Jordan had never heard of such a thing. Why play a sport if you didn't keep score? Once the game started, Jordan had to admit it was amusing to watch. The kids were pretty cute, especially the ones who ran around in circles purposefully getting dizzy until they collapsed on the court. Her favorite, though, was the Bee who seemed to be allergic to the ball. Either that or he thought they were playing dodgeball instead of basketball. He'd cost his team at least eight points so far. Yes, Jordan was secretly keeping score and happy to report that the Butterflies were up by six points, mostly due to her little brother. Chuck sank several baskets, often looking at Jordan afterward to make sure she was watching.

After the game was over, Chuck ran straight to Jordan. "You came!"

"Hey. You played awesome." She jabbed him lightly on the arm.

Chuck grinned. "I bet we won."

Jordan glanced around to make sure no one was listening, then bent down and whispered, "You guys killed the Bees. Sixteen to eight."

"Yeah, baby!" Chuck pumped his arm and gave Jordan a high-five. Rebecca walked up and placed her hands on Chuck's shoulders. "Mom, Jordan came to my game."

"I see that. Why don't you get your stuff so we can scoot out of here?"

"But Ms. Bertha brought cookies." Chuck pointed to a group of kids with a cookie in one hand and a juice box in the other.

Rebecca sneered. "Ten minutes and then we have to leave."

"Come on, Jordan." Chuck grabbed her hand, which she didn't mind in the least. She'd rather spend time with sweaty seven-year-olds than Rebecca any day.

Bertha handed them both a butterfly cookie as Chuck went to fetch them a drink.

"Well, would you look at that? Now if that isn't a spectacle." Bertha pointed at Rebecca, who was practically mauling Coach Bryant. Her hands were all over him as she jutted out her double Ds and looked like she was about to plant a smooch on his cheek.

Bertha gasped and put a hand over her mouth. "Oh, I'm sorry. That's your stepmother, isn't it?"

"Unfortunately, yes. But don't worry about it." Jordan looked at Bertha. "You know, the coach is hating every second of that. He looks panic-stricken."

"Really? You sure?" Bertha didn't look convinced.

"Absolutely. Women like Rebecca are a dime a dozen. But you're worth a million." Jordan smiled and winked, which caused Bertha to stand up a little straighter and raise her chin.

Chuck approached and handed Jordan a juice box. They sat on the bench, and each took a big bite out of a butterfly cookie.

"So did your…or rather our…dad come tonight?" Jordan asked.

"No. He had to work. He does that a lot. Do you really live in Hollywood with the famous people?"

"Yep, I do. Have you ever been?"

"Gosh, no. Do you know Mickey Mouse?"

Jordan grinned. "Not personally, but I have been to his house at Disneyland."

Chuck stopped chewing, his hazel eyes widening. "You've been to Mickey's house?"

"Sure. Maybe you could go sometime. So, Chuck—"

"Remember. Call me Chucky."

"Right. Like the scary movie. Did our parents tell you I'm a lesbian?" Jordan didn't want to pump the kid for information, but she really wanted to learn how he knew she was gay.

"No. Grandma told me."

Jordan choked on her cookie and cleared her throat before responding. "Grandma? As in our dad's mom?"

"Yeah. She told me before she died. I miss her."

Jordan's heart melted at Chuck's pathetic little sad face. "I'm sorry. Were you close to her?"

"We had fun. She'd play with me, and we'd stay up late and watch scary movies when I didn't have to go to school the next day."

Jordan resisted the urge to confirm that they were talking about the same woman. She'd never describe her grandmother as fun, nor had she ever played with Jordan when she was a kid.

"So, what did she say about me?"

Chuck shrugged. "She said you're famous and live in Hollywood with the stars, and that you're gay."

"And…did she seem upset about that?" Jordan felt a twinge of guilt about prodding her little brother, but curiosity won out.

"No, but Mom and Dad sure were when I told them."

Jordan chuckled. "Yeah, I imagine. Do you know what a lesbian is?"

Chuck rolled his eyes dramatically. "Duh! I'm not a little kid, you know. It's when women like women. Like Keith's moms." Chuck pointed to two obviously gay women. Monarch was more progressive than Jordan would have guessed.

"That's right. You're pretty smart." Jordan ruffled the top of his hair.

"Grandma said we should love everyone, especially family, no matter what."

"We *are* talking about Dad's mom, right? Frances?"

Chuck gawked at Jordan. "Duh. You're kinda slow to be so famous."

Jordan laughed. "You're probably right about that, Chucky."

CHAPTER SEVENTEEN

Elk Mountain

Sophie needed a plan. Jordan had been in Monarch for two weeks, and she'd done little to convince her not to sell. Even though Jordan had agreed not to make any decisions until February, Sophie was worried she was seeing dollar signs instead of butterfly wings.

When Sophie reached the sanctuary early Monday morning, she had a couple of hours before Jordan arrived, so she headed for the chrysalides. They had fully formed cocoons over the weekend. Carefully, she removed the twins, placed them into the hanging habitat, and filled the feeder with water to increase the humidity. Normally, she'd mist them every day, but the water should help while they were away. This trip was ill-timed when it came to the caterpillars, but Sophie couldn't cancel on the kids. After taking care of the chrysalides, she sat at her desk and stared into space. Within minutes she had an aha moment. Her posture straightened as she began to grin. The more she thought about it, the better the idea seemed. She clicked on her computer and scrolled through emails until she located one from the National Fish and Wildlife Foundation. After one quick phone call, everything would be set. Sophie had a plan, and all it required was that she and Jordan take a little detour before heading to Big Sur.

After hanging up the phone, Sophie reclined in her chair as her thoughts drifted to Jordan. Tap...tap...tap. She scanned the room, looking for the cause of the sound that had interrupted her daydream, until her eyes landed on her hand, which was frenetically striking a pen against the desk. She stopped the action midair, dropped the pen, and wrung her clammy hands. Sophie was nervous, really nervous. She was about to spend three days with Jordan—and not just any Jordan—but the new and improved lesbian-Jordan. Thank goodness she'd called the

Big Sur Inn last night and changed the accommodations to two single beds.

She should be happy that Jordan was gay. They were both single, and while Sophie wasn't sure how Jordan felt, she still had strong feelings, not to mention the fact that she was wildly attracted to the woman. But no, she felt anxious instead of delighted. Getting involved with Jordan wouldn't be a smart move. They were too different. Jordan was caught up in the rich-and-famous lifestyle. She dated beautiful French actresses named Bibi and lived in Beverly Hills. Plus, she was beyond secretive, which didn't sit well with Sophie. It was enough that they'd become friends again. Why, then, did her heart ache with the disappointment of something that would never be?

Sophie shook off the sensation, forced her attention to the computer, and worked until Jordan arrived. Damn her for looking adorably rugged in jeans, a tight-fitting olive-green T-shirt, and an LA Lakers baseball cap. The shirt in particular was a killer, the way it stretched across her chest and brought out the green specks in her hazel eyes. That shirt did things to Sophie's heart she didn't like, such as causing it to beat wildly. How had she not detected that Jordan was a lesbian? Maybe she didn't want to notice. It was safer that way.

"Hey, you put the guys in the hanging net." Jordan peered at the cocoons.

Sophie gawked at her profile. Christ, that shirt looked even better from the side than it did from the front. The way it accentuated her breasts should be illegal.

Jordan looked at Sophie when she didn't respond. "You okay?"

"Sure." Sophie rummaged through her desk drawer looking for God knows what, basically anything that would divert her attention from Jordan.

"Can I help you find something?" Jordan approached and peered into the jumbled drawer.

Sophie swished items around until she finally grabbed a package of Post-it notes. "Aha! Here they are." She looked up at Jordan, who was staring right at her. Great. Now she had to write something on the note. Sophie grabbed a pen, well aware that Jordan was watching her every move, scribbled *buy more seeds*, and stuck the yellow sticky on her computer.

"So, are you ready to go?" Jordan asked. "We should probably get on the road."

Sophie popped out of her chair like a jack-in-the-box. "Groovy! Let's boogie out of here."

Geez, what a nerd, and for heaven's sake, stop staring at her chest!

❖

Once they were cruising down the Pacific Coast Highway, Jordan reclined her seat. She hoped it made her look more relaxed, and besides, from this vantage point she could stare at Sophie undetected. Her smooth, soft-looking hands gripped the steering wheel at precisely ten and two o'clock, as her eyes—which were bluer than the ocean they were passing—never veered from the highway. As Sophie drove by a big rig, she lightly bit her lower lip, which was one hell of a sexy move. Jordan's eyes fixated on Sophie's arms, thankful that she was wearing short sleeves. At first sight they appeared dainty, but when she clenched the wheel, muscles rippled. The Disney Princess's hair was pulled back in a ponytail, revealing a slender, smooth neck that Jordan imagined nibbling. This was why she'd held off telling Sophie she was a lesbian. It kicked her mind into overdrive and made things between them seem too…possible.

Jordan cringed when Sophie turned her head, obviously busting her for gawking and possibly drooling.

"You okay back there?" Sophie asked.

Jordan shifted her seat upright and stared at the tan Chevrolet in front of them. "Sure. I can drive some, too, if you get tired." *That way maybe I'll stop fantasizing about my lips on your neck.*

"Maybe later. I'm good for now. So, did you go to your brother's basketball game last night?"

Jordan brightened at the thought of Chuck. She'd always felt like an outsider in her family, so it was nice to have a brother who didn't hate her, even if he was a seven-year-old.

"I did. And get this. He said my grandmother was the one who told him I'm gay and that she seemed fine with it."

"Really? That's surprising. Was your dad there?"

"No. I don't know how I'm going to convince him to meet me again. Did you see Nanci with an *i*?" Jordan had purposefully delayed inquiring, unsure she wanted to hear the answer.

"Yes, and her name is just Nanci. We went to that art gallery. It was okay."

"Just okay?" Jordan peered at Sophie out the corner of her eye.

"Okay is good. I haven't had okay in a while."

"Ah, so you'll see her again?"

Sophie shrugged. "Maybe. What about you? Any other Bibis waiting in the wings to date you?"

"No. I've sworn off women."

Sophie chuckled. "You've given up dating at twenty-nine? You're going to stay single for the rest of your life?"

"I'm serious. I'm not getting involved with anyone else. I just want to concentrate on SOS. It's the only thing that makes me happy."

Sophie's smile suddenly vanished, a look of gloom now on her face. "Well, that's just…sad."

Jordan was about to protest, but something in Sophie's voice made her question if maybe she wasn't pathetic after all. She was almost thirty and hadn't had a steady, healthy relationship. Was she really going to spend the rest of her life alone?

Sophie bit her lower lip, except this time she wasn't passing a truck. "Can I…ask you something?"

"Of course," Jordan said.

Sophie paused, long enough to worry Jordan about what she'd ask. "Never mind. It's not important," she said, vigorously shaking her head.

Ordinarily, Jordan would have prodded, but the petrified look on Sophie's face convinced her otherwise.

Jordan answered her cell phone as it rang. "Hello, Mr. Simms."

"Ms. Lee, I was wondering if you could come to my office this afternoon."

"Actually, Sophie and I are heading to Big Sur for a few days on business. Is something wrong?"

"Quite the contrary. I have good news. Your grandmother's estate is out of probate. I'll be issuing a deed to transfer ownership of the land and sanctuary to you, which means you can sell."

Jordan glanced at Sophie. "Wow, that was fast. Um, maybe we should talk about this later. In person. Are you free Thursday morning at ten? We should be back late Wednesday."

"Thursday would be fine. I'll see if Ms. Roberts is available as well."

"Perfect. I'll see you then."

Jordan disconnected, tucked the phone into her bag, and stared straight ahead. Sophie looked back and forth between Jordan and the highway.

"Was that the lawyer? What's up?"

"Not much. I'm meeting with him Thursday."

Jordan squirmed in her seat as Sophie eyed her suspiciously. Selling the sanctuary wasn't going to be as easy as Jordan had expected, but surely Sophie and the townspeople would understand. She was doing it for her company. It wasn't like she was spending the money on something frivolous.

They rode in silence for a while until Sophie exited off the highway. Jordan had never been to Big Sur, but she was fairly certain this wasn't the way.

"I don't think this is the right road." Jordan grabbed a map out of the glove compartment.

"We're taking a little detour first."

"Oh? And just where are we going?"

"You'll see." Sophie had such a cute smirk, it took all Jordan had not to lean over and give her a peck on the cheek. "What are you looking at? You're smiling and have a glint in your eye. You're up to something." Sophie eyed Jordan curiously.

Busted again. Jordan was usually good at hiding her thoughts, but apparently she was slipping. "*Me?* You're the one taking us on a mysterious detour."

"Patience is a virtue, my dear."

"That's a load of crap, oh wise one. No one likes to be patient."

"That's right. I forgot who I was talking to. Remember that sleepover when you coerced me into helping you open all your Christmas presents early?"

Jordan chuckled. "I forgot about that. I must say, we were like professional little thieves. Using a sharp knife was the key to our success. We could slice through the tape without tearing the paper, carefully unwrap the gift just enough to see the image on the box, and then skillfully place a piece of tape where the former one resided. My dad never had a clue."

"Yeah, except you referred to that as the worst Christmas ever since you didn't have any surprises. I think these two months will be good for you," Sophie said. "It'll teach you how to be patient. Have you…uh…thought any more about what you'll do? You know, when your time is up?"

Jordan wondered if that was what Sophie had intended to ask earlier, but she had a feeling it wasn't. "I thought we agreed not to discuss my decision until February."

"I know…I know…I'm just curious."

As Sophie slowed the Jeep and turned down a dirt road, Jordan surveyed the barren surroundings. The scene looked like the set of *The Wild Wild West*, with nothing but cacti and dry grass for miles, except for a mountain in the distance.

"Where are we?" Jordan asked.

Sophie smirked, so Jordan reclined her seat and enjoyed the view—of Sophie, that is. A spattering of trees appeared as they neared the mountain, and the farther they drove, the greener things became. Sophie turned down another dirt road, which revealed a weatherworn sign: ELK MOUNTAIN RESERVATION.

"Is this a Native American reservation? And I'm assuming that's Elk Mountain?" Jordan pointed toward the towering peak.

Sophie patted Jordan's knee. "Can't get anything past you."

Maybe Jordan had seen one too many John Wayne movies, but she had pictured a reservation to be filled with teepees, horses, campfires, and war paint. Instead, she saw dilapidated houses, stores needing a paint job, and kids riding bicycles. It looked like a small town, albeit a really run-down one.

"Have you ever been to a reservation?" Sophie asked as they crawled through town.

"No. It looks…so…so—"

"Poor?"

"I didn't want to say it, but yeah."

"Elk Mountain is actually one of the more affluent ones. On average, most tribe members are eighty percent unemployed, and fifty percent live below poverty, not that you'd ever know it by meeting them. They're some of the happiest people I've ever met."

"Really!?"

"You don't think someone can be happy unless they're living in Beverly Hills and dining at the Ivy every night?"

"No, it's not that." *Well, maybe it is that.*

"The Native Americans live in community. They take care of each other, as well as the land and nature, which is why we're here." Sophie parked in front of the Elk Mountain Elementary School.

"I'm not following you."

"We came here for the butterflies." Sophie popped the trunk, got out of the Jeep, and proceeded to unload supplies. Jordan followed, lifting a large box and setting it on the ground.

"What do butterflies have to do with an Indian reservation?" Jordan asked.

"About a year ago the National Fish and Wildlife Foundation awarded a coalition of Native American tribes a hundred thousand dollars to help restore monarch habitat on tribal land, and this is one of the reservations. They've volunteered their land for the cultivation of milkweed, not to mention spent endless hours working the fields."

"Wow. That's a lot of money for butterflies." Sophie stopped unpacking and glared at Jordan. "Sorry," Jordan said as she held up both hands in defense. "But they get paid for it, right?"

"The money is used to buy supplies and equipment." Sophie stood with her hands on her hips, which Jordan had come to learn meant business. "Not everyone is motivated by money. Some people actually believe monarch conservation is a priority. And that's why we're here. To help. Sorry you came?"

"Not at all. Bring it on, Disney Princess."

Sophie flashed Jordan a skeptical glance before carrying a load of boxes toward the school. Jordan grabbed a couple of boxes and followed. A bell rang just as they opened the front door, which probably indicated lunch since it was noon. Two little girls ran up to Sophie and hugged her legs.

"Hi, Kaia and Rachael." Sophie put the boxes on the floor, crouched down, and embraced the kids. Two more joined and dived into Sophie's arms, knocking her backward. They all giggled and piled on each other like football players. "Oh my gosh. I missed you guys so much."

"Ms. Sophie, what did you bring us?" a boy asked.

"Some milkweed seeds for us to plant, posters, and lots of coloring and activity books."

The kids yelped in unison as Sophie stood up. "Everyone, I'd like you to meet Jordan. Jordan, this is Kaia, Rachael, Gabe, and Pablo."

Wide smiles, sparkling eyes, and handshakes from the boys greeted Jordan.

"Do you work with Ms. Sophie?" one of the girls asked.

"I do," Jordan said.

"Actually, Jordan owns the butterfly sanctuary. Thanks to her we have a big field of milkweed for the caterpillars. And we all know that if there's no milkweed, there aren't any butterflies."

Jordan peered at Sophie. A little guilt wouldn't convince her to pass up two million dollars.

"Ms. Jordan, did you know that butterflies smell with their antennas and taste with the bottoms of their feet?" Gabe, or maybe Pablo, asked.

"I didn't. That's really interesting."

An older woman, who Jordan assumed was the teacher, joined them and greeted Sophie with a hug.

"Mrs. Nakos, this is my friend Jordan."

"How do you do? It's so nice to meet you. We're just about to have lunch. Come and join us."

"We don't want to intrude," Sophie said.

"Nonsense. After you called I got in contact with everyone, and they should be here shortly. We're so glad you brought more seeds to plant."

Mrs. Nakos led them into a cafeteria where at least fifty rambunctious kids were eating, talking, and laughing. After filling their plates, a tableful of girls called out to Sophie to join them. Jordan's knees practically rose to her chin as they sat in kid-sized chairs. She examined her seat, unsure if the flimsy plastic would hold her up. When Jordan looked up, Sophie was grinning at her from across the table.

"What's your name?" a cute girl with big brown eyes and braided hair asked.

"I'm Jordan. What's yours?"

"I'm Mika. Do you like butterflies?"

Jordan glanced at Sophie, who was still staring at her. "I do. They're beautiful."

"Do you know about the Native American butterfly legend?"

"I don't think so. What is it?"

"Well, see…it's like this…if you want a wish to come true, whisper it to a butterfly. Since they don't make a sound, they can't tell your wish to anyone but the Native American Spirit. So, when you let the butterfly go, it carries your wish to heaven."

"You know, now that you mention it, I have heard that before. Ms. Sophie told me about that legend when we were kids." Jordan looked at Sophie, the glint in her eye replaced with sadness, which seemed to happen often when something from the past was mentioned.

After lunch, a group of twenty-five men and women gathered outside the school. They greeted Sophie affectionately with hugs and smiles. The men grabbed the boxes filled with milkweed seeds as everyone headed to a field beside the school.

"You mean all these people volunteered to help plant milkweed? On a Monday afternoon?" Jordan asked Sophie as they walked.

"You sound surprised."

"I am. I tried to organize a beach cleanup once, and only two people showed up."

Once they reached the field, Jordan noted at least an acre of fully grown milkweed. Obviously, a lot of work had already been done. Everyone immediately grabbed a handful of seed packets and headed for the newly plowed area. They dropped to their knees and began working. Unsure of what to do, Jordan watched from afar, but then she felt a hand on her shoulder as Sophie whispered, "Just stick with me."

Jordan followed Sophie and crouched down beside her.

"It's really simple. Stick your finger in the dirt up to your knuckle, place a seed inside, and then cover it with soil." Sophie demonstrated as she explained. "Space the holes about six inches apart."

"I think I can handle that. What are those guys doing?" Jordan pointed to a group of men concocting something with wire.

"We'll put that around the plants to keep squirrels and other critters out."

Everyone worked side by side for several hours until rows of seeds were planted and the wire fence erected. Jordan stood and raised her arms overhead, attempting to stretch her back. She couldn't believe how tired she was, but more than that, she was amazed at the volunteers. Not only were they not complaining about the hard work, but oftentimes they were laughing and singing.

Sophie rose and stood beside Jordan, her cheeks rosy, eyes joyful, and dirt smeared across her forehead. How could she look so adorable?

"You have a little smudge." Jordan stepped closer and lightly stroked Sophie's skin. As their eyes met, everything disappeared except for the deep, blue sea of Sophie's gaze. They were so close it took all Jordan had not to press their lips together. Her pulse raced at the thought of kissing Sophie.

A distant voice calling Sophie's name awakened Jordan from her trance. "I think someone wants you."

"Someone wants me?" Sophie had a slight grin, like maybe she thought Jordan was the person who wanted her. When the voice grew louder, Sophie said, "Oh…yeah…right." Sophie pried her eyes from Jordan and walked away briskly, leaving Jordan with a longing in the center of her chest.

CHAPTER EIGHTEEN

Big Love in Big Sur

"What do you mean, you don't have any rooms with separate beds? I called last night, and whoever I talked to said he'd accommodate us." Sophie leaned across the counter of the Big Sur Inn, ready to strangle the clerk.

"I'm sorry. I don't know who you spoke with, but we don't have any rooms available with twin beds."

Sophie closed her eyes and shook her head. She turned around to what resembled fear in Jordan's eyes.

"Do you want to try someplace else?" Jordan asked.

"There aren't many options here, and it's late. I don't think we'd find anything. Is this okay just for tonight?"

Jordan said, "Sure," but her eyes said, "No way." While Sophie knew why she was uncomfortable about sharing a bed, she was unsure why Jordan seemed so spooked.

They grabbed their bags and headed to the room. When Sophie unlocked the door and switched on the light, the queen-size bed—large enough to romp 'n' roll and do Lord knows what in—stared them in the face. They paused in the doorway until Sophie charged into the room, moving at warp speed. She opened closets, drawers, and suitcases, hung sweaters, and stuffed undies away. Jordan, on the other hand, was still standing by the door but did have the sense to shut it, considering it had to be forty degrees in the room.

"It's freezing in here." A shiver ran down Sophie's spine. She found the thermostat and turned up the heat, then looked at Jordan, who still stood motionless clutching her suitcase. "Do you want to unpack?"

"Sure...yeah." Jordan seemed to regain the ability to walk as she laid her bag on the bed and transported clothes into an empty drawer.

Sophie stood awkwardly in the center of the room. Should she sit? Or stand? She had to do something since she was totally in the way, like an ill-placed monstrous statue that Jordan had to maneuver around. Nonchalantly, she walked to the bed and studied the hideous painting over the headboard: a beach scene a seven-year-old could have created. In fact, now that she looked around, the whole place was dreadful. The well-worn olive-green bedspread looked like it belonged in an army barracks, the pink-painted walls were something out of a *Partridge Family* episode, and a sickeningly odd scent of Pine-Sol and cigarette smoke permeated the room.

"Wow. This place sucks." Sophie chuckled.

Jordan approached the opposite side of the bed and glanced around the room as though seeing it for the first time. "No kidding. Chuck could have painted that." Jordan pointed at the picture.

"That's what I was thinking."

Their gaze bounced from the painting to the military bedspread to each other.

"Do you…want to take a shower?" Jordan asked. "I mean…you know…do you want to go first?"

"No. You go ahead. I'm going to see if I can do something about the awful smell in here."

After Jordan nodded and disappeared into the bathroom, Sophie walked around the room and flipped on every light switch she could find. The place was entirely too dark. They needed lights and lots of them. She rummaged through her bag for some Merry Berry after-bath splash and squirted a couple of shots around the room, which only made things worse. Now the place smelled like a holiday whorehouse.

A loud screech, followed by a vibrating sound, caused Sophie to jump. The water pipes shook the wall like an earthquake, which meant Jordan was in the shower…naked. Sophie sat on the edge of the bed and wrung her hands. She wasn't sure why she was so nervous. It wasn't like they were going to do anything. Just because Jordan was a lesbian didn't mean she'd jump her bones. She had *some* self-restraint. Sophie was making far too much of this. It'd be like sleeping next to a sister— albeit a super-sexy, incredibly toned, absolutely gorgeous sister, who wasn't even remotely related to her.

Sophie reclined in bed, grabbed the remote, and flipped through channels. Maybe TV would take her mind off naked Jordan. No, they didn't need a romantic movie, and God no, not reruns of *The L-Word*. Finally, Sophie found an educational program about the world's deadliest army ants. Perfect. Nothing safer than killer ants. Her heart raced at the sound of the water shutting off. The room was silent, aside from the monotonous drone of the ant narrator. Jordan was probably towel-drying her naked breasts and rubbing up and down her lean legs. That's usually what people did after showering. Within minutes, Sophie heard the bathroom door open, and Jordan peeked around the corner.

"Just going to dry my hair. Then I'll be out of your way."

"No rush. I'm enthralled with this army-ant program." *Enthralled? By ants? She's going to think I'm a total nature nerd now.*

After blow-drying her hair, Jordan came out the bathroom wearing light-gray sweatpants and a flimsy tank top. Damp auburn tendrils framed her face, which obviously didn't need makeup to look stunning. Sophie tried not to stare, but she couldn't resist. *Who looks that amazing after a shower?*

Once in the safety of the bathroom, Sophie reveled in the warmth of the water on her skin. Just moments ago, Jordan had been in that exact place running soapy hands up and down her slick, wet body. Sophie's fingers slipped between her legs as she stroked herself. Her thumb found her clit, which ached to be touched. After several breathless minutes, she stopped. She certainly didn't need to get aroused right before crawling into bed with Jordan, so she quickly showered and dried her hair.

All the lights were out, except a lamp, when she opened the door. She squinted in the darkness, relieved to see Jordan already asleep and as far over on her side of the bed as possible. In fact, one more inch and she'd topple onto the floor. Sophie pulled back the covers and slipped into bed, careful not to wake her. She settled into the mattress, sighed, and prayed she'd fall asleep quickly.

Jordan tried to move, but something heavy was holding her down. Her eyes fluttered open, the memory of where she was dawning. Arms and legs intertwined, blond hair splayed across her chest, and Sophie's nose nuzzled in the crook of her neck. Jordan sighed contentedly. There were worse places to be. She couldn't remember the last time she'd woken up with a woman. She was used to escaping before dawn, like a vampire shunning the light. What should've felt like an awkward situation instead caused a warmth to radiate in her chest. Jordan settled in closer and basked in the softness of Sophie in her arms. She would have been content to stay there all day, and she would have, if Sophie hadn't stirred. Jordan quickly closed her eyes, feigning sleep. She felt Sophie bolt upright, pause long enough to make Jordan wonder what she was doing, and roll to the other side of the bed. As Jordan squinted one eye open, Sophie stared at her with big, frightened doe eyes.

"Morning," Jordan said, hoarsely. "What time is it?"

"Seven. Did you sleep okay?"

"I must have. I don't remember a thing after lying down." Jordan yawned and rubbed her eyes.

"I hope I didn't crowd you." Sophie looked like she'd just been caught committing a crime.

"Not at all." No use making Sophie feel bad about invading her space, not that Jordan had minded.

Sophie sighed in obvious relief and sat up in bed. She looked cute in the morning, all fresh-faced and her hair tousled.

"What time do you have to be at the school today?" Jordan asked.

"Eight thirty for the first one. Then I'll hit up a couple more this afternoon. You're more than welcome to come, but if you want to investigate Big Sur, I'd understand."

Jordan sat up and leaned against the headboard. "Actually, I did want to check out a couple of hikes in the redwoods."

"You should go to Pfeiffer State Park. It's beautiful there and just down the road. I wish I had time to show you around."

"It's okay. I know this is a working trip for you."

"True, which means I better get moving." Sophie pushed the covers off and got out of bed, revealing long PJs that covered too much skin for Jordan's taste.

"Sophie?"

"Yeah?" Sophie stood over Jordan, her porcelain complexion flawless.

"I really enjoyed yesterday. At the reservation. The kids, the people. It was inspiring how everyone worked together."

A slow smile crept on Sophie's lips. "I'm glad. I liked having you there." Sophie turned and disappeared into the bathroom, leaving Jordan with a big grin on her own face.

Pfeiffer State Park was amazing. Jordan spent the morning hiking through the forest, breathing in the musty scent of foliage dampened by fog, and gazing up at towering redwood trees. One trail ended at a scene that had Jordan's mouth agape. An eighty-foot waterfall plunged down a cliff into a pool of clear turquoise water. It was one of the most beautiful sights she'd ever seen. Why had she never been to Big Sur before? Maybe she did spend too much time at work.

Jordan perched on a rock and relaxed to the sound of rushing water. The place reeked of romance. It was the kind of place where lovers kissed under the spray before plunging into the pool for a skinny-dip. Jordan wished Sophie were there to share in the experience. Not that they'd kiss and swim naked, of course, although Jordan couldn't stop the visualization that popped into her mind.

Sophie stood under the waterfall, head thrown back, a thin, white shirt plastered against her breasts, like something out of a Sports Illustrated *swimsuit edition. Sophie locked eyes with Jordan and motioned with one finger in a come-hither sort of way. Like an obedient puppy, Jordan approached and stood under the warm stream, unable to take her eyes off Sophie's rosy, aroused nipples straining against the see-through fabric. Sophie slipped her arms around Jordan's waist, pulled her close, and pressed their moist lips together.*

Jordan shook her head in an attempt to erase the sexy scene. She'd never had visualizations like that before and quickly blamed it on the waterfall. That's all it was. Anyone in their right mind would be thinking romance in a place like this.

After resting for a while, Jordan continued down the trail, which ended at a log cabin that served as the park's mini-mart. She walked around the aisles and filled a basket with various items she intended to surprise Sophie with later.

Once back at the Inn, Jordan lounged on the bed and clicked on the TV. It was too quiet without Sophie. Hopefully, she'd be back soon. Jordan flipped through the channels until she heard a soft knock on the door. She turned off the TV, jumped up, and opened the door to a face she'd missed seeing for the last eight hours more than she'd like to admit.

"I'm glad you're here. I forgot my key." Sophie slung her bag on the table and plopped down on the bed. "I'm exhausted."

"How'd things go?" Jordan leaned against the edge of the nightstand.

"Great. I love visiting the kids and teaching them about monarchs. How was your day?"

"Superb. I hiked at the park and found this huge waterfall. It was so beautiful." Jordan's face flushed as the vision of wet Sophie flashed through her mind.

Sophie shook her head. "I know which one you mean. I've been there many times." Sophie lay on the bed while Jordan fought the temptation to lie down on top of her.

"Are you tired?" Jordan asked.

"Totally. Kids are like the Energizer Bunny. They keep going and going."

"Oh. So, you probably just wanna stay in, huh?"

Sophie sat up. "What'd you have in mind?"

"We don't have to, but I thought maybe you might want to…I don't know…go somewhere with me. But if you're tired, I totally understand. We could stay here if that's what you want. It's no big deal. Just whatever."

Sophie smiled. "You're cute when you ramble."

"I ramble? Oh God, I do ramble, don't I?" Jordan was normally eloquent. She'd done hundreds of interviews and was guest speaker for many events, but for some reason Sophie made her nervous.

"Just a tad." Sophie laughed. "So, where do you want to go?"

"Well, I thought we could walk to the beach and have a picnic before the sun sets."

"I'd love to." The sparkle in Sophie's eyes ignited Jordan's heart. She loved making her happy.

With a blanket and picnic basket in hand, they walked down a trail to the ocean. Once they reached the beach, Sophie laid out a blanket in the sand, close enough so they could hear the waves, but not so close that they'd get soaked at high tide.

"What'd you bring?" Sophie rubbed her hands together as Jordan began unpacking the basket.

"We've got fried chicken, Mediterranean quinoa, Greek pasta salad, fudge brownies, and wine."

"Wow, that looks amazing. And wine, huh? You plan on getting me drunk, Ms. Lee?"

"That depends. Just what do you do when you get tipsy, Ms. Sanders?"

"Well, I guess you'll just find out, now won't you?" The mischievous twinkle in Sophie's eyes caused heat to flood Jordan's cheeks. "Did I embarrass you?" Sophie laughed.

"Nooo. Sorry about the plastic. It's not very environment-friendly," Jordan said, wanting to change the subject.

Sophie picked up a paper plate and frowned. She started to say something but then refrained. "It's okay. Just this once."

Jordan popped the cork on the wine and poured two glasses full. She held up her cup, which prompted Sophie to do the same.

"What shall we toast to?" Jordan asked.

Sophie thought for a moment. "How about renewed friendship?"

"I like that. A lot. To renewed friendship," Jordan said as they bumped plastic wineglasses.

The food wasn't half bad, even though it wasn't from a five-star restaurant. More than anything, though, Jordan loved spending time with Sophie, talking and laughing, just like old times. After dinner, they sat side by side, sipped wine, and enjoyed the sunset over the ocean. Red and orange streaked across the sky as the blazing sun inched below the horizon. As beautiful as the scene was, Jordan couldn't take her eyes off Sophie. She looked stunning. Her complexion glowed in golden hues as the colorful sky reflected in her blue eyes. She untied her ponytail and shook her head in slow motion, which was the sexiest thing ever. Jordan breathed in fresh rose petals, which she knew came from Sophie's shampoo. She'd smelled it last night when she got into bed, which had kept her awake half the night. Well, maybe it wasn't so much the shampoo as it was having Sophie inches away.

Jordan grabbed the wine bottle and refilled their glasses. She needed a task to divert her attention away from staring. It was bordering on creepy.

"You *are* trying to get me drunk," Sophie said as she seductively walked her fingers down Jordan's arm and rested her hand on her thigh. "I'm definitely tipsy."

"I think I might be a little buzzed myself. Good thing we didn't drive." Jordan stared at Sophie's fingers, which traced an invisible infinity symbol on her leg. Her head spun, but she wasn't sure if that was from the drink or Sophie's touch. Sophie brushed a strand of hair from Jordan's forehead before sweeping her fingers through Jordan's locks over and over, causing electricity to shoot to her toes. Touchy-feely Sophie was fun. They should drink more often.

Sophie cupped the nape of Jordan's neck and pulled her closer. "Do you make a habit of getting women drunk?"

It took Jordan longer than normal to respond, with Sophie's lips, eyes, breath so close. Actually, come to think of it, she didn't respond. She just stared.

"Did you get that sexy French actress drunk?" Sophie asked. "Just how many women have you been with the past ten years, huh?"

Okay, maybe Sophie was a little more than tipsy. Jordan finally found her voice once Sophie stopped stroking her hair. "Um...not many. How about you?"

"No one who meant anything. You..." Sophie slurred, as she poked Jordan hard on the shoulder. "You ruined me for all other women."

"What?" Jordan asked, perplexed.

Sophie swayed as she reached for the wine bottle and took a swig, not bothering to use the glass. "You made me love you. Just like that Patsy Cline song. I didn't want to do it, but you made me love you."

Jordan grabbed the bottle out of Sophie's hand. "Okay. I think you've had way too much to drink."

Sophie steadied herself and focused on Jordan. "I might be a little drunk, but it's the truth. I loved you." Jordan's heart raced. When she didn't respond, Sophie continued. "Remember when I said I came out in college? Well, it *was* when I came out to everyone, but not to myself. I knew I was a lesbian the day you left. It hit me when I got home after the earthquake, after you were gone. It was then that I realized how much I loved you."

Jordan stared at Sophie as the information sank in. She sounded serious and suddenly sober. "You were in love with me when we were teenagers?" Jordan asked, needing confirmation.

Sophie slowly shook her head and looked like she might cry. "It killed me when you left."

"God, Sophie." Jordan buried her face in her hands.

"I shouldn't have said anything. Now I've made you uncomfortable. Chalk this up to an embarrassing drunken tirade." Sophie started to get up but Jordan grabbed her arm.

"Wait...I was in love with you, too. I had no idea you felt the same way. You're all I thought about. You were all I wanted. I loved you so much, more than anyone I've ever known. My dad threw me out because he found out how much I cared about you. He said it was disgusting, and I thought you'd feel the same way. I couldn't tell you why I was leaving. I thought you'd hate me."

Jordan had kept her feelings locked away for more than ten years. Admitting them aloud was like breaking out of solitary confinement and standing in the warmth of the sun. She couldn't pretend any longer.

Sophie knew the truth. Jordan had never realized how that secret had been weighing her down. She felt lighter than she had in years.

Sophie's eyes swirled with emotion—confusion, shock, and maybe fear. "You left because you were in love with me?" She paused, looked at the ocean, then back at Jordan. "You mean we were in love with each other, but neither of us said anything? What would our lives have been like, where would we be, if one of us had been honest?"

A tidal wave of regret washed over Jordan. She knew exactly where they'd be, in each other's arms. Jordan would have never left Sophie's side. They could have had a life together instead of apart.

CHAPTER NINETEEN

Butterfly Kisses

They had barely said two words to each other after their confessions the night before. Sophie wasn't sure what was going through Jordan's mind, but she was still in shock. How could she not have known Jordan had been in love with her when they were teenagers? In retrospect, every emotion-filled glance, every thoughtful gesture, every word out of her mouth had screamed love. Maybe she hadn't wanted to see it at the time. She hadn't been ready to admit her own feelings, much less Jordan's.

Sophie resisted the urge to ask Jordan what she was thinking—or even scarier, what she was feeling—as they drove down the Pacific Coast Highway on their way back to Monarch. She usually liked to get everything out in the open, but now she wasn't sure what to say. Discussing it wouldn't change anything, and it wasn't like they could be together now. They had different lives, different priorities, lived in different cities. It would never work. That's what she tried to convince herself of, anyway.

One more second of silence and Sophie would scream. If they weren't going to talk, they needed a diversion. She made a sharp right, slamming on the brakes as she took a thirty-five-mile-per-hour exit going at least fifty. Jordan lunged and knocked her head on the sun visor.

"Sorry." Sophie bit her bottom lip. Jordan started to say something but stared at Sophie's mouth instead. Finally, she peeled her eyes away. "I thought we could stop off at the Preston Monarch Grove. It's just up the road."

"Sure. Whatever you want."

Jordan sounded about as excited as a kid getting socks on Christmas morning, but Sophie pulled into the parking lot anyway. Butterflies always calmed her nerves, and she could commune better with them than with Jordan at the moment. Sophie rummaged in the backseat and pulled out two water bottles, handing one to Jordan, before they headed down the trail. They walked in silence until they reached a eucalyptus grove filled with thousands of monarchs, either in the trees or flying about and whizzing past them.

"You've been here before?" Jordan asked.

Sophie lifted her chin and gazed into the branches. "A couple of times. I usually stop here on my way back from Big Sur." Sophie wrapped her arms around herself as she shivered.

"Are you cold? You should have brought your jacket." Before Sophie could respond, Jordan took off her Venice Beach sweatshirt and handed it to her.

"I can't take that. You'll freeze."

"I'll be fine. I dressed in layers."

"Thanks. You always did take good care of me." Sophie slipped the shirt over her head, touched by the gesture. The fleece surrounded her like a warm, cozy blanket, but most of all she liked wearing something that belonged to Jordan. The sweatshirt might have to get "lost" in her closet. She sat on a tree stump as several butterflies circled her head.

"Tell me what you love most about monarchs," Jordan said.

Sophie thought for a moment before she responded. "There are so many things, but I'd say the most amazing one is how they migrate to the same trees each year. It's incredible that millions of infant butterflies, who have never been to their ancestral breeding grounds, return to the very trees that their parents roosted in before they were born. It begs the question of how do they know which trees are the right ones to hibernate in."

"So, how do they know?"

"Pure instinct."

"I never understood how such a fragile creature could fly that far. To me, that's the most amazing thing about them."

"I know. They fly 2,500 miles."

"That far? No way."

"Way," Sophie said with a smile. "Similar to migrating birds, they glide on air currents to preserve energy. Monarchs are the only butterflies that make two-way migrations as birds do. It's a crime the population is declining. Twenty years ago there were five hundred million monarchs, and today there are only fifty million." Sophie liked

Jordan's interest in butterflies. The more she knew, maybe the less likely she'd be to sell the sanctuary.

"That much of a decrease?"

"People cutting down trees are destroying wintering sites, and herbicides are killing off milkweed. If we don't do something to protect the monarchs, they'll keep declining."

Jordan took a swig of water and looked deep in thought. "One less eucalyptus grove won't make a difference. Not when there are so many others."

Sophie jerked her head toward Jordan. "If you're referring to the monarch sanctuary, seven thousand butterflies migrate there every year. Granted, it's not one of the largest groves, but that's thousands of monarchs that won't have a place to go if it didn't exist."

Jordan was silent, hopefully taking in the information. Sophie wanted to say more but didn't want to push it. Instead, she inhaled the sweet scent of eucalyptus, closed her eyes, and held out her hand. Within minutes, a butterfly landed in her palm. She opened her eyes and gazed at the beautiful creature. The orange-and-black wings always reminded her of a cathedral stained-glass window.

"How do you do that? How do you get a butterfly to land in your hand?"

Sophie shrugged. "I don't know. It just happens."

"No, really. Tell me. You're like a magician."

"Well, there's a quote by Nathaniel Hawthorne that sums it up perfectly. He said, 'Happiness is like a butterfly. The more you chase it, the more it will elude you, but if you turn your attention to other things, it will come and sit softly on your shoulder.'"

"So, what does that mean, exactly?"

The butterfly in Sophie's hand flapped its wings and flew into the tree. She rose and stood beside Jordan.

"It's about letting go. Here. Turn around and give me your hand." Sophie stood close behind Jordan and wrapped both arms around her. Jordan tensed when Sophie grabbed her hand. "Relax and let go."

Sophie closed her eyes and silently sighed. The sensation of Jordan in her arms felt amazing. She rested her cheek on Jordan's shoulder and resisted the urge to hold her closer.

"What now?" Jordan asked.

Sophie's eyes fluttered open. "Mentally request that a butterfly come to you and then patiently wait. The key is not to try to make it happen. Just trust that it will."

It took less than a minute for a monarch to land in Jordan's palm. "Oh my God! I can't believe it." Jordan stood completely still, probably so as not to scare the monarch.

"See. I told you it would work." Sophie couldn't help but smile at Jordan's excitement.

"But…it probably only happened because you're here." And with that, the butterfly flew away. Jordan turned around and frowned. "It's gone."

Sophie put her hands on Jordan's shoulders and looked into her eyes. "That's because you didn't trust."

"How'd you get so smart?" Jordan hooked her fingers in Sophie's belt loops and pulled her closer. It was an impromptu move that seemed to surprise them both.

Sophie's breath hitched when Jordan's breasts brushed her own. "I…I read a lot."

Jordan's gaze dropped to Sophie's lips for what felt like an excruciatingly long time. "Reading is good. What do you read?"

"Books."

"Books are good. What else?"

Sophie didn't respond. Instead, she stared at Jordan's lips, which were plump and inviting. The desire to kiss Jordan overrode any good sense she had. In fact, she couldn't remember ever wanting anything so much before. Sophie leaned forward and pressed her lips against Jordan's, instantly melting into her warm mouth. If Jordan was shocked by the kiss, she didn't show it. She claimed Sophie's mouth possessively, which was a huge turn-on. It was like they'd been kissing for years. This was no awkward first kiss. It teemed with passion, like a hot-blooded tango, with Jordan whisking her off her feet.

Sophie's hands slid down Jordan's back as she pressed their bodies closer. She moaned when Jordan's tongue grazed her bottom lip. Wanting more of her, Sophie opened her mouth wider, kissing her deeply. Jordan's low, raspy groan when their tongues touched turned Sophie's limbs to rubber. The beating pulse between Sophie's legs wasn't surprising, but she couldn't explain why her stomach clenched and a wave of emotion cascaded upward into her chest, warming her heart. It felt like drinking hot chocolate on a wintery day, or being wrapped in a warm blanket. Sophie had made out with expert kissers before, but she'd never felt this way. But then again, she'd never kissed Jordan.

Sophie's eyes fluttered open when she felt something scrape against her cheek. Reluctantly, she moved her head back. Two monarchs flew between them and flapped their wings rapidly before soaring away.

"Great timing, guys," Sophie said, as they both released nervous chuckles.

Still wrapped in each other's arms, Sophie gazed at Jordan. In that moment, she was quite possibly the sexiest woman Sophie had ever seen. Desire radiated from her smoldering eyes, her cheeks flushed, and slightly parted, moist lips begged to be ravished yet again. Just as Sophie was about to lean close for another kiss, Jordan released her hold, stepped back, and stuck her hands into her pockets. Sophie shivered, suddenly cold. Jordan's expression was hard to read, desire mixed with fear. She took another step back, putting more distance between them, and looked at her watch.

"We should probably get going," Jordan said.

Sophie stared, not sure how to respond or what was happening. One minute Jordan was kissing the hell out of her, and the next she looked like she couldn't get away fast enough. Jordan cleared her throat, grabbed her backpack, and started down the trail. Sophie stood motionless for several seconds until she followed. They hiked back to the car and drove most of the way home in silence. Sophie was bursting with questions, but Jordan had erected an invisible electric fence between them, and she didn't particularly want to get shocked. It was frightening how quickly and efficiently Jordan could seal herself off. Talk about going from hot to cold with the snap of a finger.

Sophie spent the quiet drive home second-guessing her actions and blaming herself. Had she flung herself at Jordan? Maybe she didn't want to be kissed? But then again, she'd certainly responded. She was as clearly turned on as Sophie was. So why had she pulled away? Did Sophie do something weird with her tongue that turned her off? There had to be some reason.

It was dark by the time they reached Monarch. Sophie parked alongside Jordan's car and popped her trunk. Jordan grabbed her bags and slung them into the Jaguar. Several awkward moments of silence passed as they stood there, avoiding eye contact.

"Thanks again for your help at the reservation," Sophie said.

"You're welcome. I guess I'll see you tomorrow." Jordan hopped into her car, revved the engine, and screeched her tires as she pulled away.

Sophie stared at the red, disappearing taillights, wondering what the hell had just happened.

CHAPTER TWENTY

Winged Adults

Jordan leaned against the bathroom counter and stared at her reflection in the mirror. What was she doing kissing Sophie? That wasn't part of the plan. Women complicated things, especially smart, beautiful, totally amazing, utterly kissable women. God, could she kiss. Jordan closed her eyes and groaned. She had really screwed up. For the past ten years she'd fantasized about kissing Sophie, and now, knowing that the reality was a hundred times better made things even harder. Jordan splashed cool water on her face. She needed to focus, get back on track. Knowing how Sophie had felt about her ten years ago didn't change anything now. Jordan was in Monarch for one reason only, and that was to do her time, sell the land, and get back to LA. Sophie would always be special, and she was glad they'd become friends again, but that was as far as it could go.

Jordan showered, dressed, and headed to Mr. Simms's office for her ten a.m. appointment. Nanci was sitting in the waiting room when she arrived.

"Hello, Jordan. It's nice to see you again." Nanci stood and shook her hand firmly. "When did you and Sophie get back from your trip?"

"Late last night."

"You two seem quite close. Do I have competition?" Nanci nudged Jordan's arm.

It took her a second to understand what Nanci meant. "No, of course not. Sophie and I are just friends." *Did that sound convincing?*

"Good to know because I'd like to ask her out again."

Jordan's stomach clenched. The thought of Nanci's lips on Sophie, her hands caressing her skin, their bodies pressed together, made her ill. Nanci raised an eyebrow, which made Jordan wonder what her expression looked like. She forced a smile. "Go for it."

Nanci grinned widely and rubbed her palms together. "Excellent."

Jordan could practically see Nanci's wheels turning, probably trying to figure out how to get Sophie to second base or, worse yet, hit a home run. It was none of Jordan's business what Sophie did, but she could do way better than the real-estate lady.

Mr. Simms's receptionist opened the door to his office as they entered. He stood and motioned for them to sit.

"Ms. Lee, as I said on the phone, your grandmother's estate has been settled and I've transferred the deed in your name. You now legally own the sanctuary and land, and you're free to sell as long as you meet with your father once more and stay in Monarch another month."

Nanci chimed in, seeming excited. "Mr. Simms has given us the okay to proceed with Kelstrom since we need to move fast. They're considering another property in San Diego, so we should pin them down."

"That's great news, but remember, I can't sell until February."

Nanci cocked her head. "Jordan, there have been no other offers. If you don't jump on this, it may take years to sell the land."

Jordan looked at Mr. Simms. "Is that true? Did my grandmother receive any other offers?"

"I believe Kelstrom was the only interested party, but Ms. Roberts would know the market better than I would."

Nanci turned in her seat to face Jordan. "Do you want to sell the sanctuary?"

Of course she wanted to sell, but it wasn't that simple. She'd made a promise to Sophie. "Yes, but can't they wait another month?"

"They may not." Nanci sat back in her chair and sighed loudly. "Listen. Why don't I draft a contract for you to review and set up a meeting with Kelstrom after the holidays?"

Jordan nodded. "Okay. Let's do that." It wasn't really like going back on her promise to Sophie. What difference did it make if she made a deal in January or February?

"Speaking of the holidays, there's something I wanted to ask you, Mr. Simms. I'd really like to get away," Jordan said.

"You mean leave Monarch?" Mr. Simms frowned.

"Just next week. I'll be back New Year's Day."

"But…but that would go against your grandmother's stipulations." Mr. Simms glanced around nervously, like her grandmother's ghost might appear out of nowhere to bop him over the head.

"It's Christmas, and the sanctuary is closed all week. I won't have anything to do." Jordan flashed pathetically pleading eyes.

Mr. Simms rubbed his shiny, bald head. "This isn't in the contract."

"No, but it *is* baby Jesus's birthday." Jordan felt only slightly guilty about playing the baby Jesus card since she'd never stepped foot in a church, but she wasn't giving up that easily. Hell. She'd probably even spurt out Bible quotes, if she knew any.

"Well…you'd be back New Year's Day?"

"I promise." Jordan batted her long eyelashes and smiled sweetly.

"I suppose…since it's Christmas it would be okay." Mr. Simms seemed reluctant, but at least he agreed.

Jordan was so happy she almost bolted across the desk and planted a smooch on his cheek. She couldn't wait to get back to her Beverly Hills condo, dinner with Doug at expensive restaurants, and conversation that didn't revolve around butterflies. Finally, she'd be back where she belonged. And more than anything, Jordan needed a break from Sophie. Being around her so much had obviously skewed her judgment, considering that passionate kiss in the woods.

❖

"Oh, my God, I thought you'd never get here." Sophie bolted toward Jordan, grabbed her arm, and pulled her into the sanctuary. She turned on a video camera, which was mounted on a tripod, and pointed at the hanging net.

"What's going on?" Jordan peered into the enclosure, amazed at what she saw. The two cocoons were now transparent and revealed orange-and-black wings scrunched inside. One of the chrysalises had cracked open, and the insect was poking its thin, black legs out. They watched as he wiggled and inched his way out the cocoon. Jordan wanted to ask if the butterfly was okay, considering he had a bloated body with wet, crumpled wings, but she was too mesmerized to speak. Once the monarch was out of the cocoon, he clung to the clear chrysalis like a bat hanging upside down.

"Can he fly? Is he okay?" Fear gripped Jordan as the butterfly hung motionless.

"He's fine. He'll stay there for an hour or so until hemolymph is pumped from his body into his wings." When Jordan looked at Sophie questioningly, she added, "It's blood-like fluid that enlarges the wings and needs to harden before he can fly."

Within moments the second cocoon shook as it cracked open, and they marveled at yet another metamorphosis.

"Wow. I never get tired of seeing that," Sophie said.

"That was amazing." Jordan didn't have words to express what she'd witnessed. The twins had transformed into beautiful butterflies right before her eyes. "Amazing," she kept saying over and over.

Sophie turned off the video and took a few still shots with her camera. "We can set them free this afternoon," she said.

The thought of letting the butterflies go made Jordan sad. She'd miss them. "Couldn't we keep them a little longer? I mean, they have space to fly around."

Sophie looked at Jordan with compassion. "I know it's hard to let go, but it's not right to keep them cooped up. Their lives are so short as it is."

Jordan knew Sophie was right, but that didn't mean she couldn't pout.

Sophie snapped a few more photos, then lowered her camera and looked directly at Jordan. "So how'd the meeting with the lawyer go? Everything okay?"

Jordan considered telling Sophie about the rush to sell, but the timing wasn't right. She didn't want to ruin their last day together before she left for the holidays. "Fine. I asked him if I could go home next week, and he actually said it was okay."

"You mean you won't be here for Christmas?" Sophie looked disappointed.

"No. I need to check on SOS. I'll leave tomorrow and be back New Year's Day."

"Oh." Sophie walked to her desk and put the camera down, keeping her back to Jordan. "So you won't be here for New Year's Eve either."

"That's probably for the best…considering."

Sophie turned to face Jordan, sorrow in her eyes. "Yeah, probably."

They both looked toward the door as it opened. God. Hadn't Jordan gotten enough of Nanci today? What was she doing here?

"Hello, ladies. What are you two up to?" Nanci strolled in and stood close to Sophie.

"The two monarchs just hatched. We're going to release them this afternoon," Sophie said.

"Really? How lovely. Care if I join?"

Jordan had to think fast. Sophie was too nice to say no, and the last thing Jordan wanted was Nanci intruding. She didn't have anything to do with the twins. "Actually, we may let them go tomorrow. Right, Soph?"

"Um, yeah. Today, tomorrow, who knows?"

Jordan grinned and winked at Sophie behind Nanci's back.

"Oh well, that's okay. Actually, I wanted to see if you're free this weekend. Maybe we could check out that new Italian place."

Sophie's eyes locked with Jordan's. When she didn't respond, Nanci looked back and forth between them. "I thought you two weren't...you know...dating. Jordan said you're just friends and gave me the green light. Did I misunderstand?"

Sophie continued to stare at Jordan. "The green light? How considerate of her."

"Sooo, does that mean you're available?"

Sophie cocked her head and looked at Jordan. "Well, let's ask Jordan since she has all the answers. Am I available?"

Jordan wasn't exactly sure what was happening. She was pretty sure that any answer she gave would be the wrong one. If she said yes, then Nanci would pounce on Sophie, but if she said no, then that would cause a whole other host of problems. "Why wouldn't you be available?" Jordan regretted the words the moment they were out of her mouth.

Sophie winced and looked like she'd just stepped on a sharp tack. She peeled her eyes away from Jordan and said, "I'd love to have dinner with you, Nanci."

❖

That afternoon, they took the butterfly net down and carried it to the eucalyptus grove. The twins' wings were strong, and they were raring to be set free. Sophie put the enclosure on the ground, under their tree.

"Feels like we should say something first," Jordan said. "Like...I dunno. Isn't there a butterfly poem you should recite?"

"It's not like I have butterfly poems memorized." Sophie looked suddenly uneasy. "Actually, it might be a good time to give you your Christmas present since you won't be here."

Jordan hadn't expected to exchange gifts. "You didn't have to get me anything. I didn't—"

"I don't expect a present, so you can wipe the embarrassed look off your face. It's not much. Just something I saw that you might like."

Sophie pulled a small gray box out her back pocket and handed it to Jordan. "You can return it if you don't like it."

Jordan cocked her head. "I'd never do that." Her heart skipped a beat when she lifted the lid. It was a gold chain with a pendent of two monarchs connected at the wings. "Oh my gosh, it's the twins." Jordan's face lit up in a smile, which prompted Sophie to do the same.

"You like it? It's kinda corny, but—"

"Sophie, I love it. Would you help me put it on?"

Jordan took the necklace out of the box and turned so Sophie could hook it. Tingles went up and down her spine when fingertips grazed the back of her neck. Sophie placed her hand on Jordan's shoulder and gave it a gentle squeeze when she was done.

Jordan faced Sophie and placed a hand over the pendent. "It's perfect, and what a wonderful keepsake. Thank you."

Sophie smiled and grabbed the latch of the butterfly net.

"Wait," Jordan said. "I've been calling them guys, but do you know if they're male or female?"

"They're both female. Males have two black spots on their hind legs."

Jordan smiled. For some reason she liked the idea of that.

"Are you ready?" Sophie looked at Jordan, who nodded her approval.

Sophie untied the latch and opened the net. Within seconds the monarchs flew out, hovered in midair, then soared into the tree. Jordan's gaze followed their flight until they were lost in a sea of orange and black. She'd never tell them apart from the other thousands of butterflies, but she knew they were there, safely huddled on a branch, together. Just as it should be.

CHAPTER TWENTY-ONE

Back to Beverly Hills

Nothing says Southern California more than cruising down the Pacific Coast Highway in a red BMW convertible with the ocean on one side and multi-million-dollar mansions on the other. Jordan tied her hair back to keep it from blowing all over the place as Doug sped through Malibu. She patted his leg a few times and smiled. It'd only been three weeks, but she'd missed him.

"It's great to see you, too." Doug flashed perfect, professionally whitened teeth.

"I feel like I've been gone forever."

"I don't know how you've survived this long. Do they even have a mall there? God. Don't tell me all they have is Walmart."

"Actually, it's not so bad. It's…quaint."

Doug turned down the music. "What's this noise we're listening to?"

"Hey, that's Andrea Bocelli. I love his voice. Sophie turned me on to him." Jordan increased the volume and ignored the weird look Doug gave her.

They pulled up to the valet at the Blue Whale, which was Jordan's favorite outdoor café. It was a few feet from the beach and had the best seafood around. In the summer, rose vines filled the restaurant, and in the fall winter jasmine took over. When they got the best seat in the house, which was tucked in a corner with an unobstructed view of the ocean and mountains, Jordan shot Doug a sly look. It was an impossible table to nab.

"Well, I may have used my powers of persuasion," Doug said, which meant he'd paid a hefty price to the maître d'.

After they ordered seafood salads, Jordan stretched her arms high overhead and sighed contentedly. Then she stuck her nose into a bunch of yellow flowers next to their table and inhaled deeply. Her heart lurched when she saw two butterflies hovering over the winter jasmine.

"Oh my gosh, those are monarchs!" Jordan said excitedly.

Doug craned his neck to take a gander. "Yeah, so?"

"It's two of them. Just like the twins. Oh, I gotta tell you about this." Jordan was full of enthusiasm, like someone had just given her a shot of adrenaline. "I actually witnessed the life cycle of a monarch, from birth to caterpillar to chrysalis—that's the cocoon—to butterfly. Sophie and I took care of them, like we were their moms or something." Jordan snorted a laugh. "And then we set them free in the forest. It was so cool." Doug stared, clearly dumbfounded. "Well, maybe you had to be there."

"You're different." Doug squinted and studied Jordan closely.

"What do you mean?"

"More…relaxed, calm. Not yourself."

"Was I that stressed before?" Doug raised an eyebrow. "Okay. Maybe I was."

"Have you had any more fainting episodes?" Concern etched Doug's face.

"Actually, just one. Sophie taught me a technique that helped a lot."

"That's great. Yep, I like the new you. You're…happier."

"I was happy before," Jordan said, feeling suddenly defensive.

"Now don't get snippy. It was a compliment. But you're not turning into a butterfly freak, are you? Since when do you wear jewelry?" Doug pointed to Jordan's necklace.

"Sophie gave this to me. It's two butterflies, just like the ones we raised." Jordan lightly rubbed the monarch pendant between two fingers.

Doug eyed her suspiciously and was about to say something when the waiter walked up with their food. Jordan dove into her salad and wondered if she'd changed, as Doug said. Admittedly, she felt less stressed, but that was probably because she hadn't been working. It wasn't because of the town or Sophie or anything. And she wasn't becoming a butterfly freak. Helping to raise the monarchs had been amazing. Anyone would have thought so. She was still the hard-ass, successful Beverly Hills businesswoman she'd always been. This Monarch trip was simply a two-month detour on her way to everything she'd ever wanted for SOS.

"How's your salad?" Doug asked.

"It's great, but do you know what's *really* good?" Jordan asked with a mouthful. "Bertha's Italian sub sandwich. It's to die for."

"Who's Bertha?"

"Oh, a sweet, albeit nosy, woman who owns a coffee shop in Monarch. She and Sophie are really close. And there are these funny twins, Molly and Mabel, who own a used bookstore. They're the cutest things. Can you believe they all talked me into being the guest of honor at a butterfly festival? *Me?*" Jordan laughed. "It was actually kinda fun."

Doug furrowed his brow. "You seem to be getting attached to everyone, especially Sophie. You've mentioned her at least ten times since you've been back."

Jordan shrugged. "I thought you'd want to hear about what I've been doing the past month."

"I do...it's just...well, never mind. So, have you seen your father again?"

Jordan rolled her eyes. "No, but we do need to meet one more time. I'll contact him when I get back. Did I tell you I have a half brother? He's pretty cool, considering who his parents are."

"So, any progress on selling the land?"

"The estate is out of probate and in my name, and the real-estate lady is drawing up a contract." Jordan didn't want to tell Doug that she'd promised Sophie not to make any decisions until after February or that Kelstrom was putting on the pressure.

"That's great. Why don't you seem excited about that?"

"I am! Totally. Everything at the office going okay?" Jordan asked, wanting to change the subject. "How's Tiffany doing? Can you believe Sophie contacted me a few years ago and she never gave me the message?" That still burned Jordan up.

"Talking about Sophie again?" Doug asked with a smirk. "So, you two never...you know, hooked up?"

Jordan thought it best not to tell Doug about the kiss, which was odd since she always told him everything. "No. We're just friends. Tell me about this Christmas Eve party you're taking me to."

"It's going to be amazing! It's at the Beverly Hilton, and anyone who's anyone will be there." Wide-eyed, Doug seemed as excited as Jordan had been talking about the monarchs.

"Sounds great." Actually, it sounded crowded and boring. She'd rather stay home with a cup of hot chocolate and a good movie than be stuck hobnobbing with snooty celebrities.

Oh my, maybe I have changed.

She'd only been back one day. It'd take her a while to get back to normal. After a few more days in Tinseltown, she'd forget all about Monarch, butterflies…and Sophie. She was sure of it.

Now this was a swanky affair, nothing like the Monarch happy hour that didn't even serve liquor. This holiday party had the finest cuisine, expensive champagne, and the most famous people in Hollywood. This was proof positive Jordan had made it. No one got invited to a fancy party like this unless they were somebody. So, why wasn't she more excited? Maybe she was tired from spending the day shopping for a new outfit on Robertson Boulevard and getting her hair done, not to mention that her feet were killing her in these high heels. Or maybe she was coming down with the flu, considering all she wanted to do was crawl into bed and pull the covers over her head.

"Having fun?" Doug shoved a glass of wine into her hand. Jordan nodded and took a sip. "What's wrong?"

"Nothing. It's great. Really." She hoped that sounded convincing, not wanting to ruin the party for him. "Is that Ophelia over there?"

"Yes, and you should schmooze the hell out of her so you can get on her talk show again."

A very handsome man approached Doug from behind. "Why, I thought that was you."

Doug practically squealed as they embraced. "You devil. How long has it been?" Doug asked.

"Too long! You look amazing." The man was already tipsy, considering how he slurred and swayed.

The two men assessed each other appreciatively before Doug turned to Jordan. "Oh, I don't think you've met. This is Branson. He's a model slash actor with the Hughes Talent Agency."

That explained the good looks. Jordan shook the guy's hand before excusing herself. Doug was obviously smitten, and she didn't want to get in the way. Normally, Jordan didn't mind being at these soirees alone, but for some reason it was a little depressing that everyone was paired up except for her. She walked around the buffet table and surveyed the selection, settling on beluga caviar on crackers. She should probably talk to Ophelia, but she wasn't in the mingling mood.

Jordan stared at an angel ice sculpture in the center of the food spread and wondered what Sophie was doing. Maybe she'd gone to Bertha's, or maybe she was out with Nanci. She felt bad about leaving things on an awkward note and acting like a moron after they'd kissed. It had caught her off guard, and she hadn't expected to like it so much. In fact, she couldn't remember ever being so aroused by one kiss before. Maybe she should text her and try to make peace. It was Christmas, after all.

Jordan grabbed her cell phone and typed a message.

Merry almost Xmas. I hope you're having a good Xmas Eve.

Sophie responded almost immediately. *I am. How about you?*

I'm stuck at a fancy party. Whatcha doing?

Watching It's a Wonderful Life and drinking hot chocolate.

Wish I was there.

Jordan regretted typing that the moment she pressed send. And she *really* regretted it after the extremely long pause. Finally, her phone chimed.

Merry Christmas, Jordan.

Merry Christmas, Soph.

Jordan stuck the phone into her bag so she wouldn't be tempted to keep texting, although she did glance at it every now and then to make sure Sophie hadn't responded. She had to admit she was happy that Sophie wasn't out with Nanci. But then again, she didn't say she was alone. Maybe the real-estate maven was sitting beside Sophie drinking her special hot chocolate.

"Why, if it isn't the butterfly queen."

Oh my God. Jordan would know that fake French accent anywhere. She didn't want to turn around, but it'd be rude not to. "Bibi, how are you?"

"I thought you were stuck in that godforsaken place until February. Did they let you out for good behavior?"

"Something like that." Jordan turned to walk away but ran right into Ophelia.

"Jordan. I haven't seen you in forever." Ophelia kissed both of her cheeks.

"She's been locked away in butterfly prison," Bibi said with a snicker.

"I don't believe we've met...although you do look familiar." Ophelia extended her hand to Bibi.

"Bibi is the actress on the Leif instant-coffee commercials," Jordan said.

"Oh yes, that's it. Now what's this about butterfly prison?" Ophelia looked back and forth between them. Before Jordan could respond, Bibi chimed in.

"Jordan inherited a monarch sanctuary and two acres of land along the central coast."

Jordan shot Bibi a dirty look. She knew Jordan was private and wouldn't want her personal business spread around town.

"*You* own a butterfly sanctuary? In the wilderness?" Ophelia giggled. *What's so funny?* "I'm sorry. I don't mean to laugh, but I just can't picture you traipsing through the forest in hiking boots and carrying a butterfly net."

"It's actually a beautiful place. And they've done a lot for monarch conservation," Jordan said, feeling suddenly defensive.

"Surely you're not keeping it? I have a real-estate agent you should get in touch with. Have you had the land appraised yet?"

"Well…yes."

"Don't keep us in suspense! What's it worth?"

Most people would think that was an intrusive question, but they didn't know Ophelia. She'd never dare ask anyone their age or how much they weighed, whereas wealth was not only discussed, but also flaunted at every opportunity.

Jordan looked at Bibi. "Would you excuse us for a minute? I'd like to speak with Ophelia in private."

Bibi huffed and slithered away. Since the cat was out of the bag, she might as well tell all. It wasn't like it'd ever get back to Sophie or anyone in Monarch. They were far removed from Hollywood. And besides, when the time came, Ophelia could help promote a new office.

"It's two acres, worth two million dollars."

Ophelia looked disappointed. It wasn't a fortune to her, but it was to Jordan. "What are your plans? You are selling, aren't you? What are you going to do with the money?"

"Actually, I have an offer from a hotel chain. Doug and I plan to open another SOS office in San Francisco."

Her eyes lit up. "Oh, that's wonderful! Let me know when you do, and I'll do another story on your company."

That's what Jordan was hoping for. "That'd be terrific. Thanks so much."

"Listen. I did want to ask you a favor. I'm the head of the BPU

Charity and was wondering if SOS would like to participate in a silent auction we're having in a few weeks."

"Of course. Count me in. Unfortunately, I'm stuck in Monarch until February, but I'm sure Doug would love to represent us. What's… um…BPU?" Jordan hated asking, since it was something she should probably already know.

"It's the Bra, Panty, and Underwear Charity, you silly." Ophelia playfully slapped her arm.

"Excuse me?"

"Don't tell me you've never heard of it before. It's where celebrities donate unmentionables to be auctioned off for philanthropic causes."

"Oh. Seriously?"

"Honey, many people would pay a healthy sum of money to hold a pair of panties worn by yours truly."

Ew. This was the weirdest thing she'd ever heard, but Jordan didn't say that. Instead, she nodded and smiled. "So, did you want something of mine? Or a monetary donation, which we'd be happy to do."

"Both would be much appreciated. You could give something to Douglas, and he can drop it off later."

"Sure, but I doubt my undies would bring in as much as yours." Ophelia laughed, but Jordan could see in her eyes that she agreed. "What sort of causes does the charity support?"

"All sorts of things, such as the homeless, animal rights, save the whales, whatever the board decides."

"Do you ever take suggestions? I mean, if someone had an idea of a group to support?"

"All the time. If you have something in mind just let me know, and I'm sure I can get it approved."

After chatting with a few more people, Jordan found Doug huddled with Branson in a corner. He didn't look anywhere near ready to leave, so she feigned a headache and called a cab. Jordan held her hand to her forehead as she waited for her ride. Maybe she *was* coming down with the flu. She'd never left a party early before in her life.

❖

"When are you going to tell me what's wrong?"

Jordan turned from gazing out of her office window to see Doug standing in the doorway. She sat at her desk and looked at the computer screen, pretending to read an email. "I don't know what you mean."

He walked into the office and sat in a chair across from her desk. "You've been moping around here for almost a week. Aren't you happy to be back?"

"Of course." Jordan reclined and folded her arms across her chest. "It's just that today is New Year's Eve. You know, the tenth anniversary. And before you ask, no. I don't want to talk about it."

Doug held up his hands in defense. "All right. So, did you get a chance to talk to Ophelia at the Christmas Eve party the other night?"

"Oh, that reminds me." Jordan opened her desk drawer, took out two bras, and tossed them at Doug. They hit him in the face and landed in his lap. He stared at the undies before looking at her, definitely perplexed.

"Is this a subtle way of telling me I should be a cross-dresser?"

"You *would* make an attractive woman, but no. They're for Ophelia's BPU Charity."

"Oh, the Bra, Panty, and Underwear auction."

"You know about this? I've never heard of such a thing."

"You need to get out more, my dear."

"Well, I told her we'd help out and make a donation as well, so cut a check for whatever we can afford. The more the better. Ophelia is an excellent contact. She can really help us promote SOS, especially after we expand."

Doug examined one of the bras and arched an eyebrow. "D cup?"

"I bought those at Victoria's Secret. I wasn't going to give them one of mine. That's just…creepy."

Tiffany walked into Jordan's office, leaned against the door frame, and sighed dramatically. She was darning her customary black-leather outfit, but a blue streak had replaced the red one in her hair.

"Do you need something?" Jordan asked.

"We're out of staples." Tiffany hung her head in seeming despair. "Maybe you could…I dunno…order some? Crazy idea, but might just work."

"Well, I can't finish the paperwork without staples."

Doug turned in his chair. "Paper clips should work fine, Tiff."

Tiffany paused and stared at the ceiling. "There was some other reason I came in here." She shrugged and shuffled away.

Jordan leaned across the desk and whispered, "What's up with her? She's more scatterbrained than usual."

"She and her boyfriend broke up. Right after she got his name tattooed across her chest, so not good timing."

"You're a softie. You were supposed to fire her."

Tiffany popped her head into the office. "Oh. I remember what I was going to say. You have a call on line one. It's your dad."

Jordan stared, dumbfounded. "Did you say...my dad?"

Tiffany nodded before disappearing. Jordan stared at the phone like it was a hissing cobra ready to strike.

"Did I miss something? Are you and your father buddies now?"

"Not even close. I wonder what he wants?"

"Only one way to find out." Doug pointed at the phone.

Jordan took a deep breath and picked up the receiver. "Hello?"

"Jordan, this is your father." His tone was stern and to the point.

"Is...everything okay?"

"Yes, yes. I spoke to your mother over Christmas."

"Mom? I didn't realize you two kept in touch."

"We do on occasion. She suggested I invite you over for dinner." Jordan was silent, not sure what to say or think. "So, Rebecca and I would like to ask you to join us when you're back in town."

"Um...sure, yeah, thanks. Uh...what works for you guys?" Jordan looked at Doug and shrugged.

"Are you free this Saturday? Say seven p.m., our house?"

"That's fine."

"See you then."

Jordan slowly hung up the phone. "That was weird. He invited me to dinner. And said my mom was the one that suggested it."

"Your mom?"

"Yeah. Well, that's at least one less thing I have to worry about. This will be our second meeting, which takes care of that part of Grandma's stipulations."

The computer chimed, indicating an incoming email. Jordan glanced at the screen, surprised that it was from Bertha. She opened the message.

Jordan, can you believe Sophie gave me a computer for Christmas? It must have cost her a fortune! I can't believe I can type a letter and not even have to use a stamp to send it. Let me know if you get this. You're my first email. We miss you around here. Sophie hasn't stopped talking about you since you left. Love, Bertha

Jordan couldn't stop grinning. It was great to hear from Bertha and even better to hear that Sophie had been talking about her. She quickly typed a message back.

Bertha, email received. I hope you had a good Christmas. Tell everyone I said hi.—Jordan.

"Who was that from? I haven't seen you smile that big since... well, ever."

"It was from Bertha, the woman who owns the coffee shop in Monarch. She's technologically challenged so it's hilarious that she sent an email."

"It certainly seemed to lift your spirits. You never did tell me what happened with Sophie. Did you ever tell her you're a lesbian?"

Jordan groaned. "That's a long story, but yes, she knows. We did...sort of...kiss."

"And you didn't tell me!?" Doug sat forward in his chair. "Are you together?"

"No, it was just a kiss...and then...that was it. Actually, I was an idiot." Jordan pressed her fingertips to her temples. "I freaked and pushed her away but didn't explain why, and then we didn't talk about it, and I practically shoved her into Nanci's arms, and then I got the hell out of there as fast as I could, and—"

Doug held up his hands. "Whoa, that's a lot of info to take in all at once. Okay. Why'd you freak?"

"It's not like we can date or be together. We have different lives, and I'm about to make the thousands of butterflies she loves homeless and put her out of a job."

"Did you tell her any of that? Did you explain? Maybe you two can talk things out."

Jordan stared at Doug. "What's there to talk about?"

Doug rolled his eyes and grunted loudly. "You know I love you, right? But you're sooo frustrating sometimes. This is what you do. You close down and run away. It's the same thing you did to her ten years ago."

"What?! That was totally different."

"No, it isn't. You left without telling her what you were thinking and feeling. You're going to fuck this up before it even gets started. Just talk to her. Give it a chance."

God, was she really doing the same thing? Making the same mistakes? Had she not matured in a decade?

"Tell me how you feel about Sophie, minus all the so-called challenges."

Jordan grinned and responded immediately. "She's amazing. She's sweet, caring, sensitive. She's the most authentic person I've ever met. There's just something about her. I want to be around her all the time, and when I'm not, it just sucks. She makes me happy."

"In all the time I've known you I've never heard you talk about anyone that way. Are you in love with her?" Doug asked tentatively, probably afraid Jordan would bolt out the door at the mention of the word "love."

Jordan stood and gazed out of the window. "Honestly? I think you should ask if I've ever stopped loving her."

Doug bolted out of his chair and embraced Jordan. "I'm so happy for you!"

She was touched to see tears in his eyes. He was a sweetheart who wanted nothing more than her happiness.

Jordan pursed her lips and nodded. "You're right. I should talk to Sophie. I'm going back. Today," Jordan said with conviction.

"But I thought you were going with me and Branson to the party. It's New Year's Eve."

"I know. And that's exactly why I need to be in Monarch tonight."

Chapter Twenty-two

Shake, Rattle 'n' Roll

When Jordan had driven to Monarch a month ago, she'd purposefully gone slower than an Amish buggy, but now she couldn't get there fast enough. She wasn't sure what time Bertha's New Year's Eve party started, but she wanted to catch Sophie before she left so they'd have time alone to chat. She had no idea what she'd say. Doug had said to talk about her feelings and fears, which was easier said than done. What if they dated and it didn't work out? Relationships weren't exactly her strong point. Jordan didn't think she could survive losing Sophie again. At least now they were friends. Her resolve was melting with each mile.

It was six p.m. when Jordan pulled up to Sophie's cabin. She sat in her car for a few minutes and tried to calm her nerves with slow, deep breaths. When that didn't work she opened the door and walked to the porch, her intestines twisted in knots. Why was she so nervous? The toughest newscasters in Hollywood had interviewed her. She was a strong, confident businesswoman. Why did the thought of having one conversation freak her out so much? Well, probably because this was the first time her heart had been invested in the outcome. It was so much easier to have *the talk* with a woman she didn't love. Yes, Jordan was certain she was in love with Sophie, not that she'd blurt that out anytime soon.

Jordan pressed the doorbell and waited. When there was no answer, she pressed it again. The place looked dark and deserted, so she walked around the side of the cabin and saw that Sophie's Jeep was gone. All that worrying for nothing. She probably wouldn't even get a chance to talk to her alone tonight. Jordan got back in her car and headed for Bertha's.

"Jordan!" everyone yelled as she entered the coffee shop. The place was packed and noisy. People were chatting, laughing, and playing board games.

"Welcome to almost 2010," Molly said as she stuck a party hat on Jordan's head and hugged her.

Bertha grabbed her hand and pulled her through the crowd, with Molly following close behind. "You have to try a piece of my chocolate-fudge earthquake cake," Bertha said. She cut a big glob and handed it to Jordan. "We're so glad you made it."

"I wouldn't miss your party." Jordan took a bite and nearly melted on the spot. She gobbled it down, not realizing how hungry she was. "That was divine," she said, which elicited a satisfied smile from Bertha.

Mabel approached Jordan from behind and handed her a cup of red punch. As Jordan looked at the three women, she couldn't help but grin. To her surprise, she'd missed them. "So which one of these lucky guys will you be kissing at midnight, huh?"

They blushed and giggled. Jordan leaned closer to Bertha and whispered, "I see Coach Bryant is here." Jordan wiggled her eyebrows as Bertha playfully swatted her arm. "Why don't you go over and talk to him?"

Bertha scowled. "I look a mess. I've been baking all day and didn't have time to put anything decent on." She glanced down at her frilly butterfly apron with chocolate splatters. "Anyway, I don't think he'd be interested in talking to me."

"Are you kidding? Judging by the way he was making googly eyes at you during the basketball game, I figured he would have asked you out by now."

"Pshaw." Bertha batted her hand.

"You should listen to Jordan," Molly said. "She knows about these things."

"He does wink at you an awful lot, Bertha," Mabel said. "In church even, which oughtn't to be appropriate, but there's that."

"See? The girls agree with me. I think you should ask *him* out."

"Well, I guess I could offer to make him dinner. But I wouldn't have a thing to wear, and I'm way past due on a hair color." Bertha rested her elbows on the counter and sulked.

"I can help you with that. If there's one thing I know, it's fashion." Jordan wished they were in Beverly Hills. She'd make Bertha an appointment with Bibi's ridiculously expensive hairdresser and take her shopping on Rodeo Drive. Every woman should have at least one day of pampering.

"I don't know." Bertha shook her head and fidgeted. "Do you really think he's interested in me?"

Jordan looked Bertha directly in the eyes. "Yes. He's totally into you."

"Well, I'll think about it."

"So who will *you* be kissing at midnight?" Molly asked Jordan.

"We know a certain someone who missed you while you were away," Bertha said.

Jordan's heart raced. Was she talking about Sophie?

"It was Jordan-this, Jordan-that. We almost got sick of hearing about you," Mabel said with a chuckle.

"I'm not sure I know what you mean." Jordan didn't want to assume anything.

"We're talking about Sophie!" Bertha said. "You two would make the cutest couple."

"So…you know I'm a lesbian? And you're okay with that?"

The three women rolled their eyes in unison.

"We're not fuddy-duds, Jordan. We love Ellen. We watch her show every afternoon," Mabel said.

Jordan smiled. "Who doesn't love Ellen? But as far as Sophie and me, I'm not sure. I mean, we haven't talked about anything. And I think she might be dating Nanci."

"Balderdash. Sophie lights up like a firefly when you're around. She could give a hill of beans about Nanci," Bertha said.

"Really?" Jordan felt suddenly confident. "Is Sophie here?" She scanned the crowd.

"She was, but I saw her leave about thirty minutes ago," Bertha said. "Did you girls see her come back?"

Molly and Mabel shook their heads.

"She wasn't at the cabin. I checked there first. Where could she be?" And that's when it hit her. Jordan knew exactly where Sophie was, the only place she could be. "Listen, I need to go. I think I know where she is."

"Where?" the three women asked.

"I'll explain later." Jordan yanked the party hat off and headed to the door.

"Jordan!" The real-estate tycoon grabbed her arm. "I didn't know you were back."

"Hey, Nanci. I just got in."

"I wanted to tell you—"

"I'm sorry, but I need to be somewhere." Jordan broke from her grasp and backed away.

"Is everything okay?"

"Yes. I'm just in a rush." Jordan dashed out the door. She hated being rude, but she had a one-track mind, and all she wanted to do was find Sophie.

A sense of déjà vu washed over Jordan when she parked at the edge of the eucalyptus grove. She'd been in this exact spot ten years ago. Hopefully, tonight would have a happier ending. She shook off the odd sensation and started down the path through the forest. As she turned a curve in the trail, she saw Sophie standing by their tree, whispering something to a butterfly resting in her palm. She looked beautiful, her light complexion glowing in the moonlight, her bright blue eyes filled with wonder. Jordan's heart swelled with emotion. It was amazing how much she'd missed her, even after only a week.

After a couple of minutes, Sophie held out her hand as the butterfly flew into the tree. She inhaled sharply when her gaze landed on Jordan.

"I hope your wish comes true." Jordan approached slowly until they were a few feet apart.

"It did. Just now."

"You mean…me?" Jordan pointed at her chest.

Sophie nodded and seemed to hold her breath. Jordan knew she should say something—talk about fears, feelings, obstacles, everything she'd intended to discuss—but instead, she was overcome by an urgency to do what she'd desperately wanted to do ten years ago. Jordan stepped forward, cupped Sophie's face in her hands, and kissed her. Sophie's hot mouth instantly melted her in the chilly night air. Jordan loved the sensation of her lips, the warmth of her breath. Sophie slipped her arms into Jordan's jacket and pulled her closer. Everything disappeared except Sophie's touch, which ignited a passion within Jordan she never knew existed. She pressed Sophie's back against the tree, kissing her deeply.

Suddenly, Sophie pushed Jordan back, ending the kiss much too soon. They stared at each other, both breathing heavily.

After a few moments, Sophie spoke. "What are you doing?"

Jordan's heart plummeted. "God. I'm so sorry I threw myself at you. I didn't mean to—"

"Don't apologize. I want you to kiss me, but are you sure this is what you want? I mean…after last time."

Jordan grazed the worried crease in Sophie's forehead, wanting to ease her concern. "Yes. It's what I want. More than anything."

That must have been enough to convince Sophie, because she immediately kissed Jordan in a way that made her knees go weak.

"Jordan," Sophie mumbled, never breaking the kiss. "Let's go." At least that's what Jordan thought she said, but she didn't want to stop kissing her long enough to find out. Finally, Sophie peeled her lips away. "Let's go back to my place, where it's warm. And private."

Electricity ran down Jordan's spine at the implication of those words. Was that an invitation to sleep together? It'd been a while since she'd been propositioned, but that's certainly what it sounded like. Her desire to be with Sophie overwhelmed her, physically and emotionally. She'd never felt this strongly about anyone before, which was scarier than walking over hot coals barefoot.

Sophie didn't give Jordan a chance to respond before she grabbed her hand and briskly walked down the trail. Not wanting to spend one moment apart, they jumped into Sophie's Jeep. Jordan placed her hand on Sophie's thigh and admired her profile as she drove. Gratitude filled Jordan's heart. She had fantasized about this moment but never thought it would ever come to pass. Jordan stared out of the window and absentmindedly traced the inside seam of Sophie's jeans with her fingertips, up and down, until Sophie grabbed her hand.

"What are you doing to me?" Sophie's voice was hoarse and sexy as hell.

Jordan bit her lower lip to keep from grinning. "Don't you like it when I touch you?"

When Sophie turned, the desire in her eyes took Jordan's breath away. Sophie stepped on the gas, turning a ten-minute drive into five. When they stumbled into the cabin, Sophie pressed Jordan against the door and kissed her hungrily.

"I love kissing you," Sophie mumbled. "Your lips are so soft."

Sophie walked backward as she guided Jordan to her bedroom. They stood facing each other at the foot of the bed and held hands, moonlight filtering in through the window. A realization of where they were and what they were about to do hit Jordan. Her eyes jumped from the bed to Sophie. Everything was moving so quickly. How'd she end up in Sophie's bedroom? All she'd intended to do was talk, and now she was expected to have sex? Jordan wanted nothing more than to ravish Sophie, but Bibi's "cold fish in bed" comment echoed in her ears. Normally, she wouldn't let something an ex said bother her, except she was terribly afraid it was true. More than anything, she wanted to please Sophie, but what if she failed? What if she turned her off? What if...

"Are you okay?" Sophie asked.

"It's just...things are moving so fast...and...I'm not very good at this." Jordan cocked her head toward the bed. The corners of Sophie's mouth inched upward. She was probably about to burst out in laughter. Twenty-nine years old and Jordan still didn't know how to please a woman. "I just...I don't want to disappoint you."

"You couldn't disappoint me." Sophie sounded serious, but her smile didn't falter.

"Then why are you almost laughing?"

Sophie cupped Jordan's chin and looked directly into her eyes. "Sweetie, I'm standing here worrying that I'll disappoint *you*. You've had ten years to dream about being with me. Don't you think I'm worried about living up to that?"

Jordan blinked rapidly. "But...you're perfect."

Sophie's eyes softened, and she spoke in almost a whisper. "Jordan, I just want to be close to you. We don't even have to do anything. In my wildest dreams I never thought you'd ever be here with me. Simply having you in my arms is enough."

Jordan momentarily felt relieved. That was enough for her as well.

"Come and lie with me." Sophie guided Jordan onto the bed. She draped an arm across Jordan's stomach and rested her cheek on her chest.

Jordan basked in the sensation of their bodies melding together. Surely Sophie could feel the thumping of her heart. So much for being cool under pressure. Doing the meridian-tapping would probably kill the mood, but Jordan was tempted, since it might help her relax.

"Your pulse is racing." Sophie sat upright, grabbed Jordan's hand, and pressed it firmly over her heart. Jordan felt the pounding against her palm. "See, I'm nervous and excited, too." Jordan stared into beautiful blue eyes and nodded. "Sooo, you had a thing for me when we were kids, huh?" Sophie asked playfully, probably trying to lighten the mood.

"*Me?* I don't know where you got that idea." Jordan grinned.

"Is that right?" Sophie's eyes sparkled like the ocean glimmering in the sunlight. "And I suppose naming your company after my initials was purely a coincidence?"

"Totally accidental." Sophie raised an eyebrow and bit her lower lip in response. "Well...maybe...perhaps I was thinking about a certain blue-eyed, blond-haired Disney Princess at the time." Jordan lightly ran her fingertips across Sophie's lips. "It drives me crazy when you do that."

"Do what?"

"Bite your lower lip. Guess you didn't hear me groaning in the car on the way to Big Sur."

Sophie smiled and kissed Jordan softly, which caused her heart to swell like a helium-filled balloon soaring into the clouds. When they broke apart, Sophie sighed and looked at Jordan with emotion-filled eyes. In that moment she wanted nothing more than to shower Sophie with affection to let her know how much she meant to her. Slipping a hand behind Sophie's neck, Jordan pulled her down and captured her mouth. Sophie was quite possibly the most amazing kisser ever. Jordan melted into the mattress when Sophie lightly sucked on her lower lip and traced her mouth with her warm, wet tongue. She felt light-headed at the thought of that same tongue plunging deep inside her, tasting, licking, until she cried out in pleasure. This wasn't like Jordan. She didn't have erotic thoughts and rarely had orgasms, but for some reason Sophie inflamed her desires.

Somewhere in the middle of the kiss, it wasn't enough to simply have Sophie lie beside her, in her arms. Jordan wanted more. Much more. She slipped her hands under Sophie's shirt, caressing soft skin. When she felt the back of Sophie's bra, Jordan wanted to snap it open but didn't want to seem too eager.

Sophie moaned into Jordan's mouth and pulled away, resting their foreheads together. "You're really...really...making it hard not to touch you."

Jordan placed light kisses on Sophie's cheek and down her neck. She wanted to tell Sophie how aroused she was, how much she wanted to make love to her, but her voice faltered. All that came out was a growl.

Sophie nibbled down the sensitive skin of Jordan's neck, tugged the collar of her shirt, and planted soft kisses between her breasts. She raised her head and looked at Jordan, blue eyes darkened with desire. "You're so beautiful. Can I see all of you?"

Jordan didn't hesitate, the fear from moments ago replaced with passion for the amazing woman in her arms. Jordan lifted her shirt over her head and took off her bra. Sophie's eyes roamed up and down her torso as she licked her lips. She lightly ran her thumb over Jordan's nipple, which instantly pebbled and hardened. Sophie enclosed her mouth over Jordan's breast and sucked lightly. A fierce ache shot directly to her groin, hips arching in response. After being thoroughly stimulated, Sophie moved to her other breast, planting loving kisses on soft flesh.

"That feels so good." Jordan groaned and felt the wetness between her legs.

Sophie straddled Jordan's hips and kissed her firmly on the mouth. Needing to feel Sophie against her, Jordan slipped her shirt over her head. Sophie sat upright, unhooked her bra, and let it fall to the bed. She looked stunning, with pale breasts the color of moonlight and toned stomach that trembled under Jordan's touch.

"God, Sophie, you're perfect." Jordan swallowed hard. "Come here."

She pulled Sophie on top of her, relishing the sensation of their breasts uniting. Jordan lightly ran her hands up and down her back as they kissed. Sophie tugged at Jordan's jeans, attempting to unbutton them. When she was unsuccessful, she looked at Jordan with pleading eyes. "Off. Please."

Jordan undid her pants and slipped them down. Heat radiated through her body as Sophie lightly caressed her damp panties. When Jordan raised her hips, Sophie pressed harder, touching her through the wet fabric. Desperately craving Sophie's touch, she slipped her underwear off. In return, Sophie unbuttoned her pants, slid them down her hips, and kicked them to the floor. In one swift move, Jordan rolled Sophie over and hovered above her, taking in a breathtaking sight. Sophie couldn't have been more stunning, with gorgeous blond hair cascading down her shoulders, half-closed eyelids, slightly parted full lips, and flush-faced with desire.

"If you don't touch me soon I might actually combust." Sophie squirmed.

Jordan parted Sophie's legs, swirled fingertips through damp curls, and lightly tugged slick folds.

"Mmm…I fantasized about you touching me like this."

Jordan's hand stalled. "You fantasized about me?"

"Don't stop. Please." Sophie's plea was a huge turn-on, but Jordan didn't want to pass up an opportunity to hear this. She was pretty sure she'd never been anyone's fantasy before. Sophie opened her eyes and caressed Jordan's cheek. "Right here. In this bed. I ached for you to touch me. I need you inside me. Now."

Ecstasy washed over Sophie's face when Jordan slowly moved in and out, going deeper with each stroke. Sophie felt amazing, her swollen lips so soft and wet. Jordan wanted to stay inside her forever. As Jordan's thumb grazed Sophie's clit, she reached above her head and gripped the headboard rails. She twitched deep inside and tightened around Jordan's fingers. If it weren't for the look of desperation in Sophie's eyes, Jordan would have teased her, bringing her to the brink over and over again before allowing release.

"Yes…I'm so close…faster…" When Jordan complied, Sophie threw her head back, hips undulating wildly as her body stiffened and shuddered. The look of rapture on her face was the most arousing image Jordan had ever seen.

Jordan held Sophie close and lovingly placed tender kisses on her forehead and both cheeks. Sophie sighed contentedly and locked eyes with Jordan. In that moment, she felt like their souls were connected. The powerful emotion pulsating between them was almost tangible. Jordan had never felt so close to anyone before.

"Wow," Sophie said, laying her arm across her forehead.

"Better than the fantasy?"

"Way better." Sophie flashed a devilish grin.

"I think you should share the intimate details of your daydream." Jordan kissed around Sophie's breast, ending with a light tug of her nipple.

"Mmm…I have a better idea. How about I show you?"

Sophie slid down Jordan's body, spread her legs, and nibbled on her inner thighs. She gently played with the trimmed hair as she kissed and licked her way upward. Jordan was so turned on she'd probably come the moment Sophie touched her clit. Jordan grabbed Sophie's hand and pressed it harder against her, desperate to relieve the pulsating deep within.

"Not yet," Sophie said, a smile in her voice.

Jordan groaned and opened her legs farther, which prompted Sophie to lick the full length of her, over and over. Her tongue felt amazing on the heated, sensitive skin. Jordan ran her fingers through Sophie's silky hair, urging her closer. Finally, Sophie entered her with two fingers, which curved upward and massaged tender flesh. She moved slowly at first and then lunged in and out swiftly.

"Please, Sophie." Jordan barely recognized her own voice. It was husky, breathy.

"Please what?" Sophie's warm breath tickled Jordan's sensitive nerve endings.

"I want to come. I need to…" Jordan had never said that to anyone before, mostly because she'd never been so aroused.

When Sophie's tongue circled her clit, Jordan's hips rose sharply. The muscles in her legs and stomach tightened. Jordan lost total control when Sophie sucked lightly on the sensitive spot while sliding her fingers in and out of her wet entrance. She was on fire as she climaxed, setting off waves of pleasure. Sophie held her tight as she shuddered. It was the strongest orgasm Jordan had ever experienced, every nerve ending in her body awakened, tingling, pulsating.

Sophie planted soft kisses all over Jordan's limp body, ending at her lips. Jordan wanted to say so much, to put so many feelings into words. She'd had plenty of women in her past, but they weren't Sophie. There was something different—something exciting, intoxicating—about knowing Sophie was the one caressing her into a frenzy. With the other women, she'd had sex, but with Sophie she was making love.

Sophie gazed into Jordan's eyes and caressed her cheek. "You are the sexiest, most amazing woman I've ever been with. Stay with me tonight," Sophie whispered.

This was usually when Jordan would make her escape, vanishing well before dawn. Disappearing, though, was the last thing on her mind.

"There's no place I'd rather be." Jordan wrapped her arms around Sophie and held her close, never wanting to let go.

CHAPTER TWENTY-THREE

New Year, Second Chance

Love is strange. Sometimes it creeps up on you slowly, and other times you know exactly the moment Cupid shoots his arrow through your heart. For Sophie, it was the latter. She had fallen in love with Jordan when they were sitting under the eucalyptus tree after her mother's arrest and Jordan had made her smile. Even at ten years old, Sophie knew she'd love Jordan forever, and she was right.

Sophie lay in bed and admired Jordan's profile. Lightly, she ran a fingertip down the curve of her nose, over her lips, and down her chin. When Jordan stirred, she quickly removed her hand, not wanting to wake her just yet. Sophie let her gaze roam down Jordan's body, which looked like a picture-perfect centerfold. The sheet billowed around her in all the right places, draped under one breast and revealing the smooth skin of a beautiful long leg. Sophie swallowed hard and licked her lips, recalling the way Jordan had moaned when she feasted upon her breast. She felt light-headed as she focused on her mouth, the same mouth that had made her come over and over throughout the night. With a touch as soft as butterfly wings, she caressed Jordan's breast. Sophie felt a stirring down below when her nipple became aroused. Jordan moaned and fluttered her eyes open.

"Good morning," Sophie said as she continued to stroke Jordan.

"Mmm…come here." Jordan wrapped her arms around Sophie and kissed her deeply.

They spent the morning touching, stroking, exploring one another in heated passion, coupled with tender moments of gentle kisses and affectionate gazes. Sophie snuggled against Jordan as she lay on her back. There was no more perfect place to be.

"So tell me about your life in LA. Do you like living there?"

"Yeah. It has everything. Being here, though, reminds me to take more time off. Doug and I have worked nonstop since starting the business."

"Do you have friends?"

Jordan shrugged. "Mostly just Doug. I know a lot of people, but not sure I'd call them friends. Why do you ask?"

Sophie caressed Jordan's arm. "Just curious as to what your world is like. So I can picture where you are, who you're with when you..."

When you leave.

Jordan's body stiffened. She leaned down and kissed the tip of Sophie's nose. "Last night and this morning were amazing."

Sophie forced a smile, even though her heart was breaking at the thought of Jordan leaving Monarch. She propped on an elbow and looked into Jordan's eyes, which were the clearest and most joyful Sophie had ever seen.

"This was by far the best New Year's Eve I've ever had." Sophie froze for several seconds before she suddenly bolted upright.

"What's wrong?" Jordan asked apprehensively.

"What time is it?" Sophie nervously looked around until her eyes landed on the clock on the nightstand. "Oh my God. It's noon." She buried her face in her hands.

Jordan rubbed her back. "It's New Year's Day. No work. Plus, I'm giving you the day off for good behavior."

Sophie looked at Jordan, who had the cutest smirk on her face. "Good behavior, huh?"

"Well, maybe bad, but in a good way." Jordan pulled Sophie down and kissed her.

"No, no, no," Sophie whispered into her mouth as she regretfully pried her lips away. "I have to leave."

"You're throwing me out?" Hurt flashed across Jordan's face.

"No, sweetheart." Sophie wasn't sure where that term of endearment had come from, but it felt right so she went with it. "See, every New Year's Day the residents of Monarch have a picnic in the eucalyptus grove. It's tradition. And I'm the host. I'm the one who sets everything up. I totally blew it."

"What time does it start?" Jordan sat up in bed and put her arm around Sophie.

"Now."

"Okay, so we shower and get there in forty-five minutes. Nothing wrong with showing up fashionably late."

"You would go with me?"

"Of course. There's nothing else I'd rather do the first day of the year than spend it with you. And if I have to share you with everyone else in Monarch, then so be it."

Sophie's heart leapt as she laid Jordan back in bed and kissed her passionately.

When they paused for a breath Jordan asked, "Shouldn't we be getting ready?"

Sophie stared at Jordan's lips, moist and inviting. "Right. But if we get ready in thirty minutes, we could have fifteen to…relax."

"We could do a lot in fifteen minutes." Jordan slid her hand between Sophie's legs, her fingers lightly touching her.

Sophie's breath hitched. "Or if we got ready in fifteen minutes, we'd have even longer…to rest." Sophie closed her eyes, chest heaving rapidly, as she reveled in Jordan's touch, which had found its way deep inside her.

❖

Sophie loved the sensation of Jordan's hand in hers as they walked through the forest. She had a sudden fear, though, that Jordan might not be comfortable with public displays of affection since she was so private.

"Is this okay?" Sophie asked, motioning toward their clasped hands.

Jordan displayed a lopsided grin. "It's strange, but yeah. It's more than okay. Who'd have thought I'd be more out in a small town like this than LA."

"So it doesn't make you uncomfortable?"

Jordan stopped abruptly and faced Sophie. "I'm proud to be with you. That's not something I'd ever want to hide."

Sophie glanced around the forest, led Jordan off the trail, and pinned her back against an oak tree. The smoldering look in Jordan's eyes indicated she knew what was coming next as Sophie pressed their lips together. It was a tender kiss, one filled with affection that left Sophie feeling cared for. They broke apart slowly and rested their foreheads together. *This must be what it feels like to be with the person you love, where every moment is perfection.* Sophie wanted to climb a mountain or belt out a love song. It was the most joyous feeling she'd ever experienced, even better than being with the butterflies.

Sophie slipped her arm around Jordan's waist as they continued down the path. She'd much rather have Jordan all to herself, but she found something gratifying about being together in public. Like they were a couple. Sophie reminded herself not to get carried away. They'd slept together once, which didn't mean they were engaged, or even dating. They still lived in different worlds, and of course, there was the issue of the sanctuary. Sleeping with the boss probably wasn't the smartest thing she'd ever done, but Sophie didn't want to think about that when she was flying high.

They were clearly the last ones at the picnic. Scads of Monarch residents were sitting on blankets and in folding chairs, chowing down. A long table covered with a red-and-white-checkered tablecloth held an array of dishes. Sophie's stomach grumbled. She hadn't eaten since lunch the day before and, come to think of it, not much all week. Her appetite had diminished when Jordan left, but now she was suddenly ravenous.

Sophie hugged Bertha with one arm while still holding Jordan's hand. "I'm sooo sorry I'm late. Who set everything up?"

"Now don't you apologize. Everyone pitched it. Actually, I was hoping you might be late." Bertha smirked and eyed their joined hands.

Heat rose to Sophie's cheeks.

"It's all my fault," Jordan said, probably feeling the need to save Sophie from embarrassment. "We...uh...had a late night."

Bertha held up a hand. "Say no more. I'm happy as a puppy with two tails you two finally hooked up. It's about time. Now come on and get a plate. You must be hungry after a hard night at...work." Bertha nudged Jordan. Now they were both blushing.

As Sophie surveyed the feast, Jordan pointed to Nanci, who was leaning against a tree chomping on a drumstick. "Whatever happened with Nanci?"

"We didn't go out. I canceled the date and told her over Christmas that it wasn't going to work out."

"Ahh, well, can't really say I'm sorry about that." Jordan smiled and handed Sophie a plate.

They loaded up with fried chicken, potato salad, rolls, and more. Scanning the area for an empty blanket, Sophie located one under their tree, which was the perfect place. As they sat, Jordan leaned back against a boulder. It was the same rock Sophie had used to mark the spot where she'd buried the items for the soul-mate invocation. She smiled to herself. The chant had actually worked; Jordan was her soul mate. Sophie sighed contentedly and raised her face to the sun, feeling the warmth on her skin. It was a glorious day amongst monarchs, the scent of eucalyptus in the air, loving friends, and, most of all, the perfect woman.

"We heard about you two," Molly and Mabel said in unison as they approached. "We're so happy for you."

Wow, Bertha moved fast. Sophie wouldn't be surprised if half the people at the picnic knew by now. The girls looked adorable in matching red-and-white-checkered dresses, which looked oddly like the tablecloth. In fact, Sophie was sure it *was* the tablecloth. They'd probably made dresses with the extra fabric. The twins froze when several butterflies flew around their heads like a halo, and their eyes filled with excitement. The monarchs went around and around as though on a merry-go-round until they flew away.

"Wow. Did you see that?" Molly asked.

"Butterflies do amazing things." Sophie smiled at their excitement.

Jordan whispered, "Like even grant wishes."

"Yes, definitely that, too." Sophie put her hand on Jordan's knee and gazed into her eyes. They were a deep, rich gold, sparkling like an ancient coin and filled with wisdom and depth. She wasn't sure how long they stared at each other, but it wasn't until Mabel spoke that Sophie remembered they weren't alone.

"You two are so cute, but we don't want to intrude. We just wanted to say congratulations." The girls sped away before they could respond.

"Word gets around fast," Jordan said, with a nervous chuckle.

"That's Bertha for you."

This would have been the perfect time to talk about their relationship, but for some reason Sophie avoided doing so. She wanted to enjoy the day, pretend like they were a couple, and not discuss any reasons why they shouldn't be.

After eating, they mingled and ended the day standing by the dessert table with Bertha, sneaking chocolate-chip cookies.

"So Bertha," Jordan said through a mouthful. "Have you asked Coach Bryant out yet?"

"I haven't had a chance. You know, with the holidays and all."

"Well, he's standing over there. Now would be the perfect time."

"Playing matchmaker, I see?" Sophie asked with a grin.

"It *is* what I do best."

"Oh, I can think of a few things you do better." Sophie loved to make Jordan blush, and she was pretty sure Bertha had missed the innuendo since she was nervously glaring at the coach.

Jordan cleared her throat and regained her composure. "How about I invite him to join us?"

Bertha looked panic-stricken, but Jordan didn't give her a chance to reply. She walked over and chatted for a few minutes before he was following her back like a puppy on a leash.

"Good heavens, she actually did it," Bertha whispered.

As they approached, the coach looked just as nervous as Bertha did.

"I think everyone knows Coach Bryant," Jordan said.

Sophie shook his hand. "It's nice to see you again."

The coach took his cap off and looked at Bertha. "And how are you, Ms. Bertha?"

Bertha averted her eyes to the ground. "No complaints on this beautiful day, Coach."

"Um…you can call me Benny, if it pleases you to do so."

They looked like two shy junior-high-school kids. They'd probably be Jordan's most challenging love connection.

"Would you like a homemade cookie?" Jordan extended the tray to the coach. "Bertha made them. She's quite a cook, you know."

"Oh, I do know. I've had enough of her meals at the coffee shop." He patted his protruding belly and took a bite out of a cookie as an awkward silence settled over them.

Sophie raised an eyebrow and cocked her head at Jordan, sending her a telepathic "this isn't going to be easy."

"So, have either of you been to that new Italian place on the highway?" They both shook their heads. More silence. "Sophie and I heard it's really good."

The coach finally spoke after he'd downed the cookie. "I've been wanting to check it out."

"Bertha, didn't you say Italian was your favorite?" Jordan asked.

Bertha looked confused before she apparently had a lightbulb moment. She wasn't the quickest gazelle in the bunch. "Oh yes, I love pasta. Angel hair, fettucine, linguine, macaroni, penne—"

Jordan interrupted the never-ending noodle rampage. "You two should check it out sometime."

Coach Bryant rubbed his gray stubble, deep in thought. Finally, he took the bait. "We could…you know…go together one night if you'd like."

Bertha nodded enthusiastically. "Sure. That'd be nice."

"Are you free Friday night? Say around seven? I could pick you up."

"Okay."

The coach lifted his chin and puffed out his chest. He placed his cap on his head, winked, and said, "I'll see you then," before bouncing away.

Jordan released a satisfying sigh. "I'm proud of you." She nudged Bertha's shoulder.

Bertha, who was still staring at the coach, looked like she'd just smelled a skunk. "I haven't been on a date in over thirty years."

"Don't think of it as a date," Sophie said. "It's two people going out and having a meal together. No pressure."

Bertha looked at Jordan and Sophie with fear in her eyes. "I don't have anything decent to wear. And Lord knows what I'll do with this." She pointed to the teased mop on her head.

Jordan put her hands on Bertha's shoulders and looked her directly in the eye. "Clear your calendar, because you and I have a makeover date Thursday. You'll look like a queen by Friday night. I promise."

"Really? You'd do that for me? Thank you," Bertha said, looking relieved.

After Bertha excused herself to help the girls clean up, Sophie wrapped her arms around Jordan's waist.

"You like making people happy, don't you?" Sophie asked.

"Sure. That's why I started SOS."

"And what about you? Are you happy?"

"I'm happy right now. Here with you." Jordan glanced around to make sure no one was looking before she planted a soft kiss on Sophie's lips.

As Jordan pulled away, Sophie kept her eyes closed and sighed, feeling more content than…well, ever.

CHAPTER TWENTY-FOUR

Makeover Day

"Yippee!" Doug screamed.

Jordan held the phone away from her ear. She'd never gotten a cheer for having sex before. Ordinarily, she wasn't the kiss-and-tell type, but Doug had coaxed the news out of her.

"Now don't get carried away. It was just one night," Jordan said as she walked briskly down the sidewalk. She purposefully neglected to tell him that she and Sophie hadn't actually talked about anything yet. That was the whole reason she'd gone back to Monarch early—to talk—but other, more enticing, events had taken precedence.

"All right, all right. But I'm happy for you. And proud."

Jordan grinned. "Thanks. Listen, I gotta go—"

"Wait. Before you hang up I need to tell you something. Ophelia is doing a live show on Monday to promote her charity, and she asked me to be on it. I'm sure she'll mention SOS, so it'll be good press."

"Great. Go for it."

"It's just...I've never done an interview before. And it's *live*. You're the pro at that sort of thing."

"Nonsense. You'll be great. Just don't let her show my bra on camera, okay?" Jordan chuckled.

"You got it. And if she does, I'll swear those are your double Ds. I'll defend your honor, even if it's a lie."

"Attaboy. Talk to you later."

Jordan disconnected, rounded the corner, and bumped into a brick wall in the form of Madame Butterfly.

"Oh my, we have to stop meeting like this," Madame said. She was wearing a flowing red gown that matched the color of her fiery hair, thick green eye shadow up to her eyebrows, and an abundance of black eyeliner.

"I'm so sorry. I should watch where I'm going," Jordan said.

"You do always seem to be in a rush. Why don't you come by the shop for some tea? We haven't had much of an opportunity to chat since you've been in town."

"I'd love to," Jordan lied. "But I have several errands to run today. I'll see you later." Jordan scurried down the sidewalk, Madame matching her stride. They walked in silence until they stopped in front of the psychic parlor.

"Your *F* is missing." Jordan pointed at the sign, which read MADAME BUTTERLY.

"It's in the shop, but it's too heavy for me to hang."

Jordan felt like she should offer to help, but she really was in a hurry, and besides Madame Butterfly still gave her the creeps.

❖

Jordan slumped in a chair and rested her chin on her fist. This was the umpteenth outfit Bertha had tried on. This shopping extravaganza was getting old. Jordan looked at her watch, got up, and walked to the closed curtain of Rose's Dress Shop.

"Are you almost done in there?" Jordan asked.

"I don't know about this one. It's cut awfully low," Bertha said from behind the drape.

"Low enough to see your collarbone, cleavage, or bra?"

"Cleavage."

"Sounds perfect. Now let's see how you look."

Bertha swished open the curtain. Wow. She looked amazing. Who knew Bertha had sexy curves behind all those loose, frilly aprons she wore?

"Whoa. You're a babe. This is the one. For sure." Jordan nodded enthusiastically.

Bertha stared into the mirror at the electric-blue dress, which hugged every inch of her body. "Are you sure this isn't too suggestive?" She peered into the crevasse between her breasts.

Jordan stood behind Bertha, put her hands on her shoulders, and looked at her reflection. "Look at yourself and tell me you don't look beautiful in this."

A slow smile crept on Bertha's face. "I do look sorta…gorgeous… don't I?"

"If you were thirty years younger, and a lesbian, I'd be all over you."

"Let's plan that for the next life." Bertha sounded completely serious, which brought a smile to Jordan's lips.

"It's a date. Now let's get out of here or we'll miss your hair appointment."

After purchasing the dress, Jordan drove them to Tallon. No way was she letting Bertha go to her normal hairdresser and end up with another Aqua Net, teased rat's nest. Jordan had even convinced her to get an updated style, so when Bertha was sitting in the salon chair the hairdresser didn't have too much of a battle when she started cutting.

Jordan was flipping through a magazine in the waiting area when Bertha came out. She did a double take with her mouth agape. Bertha looked twenty years younger with a cute, sassy, casual cut. She seriously would not have recognized her.

"Oh. My. God. You look incredible. Do you like it?"

"No...I love it!" Bertha shook her head vigorously. "Look, I can do this, and it actually moves and *still* looks good afterward."

Jordan stifled a giggle. "Bertha, I swear you'll have the coach's eyes popping out of his head."

Bertha twisted around like a giddy schoolgirl. Seeing her so excited lightened Jordan's heart. They drove back to Monarch in silence, apparently both drained from the day's activities. She hadn't expected it to take so long and was disappointed she didn't get to see Sophie. Jordan wondered if she'd look needy and codependent if she offered to get together tonight. Maybe she could bribe her with some Chinese takeout. Sophie loved fortune cookies. When they stopped for a bathroom break at the Big Five Truck Stop, Jordan propped herself against the chip rack and sent Sophie a text.

Hi. How was your day?

There was a response in twenty seconds. *Lonely.*

Excellent news. Not because Jordan was mean, but because she knew she was a shoo-in.

Maybe I could help you rectify that.

I'm sure you could. Where are you?

Driving back from Tallon, but I could stop by with some Chinese, wine...and my lips.

Jordan mentally patted herself on the back. She was pretty good at this flirting stuff.

Reverse the order of that list and you're on.

Jordan really needed to stop grinning so much. Burly truckers were beginning to stare.

It's a date.

Jordan stared at her phone, anxiously awaiting a response. She waited...and waited...but nothing came. Maybe she'd gone too far with the date comment. They hadn't actually verbalized that they were going out, but what else could it be? Dinner and sex constituted dating, didn't it? Not that she expected to have sex again, but Sophie did indicate that there would be kissing. What else could you do with lips aside from that? Well, okay, lots of things, but Jordan was pretty sure Sophie was referring to kissing. She was probably just being paranoid. Maybe Sophie had something to do or was heading home. Excitement rippled through her body when her phone dinged.

Hurry.

Phew, relief washed over Jordan. Another message immediately popped up.

But drive safe! I don't want anything crushing my fortune cookie. ☺

Beautiful and witty. What a combo.

CHAPTER TWENTY-FIVE

Horror-Scopes

The great thing about living in a city of almost four million people is that you rarely run into someone you don't want to see. In Monarch, not so much.

Jordan was standing at Yui's Spicy Palace impatiently tapping the counter, waiting for her order and thinking about Sophie's lips, when she heard a voice that sent shivers down her spine.

"I figured that was your Jag parked outside." Nanci was wearing a gold blazer, navy shirt, black knit pants, and holding a leather binder with the name of her company, Chrysalis, engraved in gold. She was in full real-estate mode and all business.

"Oh, hey, Nanci."

"I saw you and Sophie at the picnic but didn't get a chance to say hi. You two looked cozy."

Awkward. The last time Jordan saw Nanci she was giving her the green light to ask Sophie out. "Yeah, about that. We weren't together when I said you could ask her out, but we seem to have hooked up New Year's Eve."

"Ah, I see. Well, I'm happy for you."

Except Nanci didn't sound happy. The sharp, curt tone in her voice, pursed lips, and twitch in her left eye tipped Jordan off.

Nanci opened the binder, slipped out a stack of stapled papers, and shoved it at Jordan. "Here's the contract I promised you." Jordan gaped at the documents. "The purchasing agreement to sell your land."

"Oh, right, of course." Jordan grabbed the contract and flipped through the pages. "It's thick."

"I'd suggest you read it over first and then get Mr. Simms to take a look. You or he can let me know if you have any questions. Also, I'd like to set up a meeting with the Kelstrom executives. What works for you?" Jordan was staring at the contract, not reading, just staring. "Jordan? When can you meet with Kelstrom?"

"What? Oh, let me check my calendar and get back to you."

"You can't keep them waiting too long," Nanci said, in a scolding manner that left Jordan feeling like a five-year-old.

"Yes, ma'am. I mean, right."

Nanci started to walk away before she turned and said, "Tell Sophie I said hi." Her eye twitched erratically. She should probably get that looked at.

Jordan stood in Yui's with the scent of spicy Kung Pao in the air and read the first paragraph of the contract. This was really going to happen. She was about to sell the sanctuary and be a millionaire. This was everything she wanted…so why wasn't she more excited?

Jordan pulled up to Sophie's cabin and stuffed the contract into her backpack, deep into her backpack. The last thing she needed was Sophie finding that particular piece of literature. They'd have to talk about things sooner or later, but Jordan was all for later. She still had a month left in Monarch to sort things out.

Jordan stood in the doorway, hypnotized, unable to do anything but stare. Sophie looked beautiful with clear blue eyes that resembled a perfect, cloudless day; glowing porcelain complexion; and a look of anticipation and joy. She was wearing the Venice Beach sweatshirt Jordan had given her when they drove back from Big Sur. It looked a hundred times better on her than it did on Jordan.

"Well, hello." Sophie's voice was low and sexy, almost a growl. She inhaled slowly and momentarily closed her eyes. "Mmm…that smells so good. Thanks for bringing dinner." She rose on her tiptoes, kissed Jordan's cheek, and lingered, which had Jordan's pulse racing. "But it isn't the Chinese food that smells so good. It's you."

Jordan gulped. "It's vanilla spice. They were giving out samples at the salon."

"My favorite combo." Sophie nuzzled Jordan's neck before placing another kiss on her cheek. "Get in here." She pulled Jordan into the cabin and led her to the kitchen.

They opened cartons of steamed rice, noodles, spring rolls, and sweet-and-sour pork. Jordan eyed Sophie as she gathered two glasses and a bottle of red wine. "You look adorable in my sweatshirt."

Sophie glanced down, as though she'd forgotten what she was wearing. "Hope you don't mind. It's quite comfy."

Jordan took the wine out of Sophie's hand, placed it on the table, and pulled her close. "Well, it *is* my favorite sweatshirt."

"Do you want me to take it off?" Sophie asked with a smirk.

Heat crept up Jordan's neck at the thought of Sophie in nothing but her bra. "What I want is for you to keep it and think about me when you wear it. And absolutely take it off later."

Jordan placed a lingering kiss on Sophie's lips. They both released a contented sigh when they broke apart.

"I missed those lips, that tongue, those eyes, that skin." Jordan ran her hands up and down Sophie's arms. They held each other's gaze until Sophie averted her eyes downward.

"It's scary how much I missed you," Sophie whispered.

Jordan lifted Sophie's chin. "Why scary?"

"Just…you know."

Unfortunately, Jordan did know. Just because they hadn't discussed the fate of the sanctuary didn't mean it wasn't always there, between them, like a pink, polka-dot elephant in the room they tiptoed around.

"Let's just take one day at a time, okay?" Jordan kissed the tip of Sophie's nose. Feeling the need to lighten the mood, she said, "I have a present for you. Do you want it now or later?"

Sophie's face lit up. "Are you kidding? Now, woman."

"Don't move." Jordan ran into the living room, grabbed an envelope stuffed in the pocket of her jacket, and returned to the kitchen.

"What is it?" Sophie took the envelope.

"You have to open it, silly."

Sophie ripped open the envelope, never taking her eyes off Jordan. She unfolded the paper, looked at it, and tilted her head to one side. "What's the Friends of Elk Mountain Reservation?" Sophie looked at Jordan with a half-smile.

"Well, you know Ophelia. She runs a charity that specializes in different causes, and I persuaded her to include the Native American reservation in her next event. They raise a lot of money, and to start things off I donated a thousand dollars in your name."

Sophie placed a hand over her heart. "Oh my God. You did that?"

"They really need it, and…I dunno…everyone was so nice, and the kids were so freaking cute."

"I think I might cry. This is so generous and thoughtful. Thank you." Sophie wrapped her arms around Jordan.

"You're welcome. It's a belated Christmas present."

Sophie released Jordan and looked into her eyes. "It's the best thing you could have ever given me."

Jordan smiled and gave Sophie a quick kiss. "I'm glad you love it. Now how about let's eat? I'm starving."

They sat close together, each grabbing bites with chopsticks out of the containers. After Sophie poured the wine, they clinked glasses before taking a sip.

"So how was makeover day?" Sophie asked.

Jordan pulled her cell phone out of her back pocket. "Take a look at this." She displayed a photo of Bertha with her newly styled hairdo.

"Oh my God. She looks ten years younger!"

Jordan's lips curled into a smile. "She wanted me to take a shot to show you. And you should see the dress she got. She looks hot."

"You're so sweet to help her out." Sophie looked at Jordan, adoringly. "What's so funny?" she asked, when Jordan chuckled.

"I don't think anyone has ever called me sweet before. I can be a ruthless businesswoman, you know. A real hard-ass when I need to be."

"I know you're very successful, but you have a good heart. That's one of the reasons I love you so much."

Jordan froze with a spring roll balanced between chopsticks in midair. The room felt suddenly thick and humid, like New Orleans in July, and so quiet she could practically hear Mr. Limpet swish through the water in the next room.

"Did I just say that out loud?" Sophie looked like she'd just stuck her finger in a mousetrap.

It was now or never, the moment of truth. What Jordan said in the next few moments would dictate their future. She could run away as she was accustomed to doing, or she could open her heart to someone for the first time in her life. Gazing at the Disney Princess, Jordan knew which path she'd take. She lowered the spring roll and laid her palm over Sophie's tightly clenched fist.

"I think…no, I know, I've been in love with you from the first moment we met," Jordan said. "Sophie Opal Sanders, you're the love of my life, my one and only soul mate."

Sophie's eyes immediately filled with tears as she threw her arms around Jordan's neck. When they broke apart, they were both giggling, probably to release nervous tension.

Sophie dabbed her eyes with a napkin. "I'd hoped so much that you felt the same way, but I wasn't sure," she said through a stuffy nose.

Jordan cupped Sophie's chin. "You're the reason I started SOS. If I couldn't be with my soul mate, I wanted to help others find theirs. In the past ten years, no other woman has come close to comparing to you…and no one ever will."

"I love you so much, Jordan. You're my heart." Sophie leaned over and kissed Jordan tenderly. When they parted, she stayed close and looked into Jordan's eyes. "Do you know what I want to do right now?"

"Hmmm…watch *The Incredible Mr. Limpet*?"

Sophie smirked and shook her head.

"Talk to the butterflies?"

She shook her head again.

"I know! You want to open fortune cookies."

Sophie started to shake her head, but then stopped and looked at the cookies on the table. "Well, actually I do. But after that I want to take you into my bedroom and show you how much you mean to me."

Waves of warmth cascaded from Jordan's chest down to her toes. She grabbed the fortune cookies and let Sophie pick which one she wanted. Sophie tore into the package, cracked open the treat, and read the fortune. She frowned and cocked her head.

"Not good?" Jordan asked.

"Well. Weird. It says the fortune you seek is in another cookie."

Jordan snickered and handed Sophie the other package.

"But that's yours."

"I'll live. And besides, this one belongs to you."

Sophie ripped the plastic and pulled out the white slip of paper. She drew her eyebrows together and clenched her jaw. The sour look on her face made Jordan suddenly uneasy.

"What's it say, Soph?"

"Some fortune cookies contain no fortune."

"Huh. Well, you can't trust something in a cookie. It's not like it's a psychic prediction."

"No. But my horoscope is."

"What do you mean?"

"It was eerily disturbing this morning."

"Read it to me. Is that the newspaper?" Jordan stretched and grabbed the *Monarch Messenger* off the kitchen counter.

Sophie pushed the paper aside. "Let's forget about it."

Jordan squinted, her curiosity rising by the minute. She snatched the paper and flipped to the horoscopes as Sophie winced.

Jordan read, "A high-intensity relationship will take a turn for the worse, dear Pisces. Passions and emotions will be strong as a power struggle ensues. This could lead to profound healing or a complete disintegration of the relationship." Jordan paused and read it again, silently. "This isn't us, you know."

"I know," Sophie said, much too quickly. "I don't live by my horoscope, but Madame Butterfly is rarely wrong." She got up, carried their glasses to the sink, and rinsed them out.

Jordan rose and stood close behind, wrapping her arms around Sophie's waist. She rested her chin on her shoulder and whispered in her ear. "Do you believe that love conquers all?"

Sophie paused before she turned to face Jordan. "I'm not sure. Do you?"

Jordan nodded. "I do. All that matters is that we love each other."

Sophie relaxed. "You're right. As long as we have love, trust, and honesty, we can handle anything that's thrown our way."

Inwardly, Jordan grimaced at the thought of the contract in her backpack. She considered telling Sophie about her plans but quickly pushed that notion aside. Instead, she took Sophie's hand and led her to the bedroom. Making love that night felt different than the first time they were together. The passion burned as strong as before, but peace replaced the nervousness. There was a moment—when they were as physically and emotionally close as two people can possibly get—when Jordan felt such love and affection that it literally took her breath away. It was the moment when Sophie looked into her eyes and whispered, "I love you. With all my heart, I love you." Jordan's eyes stung with tears, not of sorrow, but from indescribable joy.

After hours of pleasuring each other, Jordan lay awake with Sophie in her arms. She wasn't the praying type, but that night she recited a silent prayer. It was a desperate plea from the heart that what she'd told Sophie was true—that love did indeed conquer all.

CHAPTER TWENTY-SIX

Dinner at Seven

How could one look at Jordan make Sophie's heart skip a beat? She was all jittery inside, nervous and excited at the same time. She spotted Jordan walking down the sidewalk, talking on her cell phone. They were meeting at Bertha's for a Saturday lunch, but mostly to get the scoop on her hot date with the coach. Sophie rested a shoulder against a light pole and admired the view. Jordan wore fitted black yoga pants and a neon-green jacket. Even from this distance, Sophie could see that her shirt swooped low, revealing beautiful smooth skin. Jordan was probably discussing work, considering her purposeful stride and serious expression. When she spotted Sophie, she broke out in a wide smile.

"I gotta go," Jordan said as she approached. "I have a hot lunch date." She slipped an arm around Sophie's waist and gave her a squeeze. "I just wanted to call and wish you luck Monday. I'm meeting with the lawyer, but I'll tape the show and watch it later. And don't worry. You'll do great." Jordan paused and looked at Sophie. "Yeah... no way." Jordan put her hand over the receiver. "Doug wants to talk to you."

"And you said no? Why can't I speak to your very best friend in the whole wide world?"

"Because you'll embarrass me." Jordan quickly looked at Sophie and pointed at the phone. "I meant him, not you." She huffed and stared up at the clouds. "All right, all right, but be good." Jordan handed the phone to Sophie.

"Hello?" Sophie said.

"Is this the infamous Sophie?" Doug asked, a smile in his voice.

"It is. How are you?"

"It's so great to speak with you. Listen, we don't have much time because I'm sure Jordan is about to snatch the phone back. I just wanted to say you mean the world to her. I've known Jordan for ten years, and she's never, ever talked about anyone the way she does you."

It wasn't anything Jordan hadn't already said herself, but Sophie was touched by his words. "Well, I can tell you the feeling is mutual." Sophie looked into Jordan's eyes, which were light green in the sunlight.

"That's good to hear." Doug sounded relieved. "And I wouldn't be much of a friend if I didn't say if you break her heart, I will hunt you down."

Sophie laughed. "I'll keep that in mind."

Jordan reached for the phone. "I think you two have had enough phone time."

"You were right," Sophie said. "She's grabbing for the phone. So, I'll say good-bye, and maybe we can meet in person one of these days."

"Absolutely. So long."

"You still there?" Jordan asked. "Yes, she's as adorable as she sounds. Even more so." Jordan grinned. "You, too. Talk to you later." She disconnected and slipped the phone into her back pocket.

"Doug sounds nice," Sophie said.

"He's something, that's for sure. He's stressed because he's making his first public appearance on *Ophelia* Monday, and it's live. You'll be happy to know I told him about meridian tapping, and he said he'd look it up online."

"That's great. I keep meaning to ask if you've had any fainting spells lately."

"Nope. Not one. And hopefully I won't have a reoccurrence tonight when I see my dad."

"Are Rebecca and Chuck going to be there?"

"Yep, the big dysfunctional family dinner. That's probably a good thing, though. They can act as a buffer. I'm still shocked he invited me."

"I wish I could be there for you." Sophie placed her hands on Jordan's hips.

"Me, too, but under the circumstances that would make things more difficult. Plus, I don't want to subject you to a horrible night. You sure you still want me to come over afterward? I may not be in the best mood."

"Of course." Sophie moved closer, until their bodies were almost touching. "I'd be disappointed if I didn't get to see you."

Jordan bowed her head and gave Sophie a quick kiss, just a taste of sweet lips that left her wanting more.

"Are you hungry?" Jordan asked, which elicited a raised eyebrow from Sophie. "I meant for food. Come on, before I drag you back to my place."

When they entered the café they spotted Bertha propped against the counter staring into space. She didn't even notice them until they waved their hands in front of her face.

"Oh, hey." Bertha grabbed a glass and began polishing it. After that, she wiped down the counters, avoiding eye contact. Sophie and Jordan exchanged curious glances. This wasn't the usual attentive, smiling Bertha they were used to.

"Is everything okay?" Sophie asked.

"Sure." Bertha continued scrubbing the counter without looking up.

Jordon furrowed her brow. "How was the date?" When she didn't respond, Jordan prodded her. "Did something happen? Did the coach try something?" Jordan sat upright and looked like she was ready to clobber someone.

"Oh, no. He was the perfect gentleman."

"So, you had a good night?" Sophie asked tentatively.

Bertha stopped scouring the counter and looked at Sophie. "It was wonderful. It's just…I haven't been swept off my feet in a long time. I'd forgotten what it was like." Bertha paused and studied the countertop. "It's a little scary. You've got to understand. I've been alone for over thirty years. I got used to not needing anyone. Last night I got a taste of what it was like to be wanted, and I liked it. A lot. What if I get attached and then it doesn't work out?" Apprehension filled Bertha's eyes.

Sophie reached for her hand across the counter and gave it a squeeze. "What you're feeling is completely normal. Relationships can bring up all sorts of fears, but when you find someone special, someone you really connect with, it's worth taking a chance and trusting them with your heart."

Sophie wasn't sure if what she'd said was for Bertha's benefit or her own. She wanted to believe that she could trust Jordan with her heart. And more than anything, she wanted to believe that love would conquer any challenges they might face.

❖

The brass lion's head door knocker stared back at Jordan. That thing used to scare her something awful when she was a kid. Its mouth was open wide in mid-growl, revealing sharp teeth, and its devilish red-painted eyes made it look as though it'd pulled an all-night drinking binge. She probably should have suggested they meet at a restaurant, considering she hadn't stepped foot in her childhood home since they threw her out, but she'd been too shocked by the invite to even think about it. Jordan took a deep breath and pressed the doorbell. Chuck swung the door open so fast he must have been standing on the other side.

"Hey, Jordan. What's that?"

Leave it to a kid to zero in on a gift-wrapped box. She'd picked something up for him in LA over Christmas. "A present."

"For *me*?"

"Maybe." Jordan ruffled the top of his head. "Are you gonna invite me in?"

"Oh yeah." He opened the door wide. "You wanna see my room?"

"Definitely, but a little later, okay?" Jordan stepped through the foyer and into the living room, suddenly hit by the scent of bananas. She barely recognized the place. It was like she'd stepped onto the set of the *Golden Girls* or the lobby of the Ramada Inn in Ft. Lauderdale. Pastel paint was sprayed everywhere, wicker furniture galore, and so many tropical plants that she half expected to hear jungle drums in the distance.

Rebecca poked her head out the kitchen. "Hello, Jordan. Welcome to our home."

You mean what used to be my home before you tossed me out. But Jordan wasn't going there. The less they talked about the past, the better. She just wanted to get through the next couple of hours and get out of there.

"Wow, the place looks…different," Jordan said.

Rebecca came out the kitchen and into the living room. "You like? We were going for a tropical feel."

"Hmm…I think you captured it."

"We got these sea-glass lamps in Carmel and special-ordered the sofa and chair. They're made of banana bark," Rebecca said proudly.

"Oh. Looks like wicker."

Rebecca whipped her head around, and Jordan almost ducked from the poisonous darts thrown her way.

"It's banana bark." The resolute tone in her voice left no room for discussion. "And this is a Pierce." Rebecca motioned to the massive seashell painting over the fireplace. "You do know who Ramon Pierce is, don't you?"

"Haven't a clue."

"He's just the most famous artiste on the West Coast."

"Ahh." Jordan looked at Chuck and shrugged.

"Well, dinner is almost ready."

Thank God. Let's eat so I can get the hell out of here and to Sophie's sooner rather than later.

Jordan turned when she heard her father clear his throat. They stared at each other for what seemed like an eternity before Chuck broke the silence.

"Jordan brought me a present."

"Did she now?" Charles looked at the box clutched in Jordan's hand.

"Why don't you open it?" Jordan asked.

Chuck grabbed the gift and plopped down on the banana-bark sofa, which looked terribly uncomfortable. Within seconds, he'd ripped off the paper and lifted the lid, a look of shock on his face. Speechlessly, he held up a signed Kobe Bryant LA Lakers jersey and stared at it with an open mouth before clutching it to his chest.

"Wow! It's a real Lakers signed jersey." Chuck bolted off the couch and hugged Jordan's waist. She couldn't help but smile at his excitement. "Do you actually know Kobe?"

"No, but a friend of mine does. I thought you might like it."

"It's the most awesome thing ever. Wait 'til the guys on the team see this. They'll be sooo jealous."

"Dinner's ready!" Rebecca called out from the kitchen. Obviously, she was as ready to get this thing over with as Jordan was.

Halfway through the meal, even Jordan had to admit things were going smoothly. Topics of conversation revolved around Chuck's basketball team, Rebecca's interior-decorating fancy, and her father's golf swing. At first, Jordan was glad the spotlight was off her. After a while, though, she was hit with a sudden wave of sadness. It was as though she weren't even there. She contributed to the conversation every now and then but felt like an outsider in what should have been her home. This cozy dinner scene could have easily taken place without her, and surely often did. As much as Jordan professed to love her solitary lifestyle, she couldn't deny the ache in the center of her chest. She yearned to be a part of something, someplace that felt like home, and it was glaringly obvious that this wasn't the place.

After dinner, Jordan's offer to help with the dishes was met with a wave of the hand, which was fine by her since she was ready to bolt. Unfortunately, Rebecca had other ideas.

"Why don't you and your father go into his study for a nightcap?"

They stared at Rebecca as though she'd suggested they run the LA Marathon barefoot. After a few sideways glances and an awkward silence, they begrudgingly disappeared into the office, which looked to be the only room that hadn't been *Golden Girl*-ized. The scent of leather hung in the air as Jordan took in the surroundings. From what she could tell, not much had changed. It was still a dimly lit room with wood paneling, a walnut desk, bookcase, and a well-worn brown couch and chair.

"Have a seat. Would you like a drink?" Charles asked.

Jordan sat on the edge of the couch. "Water's fine, thanks."

"Not a drinker?" Ice cubes clinked as he dropped several into a glass and poured something from a decanter.

"Not much of one." Liquor usually made her say things she wouldn't normally. Better to keep her wits about her.

Charles snuck sideways glances at Jordan. "You look even more like your mother than when you were younger."

"Sometimes when I look in the mirror I see her staring back at me."

"You always were exactly like her." Charles grunted, like that wasn't necessarily a good thing. He handed Jordan a glass and sat in the chair.

She took a sip and looked around the room in an attempt to avoid eye contact. "I see you didn't let Rebecca redecorate your office."

A hint of a smile crossed his face, which was the closest he'd come to showing any pleasure all evening.

Jordan took another drink and rested the glass on her knee. "I was…uh…surprised when you invited me over tonight. And a little shocked you said it was Mom's idea. You two keep in contact?"

Charles stared into his drink. "Your mother will always be important to me." He glanced up, a surprising sadness in his eyes. "You do know it was her idea to get divorced and not mine."

Jordan had been only ten at the time, but she did recall that her father had seemed upset about the parting, whereas her mother had just wanted to escape. She was a free spirit who only cared about her career and didn't want to be tied down, and as far as Jordan knew she'd never dated anyone after the divorce. Maybe her father was right. Maybe she was a carbon copy of her mother, flitting from one relationship to the next, concentrating on nothing but her career. The thought of that was surprisingly sad. Jordan wanted something more, something different. She wanted a life with Sophie, which should have scared her, but it didn't. Instead, she felt giddy with excitement.

"I guess I did know," Jordan said, "but I didn't think you cared much for her after the divorce."

"I did. And still do." Charles's voice cracked with emotion.

Jordan wasn't sure if she was more surprised by her father's admission or the fact that they were discussing something meaningful. As she studied her father—with his stooped posture, despondent gaze, and drawn features—she actually felt sorry for him. It was painfully obvious he was still in love with her mother. Sad as it was, that was at least one thing they had in common. She'd experienced the heartache of being separated from someone she loved for the past ten years. Unlike her father, though, Jordan had a second chance at happiness.

Sophie opened the cabin door before Jordan even got out of her car, anxious to hear how dinner had gone. If the look on Jordan's face was any indication, it must have been a difficult night. Sophie immediately wrapped her arms around Jordan and hugged her tight.

"I missed you," Jordan said, slightly swaying them back and forth like they were doing a slow dance.

"Me, too. It's feels so good to be in your arms again. We're pathetic." Sophie chuckled. "We just saw each other this afternoon."

"Pathetically happy." Jordan kissed Sophie's forehead and led them into the cabin. She slumped into the sofa and stared at Mr. Limpet swimming in circles.

Sophie sat and lightly ran her fingers through Jordan's soft, chestnut hair. Sophie's heart ached at her pensive expression and troubled eyes. She wanted to wave a magic wand and make everything better.

"Do you want to talk about it?" Sophie asked.

"Yeah, but can we just rest here for a minute?" Jordan laid her head on Sophie's shoulder.

They sat in silence as Sophie stroked Jordan's hair and held her hand. As much as she hated that Jordan was upset, she loved the opportunity to coddle her. After a while, Jordan sat upright and forced a smile.

"Did you have a bad night?" Sophie asked, grazing Jordan's cheek with her fingertips.

"It wasn't as horrible as I thought it'd be. We didn't talk about what happened or anything. I'm sure if we had, it would have gotten ugly. I don't know. I just…I felt like such an outsider."

"Aww, I'm sorry, sweetheart. You know, just because you're related to someone doesn't mean you automatically have to get along with them, even when it's your father. I had to make my own family with Bertha and the girls."

"I did the same with Doug." Jordan turned and looked at Sophie. "And you. You were home to me." Jordan slipped her arm around Sophie's shoulders and pulled her close. "At least I got to see Chuck. He's a great kid. And I did have a chat with my dad in his study."

"Oh? How'd that go?"

"There was a moment when I actually felt sorry for him. He's still in love with my mom. In fact, I don't think he ever stopped. He said I was exactly like her. It made me think that maybe that was part of the reason he threw me out."

"What do you mean?"

"Maybe I was a constant reminder of what he couldn't have. I look like her, and I act like her. I'm not saying that excuses him in any way, but it may have played a part."

"You might be right. How'd the night end? Do you think you'll keep in touch with him?"

Jordan shook her head. "Not likely. I don't think he'd ever apologize for what he did or accept me. I do, though, want to be in Chuck's life. Hopefully, they're receptive to that."

"He's lucky to have a big sister like you." Sophie kissed Jordan on the cheek. She lay on the couch and guided Jordan with her. "You look exhausted. Rest with me here for a while."

It wasn't long before Jordan's rhythmic breathing indicated she was asleep. Sophie must have followed suit, because the next thing she knew she was awakened with a shiver at two a.m. She considered suggesting they go to bed, but Jordan was sleeping so peacefully she didn't want to disturb her. Instead, she reached on the back of the sofa for an afghan and wrapped it around them both, like they were safe and secure inside a cocoon where nothing could ever tear them apart.

CHAPTER TWENTY-SEVEN

Everything Hits the Fan

Aside from New Year's Eve 1999, this was quite possibly the worst day of Jordan's life. First, the meeting with Mr. Simms was a total waste of time since Nanci was a no-show, so now they'd have to set up another one to review the contract. Plus, she'd missed watching Doug on *Ophelia* because she was stuck in Mr. Simms's office trying to come up with conversation topics until Nanci arrived. Worst of all, though, was when Jordan checked her voice messages. She had parked in front of Bertha's to pick up lunch before heading to the sanctuary when she had a sudden urge to listen to a voice message from Doug.

"Hey, it's me. I didn't want to leave this on voice mail, but I wanted to give you a heads-up. Um...I think I may have screwed up. Apparently, Ophelia knows about you selling the sanctuary because she brought it up in the TV interview. I don't think it's really her fault. I mean, she was trying to talk up SOS, saying that we're going to expand after you sell the land. She put me on the spot, and I couldn't really deny it. It would have made her look bad, and it is true. Anyway, give me a call when you get this."

Jordan listened to the message again...and again. *Fuck.* Her stomach turned inside out, like she'd just stepped off the largest, loopiest roller coaster in all eternity. This wasn't the way she wanted to break the news to Sophie or anyone else in Monarch. She was planning to do it slowly, over time, and with carefully devised methods of softening the blow. She closed her eyes and rested her head against the steering wheel. She had to stay calm. It was quite possible they hadn't watched the interview. Jordan groaned. Who was she kidding? Bertha and the girls idolized Ophelia and never missed a show. The only positive was that Sophie probably had no idea. She recorded it sometimes, but right now she was at work with no TV. A wave of nausea washed over Jordan. She had to get to Bertha quick before she blabbed everything to Sophie.

The moment Jordan opened the café door it was apparent that they knew. Bertha was leaning on the counter, shaking her head and frowning. Molly and Mabel sat on barstools looking like they'd just attended the funeral of a beloved friend. Jordan approached cautiously and glanced at the TV hanging over the bar, which was broadcasting the station that aired the *Ophelia* show.

"Hey," Jordan said.

The girls stared, wide-eyed, until Bertha finally broke the silence. "Is it true? Are you really selling the sanctuary?"

Jordan's heart plummeted. She wasn't sure what to say. "Well… yes…but it's for a lot of money. Two million dollars." Jordan paused, hoping they'd ooh and aah. Instead, they were silent. "I'd be selling it to expand my company."

Bertha's eyes widened. "Does Sophie know?"

"No. Not unless you've talked to her."

"I tried calling but there was no answer."

Jordan exhaled a sigh of relief. "I'd really like to tell her myself. I'm heading there right now."

"But what about the monarchs? And the trees? And the sanctuary? Everything will be destroyed," Mabel said.

"And the milkweed field," Molly added. "The town won't be the same without the butterflies. They're everything."

The three women gawked at Jordan, looking completely devastated.

"I'm sorry." Jordan's voice sounded strained from a hard lump in her throat. It wouldn't have been so bad if they hadn't looked so hurt and disappointed. If they'd yelled and screamed, she could have fought back, but this she couldn't handle. It broke her heart to know she had caused their sadness. Jordan had grown very fond of the girls. They'd made her feel more like family than her own father did.

"I hope you don't hate me," Jordan said. Six arms reached out simultaneously to give her a hug.

"We could never hate you," Molly said. "We don't agree with your decision, but you're still our friend."

"That's right. We love you, Jordan," Bertha said.

The sentiment brought unexpected tears to Jordan's eyes. Bertha grabbed a handful of napkins and handed them to Jordan, who dabbed her cheeks and blew her nose. She scanned the faces of three unbelievable women. Here she was about to destroy something they loved, yet they still cared about her. She could only hope Sophie would react the same way.

❖

That was odd. Two strange cars were parked in front of the sanctuary. They never had visitors. It took Jordan a minute to register what she was seeing when she walked in. Three men in business suits were standing next to Nanci, who was talking animatedly with her hands. Sophie was ghostly white and looked as though a thousand volts of electricity had zapped her. It was a good thing she was sitting, because it seemed as though she'd keel over at any moment. Jordan slowly approached, never taking her eyes off Sophie.

"Oh, there's Jordan," Nanci said, excitedly. "I'd like you to meet the representatives from Kelstrom."

Nanci said their names, but Jordan didn't hear. Blood rushed to her head and a loud pulse pounded in her ears. Sophie stared straight ahead, a mixture of pain and confusion in her eyes. Jordan wanted to crawl into a cocoon and hide forever.

"Jordan?" Nanci looked perturbed and motioned to one of the guys, who had his hand out. Jordan grasped it and gave him a weak shake. When Jordan looked at Sophie, she bolted upright and headed for the door.

"Sophie, wait. I can explain." Without even tossing a glance over her shoulder, Sophie ran out and was gone.

"Jordan, you're being rude." Nanci tilted her head toward the men.

"I'm sorry. I wasn't expecting you."

They grunted and glanced at one another, obviously agitated.

"How about we have a seat and review the contract?" Nanci said, much too cheerfully considering the awkward circumstances.

"Would you excuse us for a minute?" Jordan grabbed Nanci's arm and pulled her outside, the dust from Sophie's retreating car still in the air.

"What are you doing?" Nanci shook her arm free from Jordan's grasp. "You're going to blow this deal."

"What are you doing here? You know this was supposed to be our little secret."

"You mean you *still* haven't told Sophie you're selling? I figured the cat would be out of the bag by now."

Jordan could have sworn she saw the corner of Nanci's mouth begin to turn upward in a smile before she stopped herself by pressing her lips together.

"What did you tell Sophie?"

"Just the truth. You know how much she values the truth."

A strange sensation gurgled in the pit of Jordan's stomach. Nanci had done this on purpose, maybe to get back at Jordan for dating Sophie or just to be spiteful. She'd had a bad feeling about the real-estate maven from the first moment they met.

Nanci grabbed the doorknob. "We need to get back in there."

Jordan ignored her comment and rushed to her car. Nanci yelled something, but Jordan tuned her out. She just wanted to find Sophie.

❖

The last thing Sophie wanted to do was cry. She knew Jordan would probably show up any minute, and she wanted to be strong, not bawling her eyes out. Maybe she'd been fooling herself, but she didn't think Jordan would actually sell, and certainly not before February as promised. She felt betrayed, hurt, and like a complete idiot. Sophie sat on the couch and lightly ran her hand over the cushion. What a difference a day made. Just yesterday morning Jordan had been sitting in that exact spot, where they'd awakened in each other's arms. Her heart ached. She couldn't lose Jordan again. They shared a once-in-a-lifetime soul connection that went deeper than love. How could she walk away from that?

Sophie jumped when someone forcefully knocked. She took a deep breath, walked to the door, and slowly turned the knob. Jordan looked frightened and achingly beautiful. They stared at each other for several long seconds until Sophie stepped aside. Jordan entered and stood stiffly in the center of the room. Sophie stayed a safe distance away and crossed her arms.

"I was going to tell you," Jordan said.

"Oh? When? You intended to sell from the first moment you came to Monarch, didn't you? Why did you even bother making that promise to me when you'd already made up your mind?"

Jordan ran her fingers through her hair. "Yes, I'm selling. Yes, I knew what I wanted to do before I ever got here. But I didn't break my promise. I haven't signed a contract yet."

"If you weren't hiding something, then why did you tell Nanci to keep it a secret? Did you want to get me in bed before you told me the truth?"

Jordan winced. "You know that's not true. Look, Sophie, this money can help build a prosperous future for us. For you and me."

Sophie stared at the carpet, unable to look into Jordan's eyes. "There is no us."

Jordan looked as though she might take a step forward, but then changed her mind. "Don't say that. I love you."

Sophie hated the way her heart melted from hearing those three words. She didn't want anything melting when it came to Jordan. "You don't get it, do you? I can't be with someone who would destroy something I love. It's not that I expect you to adore nature and monarchs as much as I do, but I want to be with someone who at least respects them…and me. More than money."

"What's important to you matters. But it's one grove out of hundreds. What difference would it really make? We can build a new one somewhere else."

Sophie shook her head. "We're back to square one. Nothing's changed. This is the same argument we had when you first arrived."

Jordan threw her hands up in the air, clearly exasperated. "You can't expect me to pass up two million dollars."

They were both silent for several seconds, the air between them as thick and gloomy as the early morning fog.

With a tight chest and clenched teeth, Sophie forced herself to look into Jordan's pleading eyes. "I can't do this. I can't be with you. I can't stand around and watch you tear down the sanctuary and milkweed field. The butterflies are everything to this town and to me."

"We just found each other again. I can't let you go. Not twice in one lifetime."

Sophie struggled to take a deep breath, her heart shrinking to the size of a green pea. She wanted this moment to be over. She couldn't feel Jordan's devastation and her own at the same time without crumbling into a heap. Sophie commanded her wobbly legs to walk to the front door and open it.

Jordan paused and shuffled toward Sophie, standing directly in front of her. "I'm not giving up on us. No matter what you say. I won't let you go." She glared at Sophie with determination before walking away.

Sophie closed the door, fell back against it, and cried.

CHAPTER TWENTY-EIGHT

A Flock of Butterflies

"I don't know why I let you girls talk me into this." Sophie glanced behind her at Molly and Mabel, who were scrunched in the backseat of Bertha's car.

"It'll do you good to get out and take your mind off...well, you know who." Bertha patted Sophie's leg as she drove down the highway toward Tallon. "We'll go out to lunch, do a little shopping. It'll be fun. Oh, and we should get our hair done at that salon Jordan took me...oh, I'm sorry."

It may have been sophomoric, but Sophie had warned them not to mention Jordan's name. That was several days ago, which was the last time she saw Jordan and when her world had crumbled. Since then she'd barely stepped out of the cabin, afraid to run into Jordan in town. She couldn't eat or sleep, and barely remembered to feed Mr. Limpet. Jordan had left dozens of phone messages, but Sophie deleted them all without listening. She didn't want to hear Jordan's voice. And she certainly didn't need something to remind her how much she missed her.

"Have you decided what you're going to do? For a job, I mean?" Mabel asked.

"I'm not sure. Maybe I'll teach or work at another sanctuary."

"You wouldn't leave Monarch, would you?" Bertha asked, fear in her voice.

Sophie grinned. "No. This is my home. You girls are my family. Even if I have to drive an hour to work every day, I'll never leave."

They collectively sighed in relief.

Molly leaned forward and stuck her head between the two front seats. "Jordan is miserable without you," she whispered, as though that would make bringing up the subject acceptable.

"I can't believe you'll still talk to her. She's just a lying, rich Beverly Hills snob!"

"You don't mean that," Bertha said. "You're just hurt and angry. We're as upset about this as you are, but we care about Jordan. She's a good person and has her reasons, I suppose."

"Yeah," Sophie snorted. "Money. That's her only goal. I should have never gotten involved with her."

Bertha grabbed Sophie's hand and squeezed it. From the look in Bertha's eyes, she knew Sophie hadn't meant what she'd said. Sophie gazed out the window at the blur of passing trees. Maybe she was just a romantic fool, but she thought Jordan would choose love over a mini-fortune. So yes, she was angry and planned to stay that way. It was easier than collapsing into a heap of unbearable pain and heartache from losing her soul mate, yet again. Maybe she needed to get away, at least until after Jordan sold the sanctuary and left town. She could drive up the coast or cross-country for a month. Yes, that's what she'd do, and the sooner the better.

Jordan stopped abruptly on the sidewalk. Maybe if she crossed the street and walked around the block she could avoid talking to Madame Butterfly. But the fortuneteller was struggling to heave a large *F* onto her shoulder in front of her shop, so Jordan sighed and reconsidered. The least she could do was help the woman before she broke her back.

"Can I give you a hand?" Jordan asked.

The steel *F* dropped to the ground with a clang. "Oh, Jordan, I'd be forever grateful." Madame wiped a bead of sweat from her forehead. Any more exertion and the inch of pancake makeup would be dripping down her cheeks.

"Tired of being known as Madame Butterly?"

"Normally I wouldn't care, but a stranger came into my shop the other day thinking it was a bakery." Madame cackled loudly and slapped Jordan hard on the back. When she regained her composure, she asked, "So, is it true?"

Jordan knew what Madame meant. She'd alienated almost everyone in town after word got around about the sanctuary. Thankfully, Bertha and the girls were still talking to her, but Sophie was a different story. After more than a week of phone calls and texts, Sophie was still avoiding her.

"Yes, it's true." Jordan lifted the *F*, which was none too light.

"I'm sure Sophie is devastated." Madame shook her head. "Your grandmother wanted you two to get together."

Jordan placed the steel letter back on the ground. "What do you mean?"

Madame paused and squinted at Jordan. "Why don't we finish up here and I'll make us some tea?"

Out of curiosity, Jordan agreed. After she attached the *F* to the sign, they went into the psychic parlor, where Madame motioned for her to sit at a small table while she disappeared behind a curtain. Glancing around, Jordan's eye fell on the large crystal ball in the center of the room. She recalled how she'd freaked about Madame's reading, which had been surprisingly accurate, not that she'd ever admit it.

Madame resurfaced and placed two cups on the table. She sat and stared into her tea for a full minute, which made Jordan wonder if maybe she wasn't reading tea leaves.

"Frances was a hard woman," Madame finally said.

"You can say that again," Jordan snorted.

Madame ignored her comment. "She changed after Chuck was born, and that's when we became friends. She learned what's really important in life, something she wanted to impart to you."

"Did she ever talk about me?"

"Oh, yes. All the time. It wasn't until soon before her death that she found out why you disappeared."

"You know about that? I mean, did she tell you?"

"She told me everything. She wanted you to make amends with your father, but also with Sophie. That's why one of her demands was that you work at the sanctuary. She said it was a chance to right your father's wrong."

"I wondered why that was one of her stipulations." Jordan said that more to herself than Madame. "I never thought she liked me, especially not after what happened."

"Frances felt bad about what your father did. When she found out how much you loved Sophie, she wanted to give you a second chance."

Jordan stared into space as the information sank in. "A second chance that I blew."

"Tell me something. Why did you start your matchmaking company?"

"Because I want to help women find their soul mates."

"And what about you? Have you found yours?"

"Well, yeah, that's Sophie. I knew from the first moment we met when we were kids."

"So why would you put your company over your soul mate?"

"I'm doing this for us. I want to spend the rest of my life with Sophie. I want to give her everything…a secure future, a big house, a nice car, everything she wants."

Madame reached across the table and laid her hand over Jordan's. "My dear, Sophie doesn't want any of that. She already has what she wants, and you're taking that away. It's not too late to change your mind. One of my favorite quotes is, 'If nothing ever changed, there'd be no butterflies.'" Madame patted Jordan's hand twice, rose, and disappeared behind the curtain. When she didn't reappear after several minutes, Jordan figured their visit had concluded.

After leaving the psychic parlor, Jordan drove to the eucalyptus grove. She sat under her and Sophie's tree and traced a finger over their carved initials. Reclining against the smooth bark, Jordan lightly rubbed the butterfly necklace Sophie had given her. She stared into space and marveled at everything that'd happened. Just six weeks ago she'd been ecstatic about the inheritance. Growing her company was the only important thing to her. She'd gotten exactly what she wanted, yet she felt miserable.

A piercing squawk and rustling of leaves sounded overhead. Jordan ducked as several thin branches tumbled down. If she'd felt the earth shaking, she would have sworn she was experiencing an earthquake. Instead, it appeared to be several maverick seagulls buzzing the tree. The ruckus caused thousands of monarchs, who were huddled together on branches, to spread their wings and soar into the sky. Jordan stood with her mouth agape. It was the most beautiful, glorious sight she'd ever seen, like swimming in a sea of orange and black.

She walked to the center of the grove and twirled around. Butterflies were everywhere, some landing on her shoulders and arms. It was like something out of a magical fairy tale. Jordan held out her hand, and within moments two monarchs landed in her palm, both gently flapping their wings. They were female since they didn't have black spots on their hind legs. There was a one in a million chance that they were the twin monarchs, but Jordan liked to think that they were. Maybe they'd come back to greet her or say thanks for helping raise them. Slowly, Jordan lifted her hand until they were a breath away. They were stunning, shiny wings that seemed paper thin, yet so strong. Their antennas twitched, tickling Jordan's chin, right before they ascended, disappearing together into the swarm.

When the monarchs settled and clustered on the branches again, Jordan stared at the tree, Madame's words echoing in her ear: *If nothing ever changed, there'd be no butterflies.* If anyone knew the accuracy of that statement it was Jordan. Strange how her time in Monarch had mirrored the twin caterpillars' metamorphosis. She wasn't the same person as when she'd first arrived.

Jordan surveyed the forest, the colors more brilliant than she'd ever seen. Was she insane? How could she destroy this beautiful place, the twins' home, and her and Sophie's tree? How could she exterminate seven thousand monarchs? Sophie was right. Demolishing the milkweed field and trees would displace all of these butterflies, plus any future ones. And most of all, how could she hurt the people she cared about the most? And all for the sake of money? Jordan knew in that moment she'd never sign the contract. The milkweed field, sanctuary, and butterfly grove belonged to Sophie, the Monarch residents, and the twin butterflies, not her.

CHAPTER TWENTY-NINE

Happy-Scopes

Jordan sat in her car outside Sophie's cabin. She either wasn't home or not answering the door. Jordan was desperate to find her to let her know she wasn't selling. Aside from Sophie, Jordan needed to tell one other person. She pulled out her cell phone and pressed the speed dial.

"Hey. How's it going?" Doug said.

"I need to tell you something, so I'll just come right out and say it. I can't sell the land and sanctuary." Silence. "Doug? You still there?"

"Yeah, I'm here. But…do you mean…can't or won't?"

"Well, both. I can't with a clear conscience destroy something that means everything to Sophie and the townspeople…and to me. I'm not just doing this to get Sophie back. I want to protect the monarchs and the land as well."

"Wow. Well, I guess I shouldn't be too shocked. I mean, you seem really different, but in a good way. You know what? I think it's great."

Relief washed over Jordan. "Really? You mean the world to me, and I did promise to expand the company."

"Don't even give that a second thought. It's your inheritance to do with as you see fit. And I couldn't be happier about you and Sophie."

"Well, I haven't told her yet. I hope she forgives me. She thinks I lied to her."

"She won't be able to resist you. She's in love. This doesn't mean you're moving to Monarch, does it? What about SOS?"

"I don't have any answers right now, but I can tell you with certainty I'm not walking away from our company. I'll figure something out. Listen. I'll talk to you later. I need to find Sophie. Thanks for understanding, bud."

Jordan disconnected and drove into town. If anyone knew where Sophie was it'd be Bertha.

"Can I get you the usual?" Bertha asked as she approached the counter.

"No, actually, I really need to talk to Sophie. Do you know where I can find her?" Bertha's smile dropped and she lowered her head. "She's been avoiding me for over a week. There's something I need to speak to her about."

"She told me not to tell you."

"Tell me what?" The knot in Jordan's stomach tightened. "Please, Bertha."

Compassion filled Bertha's eyes when she looked at Jordan. "Don't you dare say anything, but she's leaving. Tomorrow night."

"Where? For how long?" Jordan felt flushed, light-headed.

"I can't say."

Jordan had never seen Bertha so tight-lipped. "But where is she now?"

"I honestly don't know. I assume getting ready for her trip."

Jordan slumped on a barstool and bowed her head. She was tempted to tell Bertha she wasn't selling since it'd get back to Sophie in no time, but she wanted to do that herself.

Bertha grabbed Jordan's tightly clasped hands. "She isn't leaving until tomorrow night. You still have time."

"She won't answer my calls or texts, and I've been all but stalking her at the cabin. I don't know how to reach her." Suddenly, Jordan jerked her head upright, a glint in her eye. "I got it! There's only one way to reach Sophie and only one person who can help me."

"Who? What?" Bertha said, but it was too late. Jordan was already out the door.

Madame Butterfly was doing a card reading when Jordan entered the psychic parlor. Even though she held up a finger, indicating it would be a minute, it was more like fifteen. Jordan thought she'd jump out of her skin waiting for the spirits to stop yapping. Finally, the customer was gone and Jordan swooped in.

"Back so soon? Would you like some more tea?" Madame asked.

"I need your help. And fast."

"What's the rush? Sit. Relax."

"We don't have time for that."

"Well, what is it that you need?"

"Do you write the horoscopes for the *Monarch Messenger*?"

"I do indeed."

Jordan smiled. "Perfect."

❖

Sophie stood on a stepstool and grabbed a large suitcase off the top shelf of her closet. She placed it on her bed and stuffed it with jeans and sweaters. Next she packed toiletries and gathered Mr. Limpet's supplies for Bertha, who'd be by later to pick him up. If she stayed busy, maybe she could ignore the ache in her heart and the empty hole in the pit of her stomach. She didn't want to feel the overwhelming sorrow she'd experienced ten years ago over losing Jordan. This time, she was determined not to crumble into a heap of tears.

Sophie walked into the living room and dropped several betta flakes into the aquarium. "You be a good boy for Bertha while I'm gone. Watch your manners." The electric-blue fish flared his gills and almost seemed to nod in understanding. Sophie grabbed the newspaper off the coffee table. "How about I read our forecast? It'll be the last one for a while."

When she flipped through the paper, in place of the horoscopes she saw a full-page ad. Sophie furrowed her brow and gasped when she saw her name.

> *The daily horoscope for today is intended for one person only: Sophie Opal Sanders*
>
> *Your soul mate, dear Pisces, has a special message for you. It's taken her a while to come to this realization, but she could never destroy something that you love so dearly, which is also something she has come to love. Your happiness is what's most important to her, more than money, more than her company, more than anything. If you'd like to put the past behind and start anew, meet her by the eucalyptus tree at three p.m. today.*
>
> *If you appear, she will love you forever.*
>
> *If you don't appear, she will still love you forever.*

❖

Jordan walked around the tree and looked at her watch for the umpteenth time. She'd already done two rounds of meridian tapping trying to calm her nerves, so now she resorted to pacing. It was quite possible Sophie wouldn't show up. The last time they saw each other she'd thrown Jordan out. Sophie might still be hurt and not feel like she could trust Jordan again. The possibility of that was heart wrenching. What Jordan had written in the ad was true. Even if Sophie didn't appear, she'd love her forever.

It was ten minutes after three o'clock. Maybe Sophie hadn't seen the newspaper. No. She read her horoscope every morning. Jordan propped her back against the tree and slid down, wrapping her arms around her knees. After a few minutes she felt a tap on her shoulder. Her insides clenched and she bolted to her feet. It was Sophie, who looked like she'd been crying. This couldn't be good. Jordan held her breath, not sure what to say or think. They stared at each other for what seemed like an eternity until Sophie held out both hands, which Jordan grasped. Finally, the corners of Sophie's mouth turned upward, slowly at first, until she was smiling widely. Her eyes sparkled as tears emerged, obviously from joy and not sadness. A wave of relief washed over Jordan. She felt so light she could have soared into the sky with the monarchs.

Jordan started to speak but stopped. Words weren't necessary. They both beamed as they gazed into each other's eyes, souls connected in the knowledge that they'd never be apart again.

CHAPTER THIRTY

New Year's Day Dedication

One Year Later

Jordan rolled over in bed and was greeted with a mound of blankets instead of the warm, soft body she was expecting. As though hoping Sophie were somewhere underneath the pile, she frantically patted the covers. Momentarily disoriented, she bolted upright, looked around, and sighed in relief. She was at Sophie's cabin and not her Beverly Hills condo. Actually, Sophie insisted on calling it *their* cabin, which always warmed Jordan's heart. For the past year, she'd split her time between Monarch and Los Angeles, but that was taking a toll. Driving back and forth was exhausting, and any time spent away from Sophie just sucked.

Jordan wiggled her eyebrows when she heard the shower in the bathroom. She crawled out of bed, opened the door, and peeked behind the curtain. It didn't matter how many times she saw Sophie in the shower, in bed, or anywhere else; she always took Jordan's breath away. She stood under the spray, eyes closed, head thrown back, and fingers combing through damp hair. Jordan's gaze followed a water bead's path down Sophie's neck, between her breasts, down her stomach, and into the trimmed hair below. The sight of her caused heat to cascade down Jordan's body. When she stepped into the shower, gorgeous blue eyes popped open, followed by a broad smile.

"Good morning. Can I help you with something?" Sophie's raspy voice and a wicked glimmer in her eyes heightened Jordan's arousal.

"I didn't get my good-morning kiss." Jordan slipped her hands around Sophie and pulled her close. A low moan escaped her lips when Sophie's hands ran down her back and to her buttocks.

"Do you think you deserve a kiss without working for it first?"

Jordan shrugged, unable to speak with Sophie caressing her skin. Sophie grabbed the soap and placed it in Jordan's palm. Without diverting her gaze from beautiful sapphire eyes, Jordan worked up a lather and ran slick hands down Sophie's back, across her stomach, and around her breasts, rousing hard nipples. When Jordan's hand slipped between Sophie's legs, desire flashed across her hooded eyes right before they turned dark indigo. Jordan's stomach tightened when her fingers found Sophie's wet center. Unable to wait a moment longer, they kissed, slow and deep. This was how Jordan wanted to spend every morning—in the arms of the woman she loved.

After a long, hot shower they dried each other off and got ready for the day. Jordan sat on the bed and tied her shoes as she watched Sophie wiggle into sexy, low-rise jeans. They were Jordan's favorite pair, and the way they hugged Sophie's curves always made her heart beat a little faster. Jordan leaned back and looked Sophie up and down appreciatively, her eyes stopping on a sheer bra.

"What are you looking at?" Sophie asked with a smirk.

"Do you have any idea how much I love you?"

"I believe you showed me how much in the shower this morning."

Jordan stood, put her hands on Sophie's hips, and looked into her eyes. "I love everything about you. Not just your beautiful body."

Sophie grazed Jordan's cheek. "I know, sweetheart. Me, too." She placed a soft kiss on Jordan's lips. "As much as I hate to say it, we really need to get going. Remember last New Year's Day? We almost missed the picnic, and today everyone will be at the sanctuary for the dedication."

Jordan helped Sophie slip her shirt over her head. "All right, but next New Year's Day I want you all to myself." Knowing they'd be together in a year's time hit Jordan. She'd never dated anyone longer than six months, but Sophie wasn't just anyone.

When they arrived at the sanctuary, Bertha and Coach Bryant were setting up tables under the trees.

"We wanted to beat you here," Sophie said.

"You know what an early bird I am." Bertha hugged Jordan and Sophie as the coach shook their hands. He wasn't the hugging type, except when it came to Bertha. Everyone expected wedding bells for those two in the near future.

Jordan frowned. "Shoot. I forgot to bring the ribbon."

"It's in one of the boxes over there," Sophie said.

Jordan smiled and kissed Sophie's cheek. "What would I do without you?"

"Do you have your speech prepared?" Bertha asked Jordan as she placed platters of food on the tables.

Jordan stiffened. "Speech? I have to give a speech?"

Sophie smiled and patted Jordan's arm. "Don't worry, sweetie. You'll do fine. Just speak from your heart. Why don't you help Molly and Mabel unpack their car?" Sophie motioned toward their vehicle.

Jordan didn't like giving speeches and was out of touch with being in the public eye since Doug had taken over most of her interviewing duties.

"Hey, girls. Need some help?" Jordan lifted a box of pies out of the trunk.

"Thank you so much, Jordan." Mabel said.

The twins were dressed in matching red-and-blue-striped dresses. Jordan wanted everyone to be as happy as she was and had her sights on setting them up with some eligible Monarch bachelors.

After unloading the car, Jordan bubbled with excitement when she saw a silver Lexus approach. Chuck jumped out before Rebecca had come to a full stop.

"Hey, Jordan." Chuck hugged her waist. It was amazing how much he'd grown in just a month.

"Hey, Chucky." Jordan ruffled the top of his head.

Rebecca rolled down the window. "Have him home by four."

Jordan resisted the urge to salute. Rebecca always made her feel like she was taking orders. "You can count on it."

Rebecca nodded, rolled up the window, and sped away. Jordan no longer resented her father or Rebecca, but as Sophie always said, that didn't mean they had to be friends. If it weren't for Chuck, Jordan probably wouldn't keep in contact with them. She was just overjoyed that they let her spend time with him, which Jordan had suspected was her mother's doing. She still seemed to have quite an influence over Jordan's father.

Jordan grabbed the pigskin from Chuck. "Are you into football now?"

"Yeah. I'm going to try out for running back. Maybe we could throw it around later?"

"Absolutely. Why don't you go out for a pass right now?"

Chuck ran, cut to the left, and caught the ball that Jordan threw into his arms.

Coach Bryant approached. "Great catch. You'll make an impressive receiver."

As the coach and Chuck tossed the ball around, Jordan leaned against a tree and watched the gathering crowd. Sophie wrapped her arms around Jordan's waist from behind and rested her chin on her shoulder.

"I know it's selfish of me," Sophie said, "but I wish you were here all the time, not just a few days a week."

Jordan turned and placed a kiss on Sophie's forehead. "That's not selfish. It's hard for me, too. I don't like being away from you."

Sophie sighed. "I know. So, do you want to do the dedication now?"

Jordan glanced around. "Yeah. I was hoping Doug would have been here by now, but he may not be able to make it. He planned to stop by on his way back from San Francisco."

"We can wait."

"No. That's okay. I'm sure everyone's getting hungry."

Jordan stood behind a yellow ribbon stretched in front of the sanctuary as Sophie gathered everyone together. When forty pairs of eyes were staring directly at her, Jordan's stomach fluttered. Speak from the heart, that's what Sophie had said.

"Thank you all for coming today. I know we usually have the New Year's Day picnic in the eucalyptus grove, so I appreciate everyone gathering at the sanctuary." Jordan cleared her throat and willed her thumping heart to settle. "When I came to town a year ago, I intended to sell the sanctuary. I didn't expect to fall in love with the butterflies and all of you, and to reconnect with the love of my life." Jordan gave Sophie a sweet smile. "There's only one person to thank for bringing me here, and that's my grandmother. If it weren't for her, I'd hate to think where I'd be right now, probably alone and stressed out instead of deliriously happy." Jordan locked eyes with Sophie.

"So, on that note, I'd like to officially welcome you to the Frances Lee Monarch Sanctuary." Applause erupted from the crowd, and Jordan grabbed the giant pair of scissors. "There's someone I'd like to bring up here to cut the ribbon. Someone very important in my life and who was closer to my grandmother than anyone. Chucky, would you do the honors?"

Chuck's eyebrows shot up and he beamed. He joined Jordan, took the scissors, and cut the ribbon. Everyone cheered.

"Now let's eat!" Jordan said, which prompted the crowd to form a line by the buffet table.

Sophie and Madame Butterfly approached Jordan. "You did a good job," Sophie said as she squeezed Jordan's arm.

"Frances would be proud of you," Madame said. "Proud of you both for finding your way back to each other. I see nothing but happiness and success in your future."

Jordan smiled. "That's good to know. Thank you." Madame had definitely grown on Jordan. She still wasn't into psychic stuff and didn't particularly want her fortune told, but Madame had a good heart.

"Oh, hey, there's Doug," Jordan said. "Would you excuse us?" Jordan grabbed Sophie's hand and greeted her best friend. "You made it!"

"I'm so sorry I'm late. Did I miss the dedication?"

"Yeah, but don't worry about it."

"Hey, beautiful." Doug gave Sophie a kiss on the cheek.

"We're so glad you're here," Sophie said.

"So, is…uh…everything final?" Jordan whispered to Doug.

"All signed, sealed, and delivered."

"So that means it's a done deal?"

Sophie squinted. "What are you two up to?"

"It's final." Doug smiled with a gleam in his eyes.

Jordan turned to Sophie with a huge smile. "How would you like to have me in Monarch full-time?"

"What do you mean?" Sophie asked.

"I sold my half of SOS to Doug. I'm going to continue helping him, but on a contract basis from here. That is…if you don't mind having me around so much."

"Oh my God, seriously? Are you sure this is what you want? It's your company."

"I'm more than sure. Being with you is what's most important. I want us to be together all the time."

Sophie threw her arms around Jordan's neck. "This is by far the best news I've ever heard."

"You two are so freaking cute," Doug said. "But I'm still counting on you for help." He wagged a finger at Jordan.

"I'll do whatever you need…from here."

As the day wound down and people started to leave, Jordan looked at her watch. "I better get Chuck back. It's almost four."

"All right. We'll finish cleaning up here, and I'll meet you back home." Sophie kissed Jordan's cheek. "What? Why are you grinning?"

"It's nothing." Jordan looked down, embarrassed.

"What is it?" Sophie lifted Jordan's chin.

"When you said home, I felt it. Right here." Jordan pressed a palm over her heart. "Sophie Opal Sanders, you're my home," Jordan whispered and planted a kiss on her soul mate's lips.

About the Author

Lisa Moreau has been writing stories ever since she could hold a crayon and Big Chief tablet. She's an ultimate romantic and loves creating genuine characters who seem so real that she finds it sad they don't actually exist. When Lisa isn't writing on her laptop, in her mind, or with a crayon (old habits die hard), her absolute favorite pastime is perusing bookstores—so much so that they should really start charging her rent.

Lisa has a bachelor's degree in journalism from Midwestern State University, TX, and has completed an indefinitely large number of creative writing courses at Santa Monica College, CA. She lives in Los Angeles, CA, for the ocean, mountains, and totally awesome weather and only occasionally thinks about moving when she feels an earthquake tremble.

Visit Lisa's website: http://www.lisamoreauwriter.com.

Books Available From Bold Strokes Books

A Quiet Death by Cari Hunter. When the body of a young Pakistani girl is found out on the moors, the investigation leaves Detective Sanne Jensen facing an ordeal she may not survive. (978-1-62639-815-3)

Buried Heart by Laydin Michaels. When Drew Chambliss meets Cicely Jones, her buried past finds its way to the surface. Will they survive its discovery or will their chance at love turn to dust? (978-1-62639-801-6)

Escape: Exodus Book Three by Gun Brooke. Aboard the Exodus ship *Pathfinder*, President Thea Tylio still holds Caya Lindemay, a clairvoyant changer, in protective custody, which has devastating consequences endangering their relationship and the entire Exodus mission. (978-1-62639-635-7)

Genuine Gold by Ann Aptaker. New York, 1952. Outlaw Cantor Gold is thrown back into her honky-tonk Coney Island past, where crime and passion simmer in a neon glare. (978-1-62639-730-9)

Into Thin Air by Jeannie Levig. When her girlfriend disappears, Hannah Lewis discovers her world isn't as orderly as she thought it was. (978-1-62639-722-4)

Night Voice by CF Frizzell. When talk show host Sable finally acknowledges her risqué radio relationship with a mysterious caller, she welcomes a *real* relationship with local tradeswoman Riley Burke. (978-1-62639-813-9)

Raging at the Stars by Lesley Davis. When the unbelievable theories start revealing themselves as truths, can you trust in the ones who have conspired against you from the start? (978-1-62639-720-0)

She Wolf by Sheri Lewis Wohl. When the hunter becomes the hunted, more than love might be lost. (978-1-62639-741-5)

Smothered and Covered by Missouri Vaun. The last person Nash Wiley expects to bump into over a two a.m. breakfast at Waffle House is her college crush, decked out in a curve-hugging law enforcement uniform. (978-1-62639-704-0)

The Butterfly Whisperer by Lisa Moreau. Reunited after ten years, can Jordan and Sophie heal the past and rediscover love or will differing desires keep them apart? (978-1-62639-791-0)

The Devil's Due by Ali Vali. Cain and Emma Casey are awaiting the birth of their third child, but as always in Cain's world, there are new and old enemies to face in Katrina-ravaged New Orleans. (978-1-62639-591-6)

Widows of the Sun-Moon by Barbara Ann Wright. With immortality now out of their grasp, the gods of Calamity fight amongst themselves, egged on by the mad goddess they thought they'd left behind. (978-1-62639-777-4)

Arrested Hearts by Holly Stratimore. A reckless cop who hates her life and a health nut who is afraid to die might be a perfect combination for love. (978-1-62639-809-2)

Capturing Jessica by Jane Hardee. Hyperrealist sculptor Michael tries desperately to conceal the love she holds for best friend, Jess, unaware Jess's feelings for her are changing. (978-1-62639-836-8)

Counting to Zero by AJ Quinn. NSA agent Emma Thorpe and computer hacker Paxton James must learn to trust each other as they work to stop a threat clock that's rapidly counting down to zero. (978-1-62639-783-5)

Courageous Love by KC Richardson. Two women fight a devastating disease, and their own demons, while trying to fall in love. (978-1-62639-797-2)

One More Reason to Leave Orlando by Missouri Vaun. Nash Wiley thought a threesome sounded exotic and exciting, but as it turns out the reality of sleeping with two women at the same time is just really complicated. (978-1-62639-703-3)

Pathogen by Jessica L. Webb. Can Dr. Kate Morrison navigate a deadly virus and the threat of bioterrorism, as well as her new relationship with Sergeant Andy Wyles and her own troubled past? (978-1-62639-833-7)

Rainbow Gap by Lee Lynch. Jaudon Vickers and Berry Garland, polar opposites, dream and love in this tale of lesbian lives set in Central Florida against the tapestry of societal change and the Vietnam War. (978-1-62639-799-6)

Steel and Promise by Alexa Black. Lady Nivrai's cruel desires and modified body make most of the galaxy fear her, but courtesan Cailyn Derys soon discovers the real monsters are the ones without the claws. (978-1-62639-805-4)

Swelter by D. Jackson Leigh. Teal Giovanni's mistake shines an unwanted spotlight on a small Texas ranch where August Reese is secluded until she can testify against a powerful drug kingpin. (978-1-62639-795-8)

Without Justice by Carsen Taite. Cade Kelly and Emily Sinclair must battle each other in the pursuit of justice, but can they fight their undeniable attraction outside the walls of the courtroom? (978-1-62639-560-2)

21 Questions by Mason Dixon. To find love, start by asking the right questions. (978-1-62639-724-8)

A Palette for Love by Charlotte Greene. When newly minted Ph.D. Chloé Devereaux returns to New Orleans, she doesn't expect her new job and her powerful employer—Amelia Winters—to be so appealing. (978-1-62639-758-3)

By the Dark of Her Eyes by Cameron MacElvee. When Brenna Taylor inherits a decrepit property haunted by tormented ghosts, Alejandra Santana must not only restore Brenna's house and property but also save her soul. (978-1-62639-834-4)

Death by Cocktail Straw by Missouri Vaun. She just wanted to meet girls, but an outing at the local lesbian bar goes comically off the rails, landing Nash Wiley and her best pal in the ER. (978-1-62639-702-6)

Cash Braddock by Ashley Bartlett. Cash Braddock just wants to hang with her cat, fall in love, and deal drugs. What's the problem with that? (978-1-62639-706-4)

Lone Ranger by VK Powell. Reporter Emma Ferguson stirs up a thirty-year-old mystery that threatens Park Ranger Carter West's family and jeopardizes any hope for a relationship between the two women. (978-1-62639-767-5)

Never Enough by Robyn Nyx. Can two women put aside their pasts to find love before it's too late? (978-1-62639-629-6)

Love on Call by Radclyffe. Ex-Army medic Glenn Archer and recent LA transplant Mariana Mateo fight their mutual desire in the face of past losses as they work together in the Rivers Community Hospital ER. (978-1-62639-843-6)

Two Souls by Kathleen Knowles. Can love blossom in the wake of tragedy? (978-1-62639-641-8)

Camp Rewind by Meghan O'Brien. A summer camp for grown-ups becomes the site of an unlikely romance between a shy, introverted divorcee and one of the Internet's most infamous cultural critics— who attends undercover. (978-1-62639-793-4)

Cross Purposes by Gina L. Dartt. In pursuit of a lost Acadian treasure, three women must work out not only the clues, but also the complicated tangle of emotion and attraction developing between them. (978-1-62639-713-2)

Imperfect Truth by C.A. Popovich. Can an imperfect truth stand in the way of love? (978-1-62639-787-3)

Serious Potential by Maggie Cummings. Pro golfer Tracy Allen plans to forget her ex during a visit to Bay West, a lesbian condo community in NYC, but when she meets Dr. Jennifer Betsy, she gets more than she bargained for. (978-1-62639-633-3)

Life in Death by M. Ullrich. Sometimes the devastating end is your only chance for a new beginning. (978-1-62639-773-6)

Love on Liberty by MJ Williamz. Hearts collide when politics clash. (978-1-62639-639-5)

Taste by Kris Bryant. Accomplished chef Taryn has walked away from her promising career in the city's top restaurant to devote her life to her six-year-old daughter and is content until Ki Blake comes along. (978-1-62639-718-7)

Valley of Fire by Missouri Vaun. Taken captive in a desert outpost after their small aircraft is hijacked, Ava and her captivating passenger discover things about each other and themselves that will change them both forever. (978-1-62639-496-4)

The Second Wave by Jean Copeland. Can star-crossed lovers have a second chance after decades apart, or does the love of a lifetime only happen once? (978-1-62639-830-6)

Coils by Barbara Ann Wright. A modern young woman follows her aunt into the Greek Underworld and makes a pact with Medusa to win her freedom by killing a hero of legend. (978-1-62639-598-5)

Courting the Countess by Jenny Frame. When relationship-phobic Lady Henrietta Knight starts to care about housekeeper Annie Brannigan and her daughter, can she overcome her fears and promise Annie the forever that she demands? (978-1-62639-785-9)

Dapper by Jenny Frame. Amelia Honey meets the mysterious Byron De Brek and is faced with her darkest fantasies, but will her strict moral upbringing stop her from exploring what she truly wants? (978-1-62639-898-6)

Delayed Gratification: The Honeymoon by Meghan O'Brien. A dream European honeymoon turns into a winter storm nightmare involving a delayed flight, a ditched rental car, and eventually, a surprisingly happy ending. (978-1-62639-766-8)